A Family
Secret

Also by Josephine Cox

JOSEPHINE
COX
A Family
Secret

HarperCollins*Publishers*

HarperCollins*Publishers*
1 London Bridge Street,
London SE1 9GF

www.harpercollins.co.uk

Published by HarperCollins*Publishers* 2017
1

A catalogue record for this book is available from the British Library

ISBN: 978-0-00-742000-1

Set in ITC New Baskerville Std 12.75/16.75 pt
by Palimpsest Book Production Limited, Falkirk, Stirlingshire

Printed and bound in Great Britain by Clays Ltd, St Ives plc

MIX
Paper from
responsible sources
FSC www.fsc.org **FSC™ C007454**

FSC™ is a non-profit international organisation established to promote
the responsible management of the world's forests. Products carrying the
FSC label are independently certified to assure consumers that they come
from forests that are managed to meet the social, economic and
ecological needs of present and future generations,
and other controlled sources.

Find out more about HarperCollins and the environment at
www.harpercollins.co.uk/green

For my Ken — as always

ACKNOWLEDGEMENTS

My huge love and devotion as ever, to our much-cherished sons, Wayne and Spencer, including also Jane and my delightful two granddaughters, Chloe and Milly. Also the wider family. All my love and devotion always.

I would also like to recognise the dedicated HarperCollins team who work tirelessly behind the scenes in order to bring my stories to my readers, whose wonderful, heartfelt letters are hugely precious to me.

As always I send my best wishes and warmest thanks to all of you.

*N*one of us can foresee the future, and maybe that is a good thing, because each and every one of us is driven by whatever certain circumstances might well influence our lives, as we work towards the precious things in life, good or bad. We are often made to deal with life as it takes us forward to an unknown future, be it a sorry, empty fate or a kind and fulfilling happy life with the people we cherish.

In the beginning of my story we can picture Marie, happily playing on the seaside beaches with her beloved child, Anne.

In contrast, as time passes and the child becomes the adult, circumstances within Marie's beloved family may inevitably change and dark secrets throw a shadow over Marie's family.

How will she cope when the truth is made known?

It was a simple, heart-warming scene, long before the joy of friendship turned into badness, which was bound to touch and scar everyone in that happy holidaying mood on this particular lovely day.

1

No one could have seen what sadness might touch straight and decent people – a family so far without secrets to fear. Life was good and the friendship strong. Today, they were happy, enjoying an innocent ramble along the busy beach. Sadly the small happy band of people could never have envisaged the lies and deceit that would touch them in different ways. How will they deal with what awaits them? Only time will tell.

PROLOGUE

Blackpool, North-West England, 1935

'WAS THERE EVER a more splendid sandcastle?' said Marie, beaming on her daughter, Anne. 'Those little flags on the sand-pies round the moat make a castle fit for the King.'

'I like this one best,' said Anne, pointing to the paper Union Flag, fluttering furiously in the strong April breeze blowing straight off the Irish Sea. 'It matches my bathers.'

'That blue matches your skin all right,' laughed Derek. 'Tony and Eileen have got the right idea – going for a stroll along the Promenade. Tony said he'd look what's on at the Winter Gardens; said he'd treat us to a night on the town if we can get the landlady to babysit Anne.'

'Yes, he's a good friend,' Marie said, leaning forward in her deck chair to unscrew the lid of the

Thermos and pour a steaming cup of tea. 'They both are. Tony's such a generous sort, kind-hearted and so sweet with Eileen.' She lowered her voice. 'She told me she'd like a little one, too, but they've not been blessed yet. Still, there's time . . . Here, love, have some of this.' She passed Derek the cup and poured another for herself. 'When I've drunk this I think I'll take a stroll, too, if you'll keep an eye on Anne? This saggy old deck chair is starting to lose its appeal.'

Having drunk her tea, she climbed up the steps to the Promenade, stopped at the railings to wave to her husband and daughter, then set off in the direction of the Tower, hoping she might bump into Tony and Eileen returning from their walk.

~

Two workmen, canvas bags containing paint pots and brushes at their feet, were leaning over the railings a few yards down from where the pretty, dark-haired young mother had emerged up the steps and onto the Promenade.

One was a striking figure, a handsome towering giant of a man with a fine pair of shoulders so broad they looked as if they could carry a horse. A huge dark beard covered almost the whole of his lower face and thick neck, and his narrow dark eyes constantly danced, missing nothing.

In contrast, his colleague was slight of build, with small features, fair colouring and bright blue eyes, and when he turned to address his mate his voice had a musical Irish lilt.

'The first of this year's Blackpool Beauties,' he said, watching the young woman walk elegantly away.

'Aye, gives you something to hope for,' said the big fella, his voice betraying his Scots heritage. 'I tell you, Danny Boy, it's not just better weather I'm looking forward to. It's the sight of the ladies sunbathing on the beach that makes my hard working day worthwhile.'

'I'll drink to that, Big John,' said Danny Magee.

'There's a fair few things you'll drink to,' grinned John Ferguson. 'Comes of being Irish, I reckon.'

'So what's your excuse?' laughed Danny, slapping him on the back.

'Luckily we're going her way,' said John, nodding at the receding figure of the pretty young woman who had been on the beach. 'First pint's on me if you can find out her name. Your round if she tells me.'

'Yer've got money to lose, big man.'

~

Marie started along the Promenade in the direction of the Tower, the cold wind lifting the skirt of her coat. She glanced back and waved to Derek, and to Anne, now snuggling into a towel, filling Marie's heart with joy. What fun to be on holiday with the four people who meant most to her in the world: her darling daughter, her handsome husband, and her dearest life-long friends. The Blackpool holiday had become an annual treat by now, sometimes at Easter and some years in summer, when the weather was more predictable and the beaches were packed with workers from the industrial towns on their break. She spotted Eileen and Tony sitting on the Blue Bench, the renowned meeting place for visitors and locals alike, a refuge for lost children, a trysting place for young sweethearts and place for weary travellers to rest. Since last century the bench had occupied this prominent position facing the sea and had passed into local folklore. No one could remember now how the bench had come to be there in the first place, and today, Marie saw, it was beginning to betray its age. Although it had been repainted every year, the iron-work was showing through with rusty stains. Marie thought that so far this year the Corporation hadn't got round to repainting it and she hoped it wasn't going to be neglected and allowed to fall into disrepair.

'Hello! Eileen, Tony, how was your stroll?' Marie called as she approached.

'Marie, we guessed if we sat here for a bit you might come to find us,' grinned Tony, shuffling along to make room for Marie on the bench next to Eileen. 'Didn't think you had the staying power.'

'Oh, it's not *that* cold,' Marie protested. 'Although

Anne insisted on wearing her bathers and I left her looking bright blue.'

All three laughed and Eileen passed across a brown paper bag of humbugs. 'Here, love, help yourself. Neither my waistline nor my fillings will stand another one.'

For a while Anne sat sucking the sweet while Tony related what he'd seen of the programme at the Winter Gardens and Eileen commented on the choice.

'We'll simply have to go to hear this new Wurlitzer organ that's been installed in the Empress Ballroom,' she enthused. 'There's a new organist – Horace Finch his name is – and he's supposed to be brilliant. To me, that's the sound of the seaside.'

'The sound of the seaside to me is the howling of a gale,' said Tony, deadpan.

The women burst out laughing and by the time their chatter had receded they saw that there were two young men in overalls standing before them. From the look of the bags they were carrying their business was with the bench the friends were sitting on.

'Good afternoon,' said the short wiry man with the fair curly hair. 'And a fine afternoon it is indeed.'

'Good afternoon to you,' Tony responded. 'I'm guessing you're here to smarten up the Blue Bench?'

'Right you are,' answered the Irishman, 'but it seems downright rude to turf the ladies off when they look so comfortable. I'm guessing you're on holiday, is that so?'

'I think that's a fairly safe bet,' said Marie with a smile.

'Smart as well as pretty,' said the irrepressible workman, lifting his flat cap politely. 'Though it just happens I do have a bit of a gift – being the seventh son of a seventh daughter – and I can tell ye a thing or two about yerself ye wouldn't expect me to know.'

The other workman rolled his dark eyes in mock exasperation. 'Just listen to his blarney,' he said as Eileen dug Marie in the ribs with her elbow and they whispered and giggled.

'All right, you're on,' said Marie, 'but I'm not crossing your palm with silver.'

'No need, dear lady,' answered the little fella. 'My gift is free to a beauty like you.'

'Hark at him,' guffawed the big man, who had a Scots accent.

'All right, then, where are we from?' asked Eileen.

Fortunately for Danny, Eileen had the distinctive accent of the area, and Danny had a good ear for the various Lancashire and Cheshire voices that were so often heard among the Blackpool holidaymakers. When he'd guessed right, his answer greeted with oohs of admiration, he decided to direct the conversation back to the young mother before he got out of his depth.

'Now, give me your hand,' he said, and Marie half-reluctantly extended her left hand into his none-too-clean, rough and work-worn one with a slightly nervous smile.

He studied her hand carefully for half a minute, then said, 'Now I can see that you're married, am I right?'

Marie, Eileen and Tony caught each other's eyes and rocked with mirth.

'I think the wedding ring is a bit of a clue,' Marie spluttered, and this time all of them were laughing.

'All right . . . all right . . . Let me see . . . I see a handsome husband, a tall man with dark hair. He's a bit older than you are. Would I be right?'

'Yes!' said Marie. 'How did you know that?'

'It's the gift,' said the workman. 'And . . . what's this? A child, a little girl . . . maybe four or five years old?'

'Right again,' gasped Marie. 'Anne is four. How did you know that? You really do have a gift, don't you?'

'The gift of the gab,' said the big fella. 'Only saw you on the beach earlier, didn't we?'

Marie snatched her hand away, tutting at her own gullibility, but she couldn't be cross at the charming rogue with the twinkly blue eyes.

'You had me for a moment there,' she smiled.

'Me, too,' said Tony, impressed with the friendliness of these two likely lads. 'Do you always try your "gift" with the visitors?'

'Only the pretty ones,' the big Scot answered. 'I'm John Ferguson, by the way, known as Big John round these parts, and this is my workmate and partner in mischief, Danny Magee, known as Danny Boy.'

'Tony and Eileen Withers.'

9

'And I'm Marie Foster.'

'Your round, I think,' said Big John to Danny, inexplicably to the others.

The young workmen appeared to be in absolutely no hurry to begin their painting and settled down on the path in front of the bench where they continued to chat. They asked about the visitors' holiday plans and what they had seen so far. Eileen passed round the bag of humbugs and John and Danny moved on to entertaining anecdotes about their various tasks as handymen for Blackpool Corporation. It was clear they were often in trouble with their boss and had probably held on to their jobs partly through a combination of low cunning and charm, and partly by being rather good at what they did – when they were actually doing it.

'Right . . .' said Danny, rubbing his hands together in a show of enthusiasm for the task ahead, 'I think you and I had better be starting on this here Blue Bench, if these lovely people don't mind?'

'No, of course you must get on. And so must we,' said Eileen. 'Heavens, Marie, have you seen the time? Derek and Anne will think we've gone back to Cheshire and left them.'

'Oh, good grief!' Marie exclaimed, looking at her watch. 'I said I wouldn't be long, I'd better run ahead. Goodbye, Danny, goodbye Big John. I hope we'll see you around. We've got a couple more days here so I'll look out for you.'

'We all will,' said Tony, shaking hands with the work-men. 'See you soon.'

'I hope so,' said Danny, looking especially at Marie. 'And if not this year, then maybe next year?'

'If I'm not on the other side of the world,' said John.

'Or in the clink,' said Danny, and as he watched the three friends happily making their way down to the beach he thought that Marie really did have the prettiest laugh he'd ever heard.

PART ONE

Old Secrets

CHAPTER ONE

Blackpool, July 1970

ILEEN PRIMPED HER perm with the large-tooth comb then patted her bubbly new hairstyle in place. She put the comb on the hotel bedroom dressing table and, peering into the looking-glass, applied a slick of coral lipstick.

'Will I do?' she asked Tony.

Tony heaved himself out of the armchair and came closer to admire his wife. She'd kept her slim figure and always made an effort to look good, but over the last twenty years her face had grown sharper, the line of her mouth disappointed. Not that he was looking so dapper himself these days, what with the extra weight and the thinning hair. Once she'd told him he was love's young dream – that seemed a long time ago. He knew the lines of disappointment on Eileen's once-pretty face were there because of him.

'As proud to have you on my arm as always. You'd give any of those dolly birds on the beach a run for their money.'

'Even though I'm old enough to be their grandma?'

'To me you look as good as the day I married you.' Tony beamed at her, pleased to make her happy this evening. 'I've booked our favourite restaurant on the Promenade for seven o'clock.'

'Oh, Tony, you are spoiling me. We've had such a lovely holiday that I shan't want to go home.'

'Me neither, love.' For a moment he looked stricken, an expression on his face that Eileen had seen a few times over the last few days.

'Tony, you are all right, aren't you?' she asked.

Tony was looking distinctly uncomfortable now. 'It's just that . . . well . . . I've had a letter.'

'Bad news? It's nothing to do with Beth or her brother, is it? I've never liked that fella she's married to and it wouldn't surprise me if he doesn't treat her right. I know she's only a friend and I should mind my own business, but she's such a lovely girl and I've grown that fond of her I feel that she *is* my business, if you know what I mean?'

'No, it's nothing to do with Beth or Ronnie.'

'Then what? Come on, Tony, I'm dying of suspense.'

'If you'd just let me say—'

'*What?*'

'Marie. It's Marie who's written to me. She's asked to see us and she's coming here.'

'What? Now? Marie's coming out to dinner with us?'

'Course not, love. No, she wrote last week asking to meet us. Suggested tomorrow, as it happens. She knows we're here for our annual holiday and she . . . she just thought that after all the happy times we had together it would be a nice place to meet up – sort of neutral ground.'

'Well she knows she'd never be welcome at our home again, not after what she did. I really don't want to set eyes on her again. But why follow us here? The cheek of the woman writing to you—'

Tony reached out and took Eileen's hand as her voice became shrill and her face darkened with anger. 'Listen, love, it was my fault as much as hers – possibly more. You've forgiven me –' forgiven but not forgotten, he might have added – 'and maybe she wants to try to put things right, to be friends again. And I suppose over the years we had so many lively, lovely holidays up in Blackpool she felt it would be easier here than home? Marie's not getting any younger either; perhaps she's the one who's not well. I think we should meet her and hear her out.'

'Oh, do you indeed!'

Eileen turned away and was silent for so long that Tony looked at his watch, thinking of the restaurant reservation. He silently berated himself for tackling the subject of Marie and her letter only now. He'd thought the prospect of an evening out would have offset the news he had to break to Eileen. Of course, this wasn't the first time he'd totally misjudged the situation, he reflected ruefully.

When Eileen turned back Tony was not entirely comforted by the expression on her face, though her words could be interpreted as conciliatory.

'All right, we'll see her. Let's hear what she has to say after all this time.'

'Thank you, love. That's very generous of you. She said she'd meet us late morning, at the Blue Bench. But actually, she said she'd be staying here tonight.'

'Good grief, it gets worse! Why on earth . . .?'

'I don't know, Eileen. Maybe she didn't want to miss us if I'd said no to the meeting or if we didn't show.'

'Sounds a bit desperate to me.'

'Aye, well, I think you're right there, love, but let's just see what she has to say, eh?'

Eileen sighed heavily. 'All right, Tony. Whatever you want.'

'Good girl.' He kissed her cheek, glanced again at his watch and started to gather his loose change into his pocket. 'Time we were off. We might be a few minutes late, even.'

'You go down, Tony, and perhaps you'd better phone the restaurant from the foyer to say we're running late while I check I've got what I need in my handbag.'

As soon as Tony had closed the door behind him

Eileen grabbed a sheet of the hotel stationery and quickly wrote a few words. Then she took one of the smart blue envelopes and addressed it to 'Mrs Marie Foster'. If she were quick she'd be able to leave it at Reception while Tony was busy telephoning.

CHAPTER TWO

O N WHAT PROMISED to be a glorious summer's day, two workmen strode purposely back along Central Pier, the echoing thud of their heavy work-boots resounding a soulful rhythm against the ancient, wooden boards, their shoulders hefting their canvas tool bags.

On this gloriously warm morning the first priority was a true labour of love; the task being the ongoing restoration of the famous Blue Bench, one of the oldest and much-loved landmarks along the entire coast.

Painstakingly painted year after year in a shade as blue as the skies above, the old bench was instantly recognised and cherished by those who had often found comfort and peace when seeking to rest awhile.

For over eighty years, as far as the records implied, the small, upright bench had proudly stood in the same place, from where it offered much-needed refuge for both locals and the many hordes of holidaymakers who arrived at the resort, year after year. Danny shook his head in admiration. It's a great pity but we may never find out where she came from, he thought to himself. I'd love to know who put her there, standing forever strong against whatever the weather throws at her. Sometimes feel a bit sorry for the old thing, when the holidaymakers have gone, the Blue Bench could look sad and lonely, her paint would start to crack and peel and her arms would creak and rust. That bench must have witnessed many unforgettable sights, silently keeping the secrets of many sad souls who used her as refuge. He hoped she would stand there facing the elements long after he and John were departed, he thought, with a gentle smile lighting up his eyes.

'Hey, Danny Boy!' John Ferguson called out to his colleague, who had hurried ahead of him. 'Slow down, man! There's no need to rush about to start another hard day's work? Especially in this damned heat!' He gave a low, agonising groan. 'If there was any justice, the two of us would be flat out on the beach right now, sunning ourselves!'

'Fat chance o' that, me old mate!' Danny kept up his pace. 'We're not here to lie on the beach. Like it or not, you and I, Big John, are just two working men, bought and paid for. We've looked at those handrails, now we'd better see what else is to do. And I, for one, think the pair of us should be grateful to be still earning a wage at our time o' life!'

Having spoken his piece, Danny pressed on along the pier, with Big John ranting on as he followed. 'Slow down! Why the big rush? I dare say that useless bench will outlive us, you see if I'm not right!' Once John climbed onto his soapbox, there was no shutting him up. 'I mean it, Danny Boy! It's time we took it a bit easier. Like I said, we're at a certain age now. We're no longer two young men just larking about. We've grown old, and that's the truth of it!'

Their attention was duly diverted to watch some children scampering over the wide stone steps leading to the sea front and to the ice cream shop. 'It's a wonder the little devils don't get seriously hurt . . . fighting and shoving like that.' Shaking his head, John looked away and moved on.

Danny took a moment to watch the children. 'It's like a Christmas sale at the Co-op!' he chuckled. 'Hordes of frantic women knocking seven bells out of each other, fighting like cat and dog in order to reach the bargains before anyone else. It's downright mayhem, so it is!'

John laughed, 'Is that so? And how would you know that, eh? Unless you were there in the queues yourself?'

Grabbing Danny's shoulder, he pushed him forward. 'Stop your idling now, and employ your mind to something useful. Come on, eyes front, before the boss catches us wasting precious time.'

Having said his piece he increased his pace and

strode steadily onward. Danny measured his step so as to walk alongside the big man, who appeared to have slipped into a silent world of his own. But Danny continued to chatter along.

'We've had some good years haven't we? Lived for the moment, with our boozing til dawn, backing the horses good and bad, mostly losing our shirt into the bargain! Enjoying ourselves come what may, never giving a thought to the consequences.'

Their wayward antics over the years had now begun to hit them hard as age caught up with them, but each man always looked at the bright side, no matter the woe or the weather.

John nudged his pal, 'We were good at the game though and still are. When we're not worn and knack-ered from a hard day's work, that is.'

That's what Danny Boy could do to him, always put a smile on his face. The twinkle in his eye grew bright as his thoughts wandered back to good times.

Ever practical, John remained a straight-talking fellow. In the main a hard-working man, he liked to work and earn a wage, and he enjoyed the treats that money could buy. Now in his sixties, he was thankful to be healthy and able, although he deeply regretted the years passing by so quickly. A man could still dream his dreams, but he did so now with a heavy heart.

He was as huge and as handsome as he'd been in his prime and his heavy-booted feet still made the walkways tremble as he thumped along.

A FAMILY SECRET

Danny Magee and John Ferguson had been close friends and workmates for more years than either of them cared to remember. By now, they were more like brothers than workmates. Each man had earned the respect of the other, having been tried and tested through good times and bad. They rarely rowed, but when they did – usually about work and women – it was fast and furious, then soon forgotten. In some ways theirs was an unlikely alliance, each man having strongly held views and differing opinions on many subjects, though they shared a powerful passion for the after-work leisure, especially football. If George Best was their hero, Stanley Matthews had been their god. More often than not these days, this leisure time would find them growing increasingly rowdy and comical as they relayed stories of their heyday, while they supped their pints of beer, played their shots at the billiard table, and still made time to ogle the good-looking women.

Danny Boy, grown slighter and shorter with the years, his hair now thinning, turned back to address his mate in the musical, Irish lilt he'd retained. 'John, me old friend, will ye move yerself! Don't forget, we planned to sneak away early tonight and there's work to be done.'

'D'you think I don't know that?' Big John spat on the ground. 'You don't need to tell me how it is and I know we should be grateful to have work to go to. I understand that.'

'Good. And let's not forget Blackpool in summer does have its compensations,' Danny gently reminded him. He gave a wide grin as he stole a peep over the railings and down to the beach. 'Hey!' He pointed excitedly. 'Take a look at that little beauty stretched out. There, the one against the wall on the pink towel!' He made a whooping sound. 'It's a crying shame we're not down there, taking it easy and chatting up these dolly birds.'

John treated himself to a peek at the blonde and gave a cheeky wink. 'Let's not forget that we're a bit long in the tooth for chasing the young'uns. It might improve our chances if we had money to throw about, but neither of us has ever been fortunate in that respect.'

'That's very true, more's the pity,' Danny sighed. 'The sad truth is we're meant to work till we drop.' There was real regret in his voice as thoughts of various women who had passed through his life, and one in particular, crowded his mind.

As his mood lowered, he forged ahead, calling back to his mate, 'Move yourself, will you? And don't think I can't see you sneaking another glance at the half-clad women down there. We're agreed we both need this job, at least for a few more years. So let's get on with it . . .'

John tried to raise the mood with some banter. 'As for you, Danny Boy, you try to keep your eyes ahead, too. Forget the beautiful women, 'cos they're not looking at you, are they?' He gave a snigger. 'While they would happily spend a night with a fine man like myself, I'm not altogether sure they would really appreciate a crinkly-faced little squirt like you.'

Danny took the harmless dig in the spirit in which it was given. 'I'll have you know there's a heap o' life in this old dog yet. I'm nowhere near ready for the knacker's yard.'

John gave a mischievous wink. 'Me neither. And though I say it myself, there is still a good tune left in this old fiddle.' Giggling like two naughty schoolboys, they each recalled the wild and naughty antics in a misspent youth, when their manly prowess and lust for the girls was at full throttle. Life had been theirs for living to the full, and pretty girls had flocked round them like bees to a honey-pot.

Eventually the big man broke the mood with a great sigh. 'Well, Danny Boy, we really did have some great times back in the day, didn't we, eh? How desperately I wish we were young and virile again!'

Danny gave a sorry little snort. 'You mean when we had more hair on our heads, and naughty tattoos proudly across our chests and a woman on each arm?' He sighed at the memories. 'Now the girls have moved on, and the tattoos are sagging.' His voice dropped as he added sombrely, 'Just like everything else if you know what I mean?'

'Oh, but I do.' John lapsed into silence. 'I really am worried about the future,' he admitted eventually.

'How could we have been so stupid? We should have made plans for our old age. We've been enjoying ourselves too much, that's why!'

'We've only ourselves to blame. We've never earned much but what we had we spent. Still, what's done is done and we can't ever turn the clock back. It's no use grumbling about it! Instead, we should be thanking our lucky stars that we've been able to enjoy life and still be as healthy as we are. Look on the bright side, we've got good jobs and a regular wage. And though we've left it a bit late we are now, at last, starting to think about the future.'

'Not every working man is as fortunate as us. Look at poor Len Waterman. He's a year or two younger than us, but he's so crippled with arthritis he can hardly get along. Fate can be so cruel. If he hadn't fallen off that roof, he might have been working alongside us even yet. But he seems to get worse as the days pass. More's the pity.'

'But by God, don't the years just fly by. Even when we were in our forties we had enough knowledge to start our own business. We should have taken the bull by the horns back then,' John said quietly. 'You're right, Danny Boy. We'll just have to concentrate on what we've actually achieved and not dwell on what we've lost. Who knows, we might yet give another thought to the idea of setting up in our own business? We can make a success of it if that's what we aim for. '

Both men felt uplifted to have discussed most of the matters that had been weighing heavily on their minds. They squared their shoulders and put a spring in their step as they continued along the Promenade, ready and raring to set about the day's workload.

Taking a grubby old handkerchief from his trouser pocket, John slapped it across his nose and blew hard. 'Dammit, I reckon I've got a cold coming on.' He moaned under his breath, before blowing his nose again. 'Look there! Do you see that tired old woman across the way? Poor old bugger, she's been lumbered with that huge bag . . . no doubt filled to the brim with kids' stuff, all dumped on her by her family. Really struggling she is.'

Danny stole a glance at the woman. 'Bless her old heart. I'm sorely tempted to go and help her. She looks well and truly done in, so she does.'

John produced from his overalls pocket a piece of paper on which was scrawled a list of tasks for the week, some already crossed off. 'Come on, matey! We'd best crack on. No time for rescuing damsels in distress, and look her family are catching her now. I wouldn't mind betting she's got a little dram o'whisky hidden inside that bag. The crafty old devil.' He gave a deep-throated chuckle, before waving the list under Danny's nose. 'I expect you'll want to start on her first?' He gestured in the direction of the Blue Bench. 'She's looking a bit weathered of late, don't you think?' John strode on, clutching his list and grumbling as he went to his own tasks, leaving the bench to Danny.

He paused to admire her, 'She's like an old friend,' he murmured, 'this place would never be the same without her. And you're right . . . she does seem to be looking a bit worse for wear, but you can't blame the old girl for looking worn out. Not when she's facing the elements twenty-four hours a day, year in year out.' He chuckled loudly, 'In some ways, she's a bit like us, don't you think? Forging onwards, whatever the weather throws at us, and just like her, we've learned to stand strong against the elements. I'd love to know what her story is.'

When Danny looked up at the Blue Bench, his ready smile faltered and his heart seemed to flip over. It couldn't be . . . Surely not! The lovely Marie Foster sitting on the bench – alone.

CHAPTER THREE

MARIE HAD ARRIVED at the Blue Bench very early this morning. After she'd received Eileen's note she decided to skip breakfast at the hotel in case she bumped into Eileen and Tony in the dining room. Instead, she'd bought a cup of tea at a seafront stall and would have enjoyed the stroll along the Promenade had it not been for her nervousness.

Why had she put off suggesting this meeting all these years? The longer she'd left it, the harder it had become to make this move. Even now she was halfway to thinking she'd just scarper and forget all about it, especially as Eileen's note didn't have what you might call a friendly tone.

~

Tony has agreed to meet you so I suppose I had better come along, too. I don't know what

your game is, Marie, but don't you dare ever,
ever tell him our secret.

~

Well, that left no room for doubt.

And just what was her 'game', Marie asked herself
as she sat down on the Blue Bench, clutching her tea
tightly. What on earth had possessed her to come to
Blackpool by herself, hoping to be reconciled with
Eileen and Tony and to share with them an important
part of her life? Her conscience had troubled her for
years and she wanted to be free of that burden now,
while she was still physically and mentally able. But
what had seemed like a sound idea at home – to meet
Eileen and Tony in Blackpool while they were relaxed
on their holiday, a place they had shared so much
laughter, so many good memories – now seemed
fraught with potential disaster. Should she just go now
– get up and leave and pretend to herself she'd never
sought this meeting? Her life-long demon was even
now sitting on her shoulder, whispering in her ear
that this whole stupid plan was doomed from the start.

But that demon had always led her by the nose,
and now, twenty years after Derek's death, she owed
it to her family to shrug it off and be a better person.

Derek – every day it was hard to believe he'd been
gone for so many years. Dead of a heart attack and
only in his forties. So Marie had lived on without

him, though she still had Anne, and her lovely husband, Dave . . . and of course Cathy, that dear girl. Cathy, the light of their lives, an unlooked-for joy, was now on the brink of womanhood, and Marie owed it to her – to all of them – to reveal the truth at last. What if she herself were to die suddenly, as Derek had done, and never tell what it was her duty – *her* duty, not Anne or Dave's – to tell? How would Cathy think of her then?

Marie could still picture Eileen's face that night, they'd been sitting at the same kitchen table they'd sat and talked over for years. When it became clear to Marie that Eileen had discovered their one night together, she felt she had to confess all. But in that moment, fearful that Eileen and Tony might want to claim her baby as their own, she told the most awful, shameful lie. It had been a wicked thing to say and she'd regretted it every moment.

And now, she felt she needed to go back to the beginning, where it all started. She looked out over the Promenade to where the gentle waves washed the beach. Already there were families set up on the sand, colourful towels laid out, deck chairs in clusters, brightly striped windbreaks – more for privacy than to keep any breeze at bay on this glorious morning – and, as always in summer, the piping voices of excited children.

Marie was immediately transported back to the long-ago holidays here with Derek and Anne, such happy holidays when Tony and Eileen had been dear friends. Then there had been the war, of course, when seaside holidays were not possible, and then afterwards . . . after Derek had died . . . everything had changed. There had been other trips, but more often to Southport rather than Blackpool. Marie had not wanted to risk bumping into Tony and Eileen. Little Cathy had loved those holidays. Three generations playing on the beach together – that's what anyone watching the little family would have seen.

Could she live the lie any longer? It wasn't hurting anyone, was it, it just weighed heavier on her shoulders every year. Wise women say secrets would out, and Marie knew she must try hard to gather her courage, to do what in her heart she knew was right, before it was too late.

A lyrical voice she vaguely knew came at her from a few yards down the Promenade.

'And a beautiful day it is, too, for a picnic on the Blue Bench.'

Marie looked to her left and there . . . Good heavens, after all this time! The man with the Irish lilt was none other than Danny Magee.

'Danny! It really is you! What a marvellous surprise.' And indeed his appearance, as she once again deliberated, was very welcome. She stood and found herself hugging him with delight.

'Marie, ye're a sight for sore eyes on this fine morning. I'd quite given up on ever seeing my best girl again. It's been some good years since ye last graced these parts with yer beauty. And ye don't look a day older than when we last met.'

Still the same old Danny, a charmer with a touch of the blarney.

Marie laughed and stood back to survey him properly. He was so recognisably the same and yet, of course, older – thinner, greyer . . . balder, with deeper laughter lines around those blue, blue eyes. Yes, he looked worn, like a man who had lived.

'You're looking good yourself,' she said, and realised that there was at least some element of truth in that. 'It's so lovely to see you.'

'Derek and Anne not with ye?' he asked.

Marie gathered herself, as she had done for the last twenty years whenever anyone had asked about Derek.

'Let's sit down – if you've got a minute? – and I'll tell you all my news,' she said, summoning a smile and patting the bench beside her as she resumed her seat.

~

Well, it was hardly 'all her news', Marie reflected as she watched Danny walk away. She'd given him a much-edited version of the last twenty years, an account that actually held one very important lie.

She waved and smiled as he turned back and blew

her a kiss. Off to his work, he'd said, and his main-tenance of the Blue Bench could wait awhile as she was sitting on it. Such a kind man, though she knew he no doubt flirted with all the female visitors. It was a wonder he got any work done at all.

Danny, too, was thinking about the meeting. He'd felt what was almost a surge of joy when he'd clapped eyes on Marie, sitting there all alone, and though his heart had gone out to her as she related the sad event of her widowhood, he couldn't help reflecting – and may the Good Lord forgive him – that now she was a free woman. Of course, she lived in Cheshire, but he'd really like to see her again if it were possible.

You're a silly old fool, so ye are, he chastised himself. If she only knew what ye were thinking no doubt she would run a mile in the opposite direction. And how is anything to come of ye wishing to know the darlin' woman better anyway?

Still, he was ever the optimist, as evidenced by his love of a bet on the horses, and stranger things had happened than two lonely people getting together in their later years.

~

Danny had not been long gone about his business when Eileen and Tony appeared arm in arm. Marie recognised them at once – she had occasionally seen

36

them around town at home – but she particularly noticed now how plump Tony had grown, his once-handsome face jowly and sagging, and how formidable Eileen looked despite the fashionable brightly coloured dress and curly hairdo.

'Hello, Marie,' said Eileen frostily.

'Eileen . . . Tony.' Marie stood and half went to hug them like in the old days, then thought better of it and retreated.

'Shall we sit?' said Tony with an apologetic smile at Marie, and Eileen immediately seated herself in the middle of the bench so that she would be between Tony and Marie.

There was an uncomfortable silence and Marie knew – just *knew* with all her heart – that this meeting had been a bad idea. How could she have thought to say what she had so foolishly planned? And out here, in the open air, when anyone passing would see them, might even hear? The air around them seemed crowded with happy memories of long-ago meetings at the Blue Bench, when fish and chips wrapped in newspaper were passed between them, or a bag of humbugs shared as jokes were told and plans for the following day made.

Don't do it! whispered the demon on her shoulder, and this time her common sense was in agreement: better to test the water first. She took a deep breath and began.

'I'm in Blackpool for a night or two and found

myself staying in the same hotel as you. It seemed silly not to say hello.'

Tony smiled. 'It's good to see you again, Marie.'

Eileen said nothing.

Marie swallowed nervously. Oh Lord, this was not going well.

'So I just thought . . .'

'That you'd say hello. Yes, you said,' said Eileen quietly.

'. . . that whatever happened between us, we could maybe put it behind us. That we might . . . we might . . .'

'Forget about it?' asked Eileen, with a raised eyebrow.

'Yes . . . no! Oh, please, I just hoped—'

'Believe me, Marie, I shall never, ever forget.' Eileen rose to her feet, turning her stiff back on Marie. 'Come on, Tony, let's go and find somewhere nice for lunch.' And without another word she took his arm and propelled him away, Tony shooting Marie an apologetic glance over his shoulder.

Marie watched them go, feeling very small and very alone. Tears ran down her face. Either she'd gone about that all wrong or – just possibly – it was the worst idea she'd ever had. She owed it to her family to see this through but, with such a reception at the outset, what on earth was she going to do now?

～

Danny had caught up with John, who wasn't very far along the railings.

'I'm slowing down, old boy!'

Danny had to agree, 'Okay, so we're just a bit slower and we make the occasional mistake, but who doesn't?'

John though, remained adamant. 'I know what you're saying, and you're right. But I still worry that no one else would be keen to take us on, because of our age. And even if they did take us on, I very much doubt that we would be offered the same money that we get now.'

Danny had to admit that yes, it was possible they might lose a sizeable part of their income. 'I under-stand what you're saying. But, there's always a chance they would match what we've been earning, especially if we were to show them how good and reliable we are. Like I said, look on the bright side.'

Another unsettling thought crept into John's worrying thoughts. 'If our current boss decided not to give us the recommendation we deserve, we might never find anyone to employ us. Or, if we did find work, what if the new boss was a nasty piece of work? I don't know if I could put up with that, I'm a bit stuck on my ways now. All right, our boss can be a bit mouthy and overbearing at times, but he's a decent enough sort so long as we get the work done.'

'Oh, he's all right.' Danny was willing to forgive. 'The thing is, we're used to his ways. I wouldn't want to work under a tyrant, whatever the wages might be.'

He bristled, 'Like as not, I'd probably lose my temper and give him a hiding he wouldn't forget.'

John couldn't help but laugh out loud. 'So! You might give him a hiding, eh? You little runt!'

'Hmph!' Moving closer, Danny bunched his fists, pretending to prepare for a fight. 'Don't mess with me!' He had an impish gleam in his eyes. 'Don't make the mistake of thinking that small is weak, and old is over, because I'll have you know – I'm like a raging tiger when I get going—'

'Is that so? Well, you can get going now, because I just heard someone call out, and it sounded much like the bossman!' He gave Danny a playful shove that sent him nearer to the tool-shed. 'If he asks where we've been, tell him we had to check the bench, because some old woman told us it was a bit wobbly and we don't want the old dear getting hurt, do we now?'

'Hey! You two! What the hell are you playing at?'

Emerging from behind the big tool-shed, the man frantically waved his arms. Tall, balding and thin as a lamppost, George Mason possessed a surprisingly thick and gravelly voice. 'What's wrong with you two? You never can seem to get here on time. Where've you been?'

Coming to a halt, he leaned on the shed wall, while continuing to shake his fist, and threaten the two men at the top of his voice, 'Where the devil have you been? There's a long list o'work to get through, and as far as I can see you haven't even started it yet?'

Hurrying into the shed, the two of them were met with yet another torrent of abuse as the boss turned on them as though they were teenagers. 'YOU SHOULD HAVE CLOCKED IN, OVER HALF AN HOUR BACK. I'VE A DAMNED GOOD MIND TO DOCK YOU AN HOUR'S PAY FROM YOUR WAGES AT THE END OF THE WEEK.'

Stepping forward, John made an effort to smooth matters. 'We're sorry, boss, but it took us a few extra minutes to check the railings, and we reckon there are six dodgy uprights that need replacing, two more than were down on the list. Oh and we also took a few minutes to check the Blue Bench . . . we had a complaint you see. A woman approached us in a bit of a state. She complained that when she sat down, she felt the bench kind of shudder . . . She actually said one of the legs felt a bit wobbly. So of course, we realised that you would want us to check it out . . . which we did.'

'I should think so, being as you get paid good money for keeping everything ship-shape and suit-able!' Clearing his throat the boss asserted his authority. 'Right then! Time's a wasting, so you'd best get cracking. I know I can trust you to make a good job of it. Go on with you.'

As the boss hurried away, Danny commented with a chuckle, 'Well, well! I told you, didn't I? We're too damned good at what we do, and he knows it! He also knows that if he was ever to let us go, he would never find anyone else as hard-working or downright thorough.'

Smiling smugly he finished with a cheeky grin, 'Men like us are few and far between.' By the time Danny had finished praising their skills and unique dedication to duty, each man was lifted by his own worth.

Danny's thoughts went back to the meeting on the Blue Bench earlier. He held the image of Marie in his mind's eye, and it wasn't long before he was softly murmuring to himself, 'I had a real feeling that there was something going on there, she always seemed such a happy woman all those years ago, but now the warmth in her eyes has faded a little. But then haven't we all faded a little over the years.' Reliving the time he'd spent in her company, the niggling suspicion lingered, as he tried to make sense of it all. Danny realised the curious sense of longing for the past.

It was a sorry truth but over these past years he had been lacking a pretty woman in his arms, and his lonely heart felt incredibly empty. The thought of Marie in his life made his heart skip just a beat. 'You're a silly old fool, so ye are. Stranger things have happened than two lonely people getting together in their later years . . . If she knew what you were thinking she'd laugh at you,' he chastised himself. Being a practical man he truly believed nothing could come of his little dream to get to know Marie better again, nevertheless he enjoyed thinking of her.

'Now John, you'll never guess who I met . . .'

CHAPTER FOUR

THE HOLIDAY WAS over, and it was time to say goodbye before the taxi arrived to take Marie to the railway station.

Eileen was sorry to be leaving, yet also relieved to be going home after Marie had turned up.

Sitting in the hotel foyer, her bags around her feet while Tony went to fetch the heavy cases, Eileen wondered again about Marie's motive in following them here. Marie was also in the tiny reception, her handbag and small suitcase also at her feet, waiting for her taxi.

In this most uncomfortable moment before they all went their separate ways, Eileen wondered whether to confront Marie now . . . before she climbed into the cab and was gone.

With regards to the hotel, it was clear Marie had guessed where they might be staying and had booked herself in too. Years ago, the friends had sometimes stayed in this same hotel together, but that was when the three of them were the best of friends, before Marie and Tony had broken Eileen's trust, and destroyed the close and cherished friendship between the two women who had been as close as sisters some twenty years ago.

What had happened was a very hard blow for Eileen to bear. She had found it in her heart to forgive Tony for the liaison and maybe she would have forgiven her friend, if only Marie had not confessed to something that Eileen could never accept. After that, forgiveness of Marie was something that Eileen could never undertake. It was quite simply out of the question.

So, why was Marie here now – after all this time? What devious game was she playing?

Since the meeting at the Blue Bench the previous morning, Eileen had forced herself to respond as normally as possible in the hotel to Marie, both for Tony's sake and because she didn't want to spoil her own holiday. But since Marie had confessed her shocking secret, some weeks after her affair with Tony, Eileen had found it difficult even to think of Marie.

Eileen could remember that day as vividly as if it was yesterday. Marie had gone to visit her – she had been out of her mind with guilt and worry. She confessed she'd become pregnant by Tony and, for all their sakes, she had taken the drastic and criminal decision to bring an end to the entire, unfortunate matter.

Eileen had been utterly distraught and to this day had avoided ever seeing Marie again. Now Marie was back in their lives, bringing the past back like a ghost. What exactly did she want? The unanswered questions haunted Eileen. The worry she'd kept the secret from her own husband all these years troubled her.

It was true that there was a time when Eileen would have welcomed Marie with open arms; but not now. Not after what she had done.

Over the past two days, Eileen had actually come to wonder whether Marie was here for one purpose only: to entice Tony into her arms for a second time! But, no, she'd hardly have written asking to meet them both if that were the case. Nor would she try to seduce Tony while he was on holiday with his wife. The only way to get at the truth, Eileen decided, was to ask Marie directly. But, before she could put her question, Marie turned to her. 'Eileen, I want to ask you something.' She paused to take a nervous breath before going on. 'Promise you won't get upset, because I honestly don't want to cause any trouble.'

'Oh, really?' Eileen looked her in the eye. 'Don't you think that's a bit late after what you did?'

'I just want to say how sorry I am, about what happened between me and, well, you know what I'm saying, don't you?' Under Eileen's hard and disapproving stare, Marie was losing her nerve again.

'Well, come on then!' Eileen knew exactly what Marie was trying to say. 'Let's get it over with. You mean you're sorry for having a fling with my husband. But you already told me that long ago, and I don't want to hear it again. Tony was a fool, a man flattered by your attentions. He had no love for you. Yes, he did a foolish, and disgraceful thing, but it was you who threw yourself at him, didn't you? You saw how much he loved me, and you wanted him all for yourself.'

Leaning closer to Marie, she lowered her voice to a whisper. 'It took me a long time, but I forgave him because he was a man swayed by a woman who knew what she wanted and used her womanly wiles to get it . . . whatever the damage it might cause to my marriage!'

Shaking her head, she moved forward and continued in a whisper, 'Tony was snared by you. You saw him, and you took him, and you didn't give a damn whether my marriage or our friendship was torn apart or not!'

When Marie tried to speak, Eileen firmly shook her head. 'I don't want to hear your excuses. It took a while but I finally believed him when he insisted that he was sorry. That he was ashamed and needed my forgiveness.'

When Marie lowered her gaze, Eileen hissed in her ear, 'Tony will be back any minute with the rest of our luggage, and I don't want him to hear what we're talking about. He is a good man. All right, he did a bad thing, he made one mistake, but you went for him, you set your cap at him, and you meant to take him away from me. Be honest . . . wasn't that the case?'

'No! Believe me, Eileen, I never intended to take him away from you. It was an emotional moment, a mad moment of loneliness. My Derek had died just two months before and I was a mess. I needed to talk to you. It was you I came to see, Eileen – my one and only friend – and I so needed you. But you weren't there, and Tony was, and I was distraught.'

Recalling the occasion with embarrassment and guilt, she fought back the tears. 'I'm so sorry . . . I truly am. Please, Eileen . . . please believe me, it was a moment of grief and emotion . . . I was in a bad place. Oh, Eileen! If I could turn the clock back, I would, I swear!

'But I needed help, and Tony comforted me, and yes, I held onto him. It was a fleeting, crazy thing we did, but at the end of the day it meant nothing. It was wrong, it was never meant to happen.' When she reached out to take Eileen's hand, Eileen moved it away.

Looking Marie in the eye, she told her firmly, 'Tony is my world. I know how a woman can seduce a man if she wants him badly enough. I forgave Tony, eventually, but we were miles apart for a long time. We nearly broke up. For months I agonised about you and Tony, but because I love him I was desperate to put it all behind us which we have now.' In a low, trembling voice, she admitted, 'I honestly did try to forgive you too, but in the end I couldn't do it because of what you confessed to me about the baby and how you dealt with it . . . I never imagined you could ever do that!'

After a moment, her voice shaking with emotion, she went on softly, 'Even though it was a long time ago . . . it still shocks me! I really did think about whether we could mend bridges on this holiday, but your confession kept coming back to haunt me – about the pregnancy and the decision to end your unborn child's life. How could you do it, Marie? How could you? It was Tony's child too! You at least should have talked it through with him. Why didn't you come to me before you did it? Why didn't you tell me what you were planning to do? We were friends.'

'I wanted to tell you, but I was so afraid, so hopelessly mixed up. I was going out of my mind, Eileen. It was never meant to happen. I was a woman over forty. I had lost my Derek just months before. One minute he was there – my haven – and then he was gone, and I was hopelessly lost. My whole life was suddenly turned upside down. I couldn't sleep, I couldn't work. I got behind with the mortgage. I was ashamed to tell my daughter. And then I could not even afford to keep the house.'

All the bad memories came rushing back. 'I tried and struggled, and there was nowhere to turn. And then, not realising I was pregnant, but knowing I was finding things increasingly difficult, my daughter and son-in-law offered to take me in to live with them. So, I sold my cottage, and did that. I have never regretted it, but I missed my Derek so much! Life seemed unbearably lonely, but I counted myself fortunate in having a loving family about me, and I was hugely grateful for that.'

Choking back a sob, she went on, 'Then I discovered I was pregnant. I was afraid and ashamed. It was an impossible situation, but I had to deal with it in the only way I could. My head was bursting. I felt suicidal. I had to make a decision, Eileen, and it had to be settled quickly. I simply had no choice but to do what I did.' She fell silent, because that was as far as she dared go with that particular subject.

Eileen hissed, 'I do not want Tony to know the truth about the pregnancy, and what you did. Do you understand?' She continued quietly, 'It's far too late for regrets. And as we're being honest with each other there is something you need to be made aware of.' She leaned closer to Marie. 'After we leave here, I never want to see you again. Do you understand?'

Sad to the heart, Marie nodded.

Eileen stole a glance towards the lift, but Tony had not yet reappeared. 'What I am telling you now, Marie, must never be repeated. Not to anyone. Will you promise?'

Marie nodded. 'Yes . . . I promise.'

Eileen leaned closer to Marie. 'I have never told anyone this, but I need you to know so maybe you can fully understand my pain and disgust at what you did.'

Taking a deep breath, she addressed Marie in the softest whisper. 'I knew Tony was bitterly disappointed that we were never blessed with children. I felt I'd let him down, but as the years rolled on he seems finally to have got over his disappointment at not being a father, but it was always secretly his dearest wish.'

Her voice wavered as she went on and she forced a smile. 'The truth is, I'm used to it. I like my life as it is now, just the two of us. So, that is why I never want Tony to know you were left with his child and you did away with it. Always remember, Marie, that it was your wickedness, not mine! I can't even begin to imagine what pain it would cause him! Do you understand what I'm saying?'

'I understand.' She knew she'd robbed him of a different kind of future. 'And I promise he will never know it from me. Not ever!'

Marie had come here to unburden herself of her deepest secret and try to do the right thing but in just two days she had come to realise that her life – and that of her family – was a far more tangled web than she'd naively thought.

'He won't know from me,' Marie repeated. How quickly she had changed her mind. 'You have my absolute word he will never know from me. I'm sorry. I really wish I had never confided in you,' she added.

She felt both cursed and blessed. And now she made a silent prayer that, in the end, all would be right without pain or hardship to the people she respected and loved.

A taxi was seen drawing up to the kerb and now the driver was in the hotel foyer calling, 'Taxi to the station for Marie Foster.'

Marie waved her hand. 'That's me! Thank you . . . I'll just be a minute.'

In a low whisper, Marie put a tearful question to her former friend. 'Eileen, please. Will there ever be the smallest chance, that one day you will forgive me? For what it's worth, I'm truly sorry,' she promised earnestly, 'and if there was any way I could turn back the clock I would do it in a heartbeat.'

When Eileen's silence was the only reply, Marie could not blame her old friend. However, even now, in her deepest heart, Marie was convinced that although people, including herself, had been hurt, she had done the best she could in a bad situation.

'Don't hate me, Eileen . . . please?' she asked with a shaky smile.

'I can't help how I feel, Marie, but before we part I need to emphasise what I said in the note I left for you the other night. I could never bring myself to tell Tony that you aborted his child. What purpose would it have served when the deed was already done? What difference would it have made to tell him then? None whatsoever! So I made a decision that I would never tell him. I did not want him to know then, and I do not want him to learn of it now. Not ever. Do you understand? Tony must never know about the child he might have had! You did him a huge wrong, but it's no use raking over old coals now. Go home to your family, Marie! As for me, I am deeply grateful that I have the love of my husband to keep me warm and safe, whereas you, Marie – who do you confide in? I pity you because you have no one to listen and comfort you in the middle of the night when you wake troubled over what you did. I might have listened at the time if only you had come to me. Maybe we two might have come up with some kind of plan that would have helped everyone. But you didn't let me in until it was too late, and the child was no more. And now I don't want anything else to do with you.'

'I understand,' Marie replied in the smallest whisper. 'I am sad to have lost your friendship, Eileen. Ever since we were children, we were always together like sisters, and now I fear I may never see or hear from you ever again.'

Eileen made no reply. 'Excuse me, do you need a taxi or not?' The driver was growing irritable.

'I'm sorry, I'm just coming.' Marie waved a hand.

'Oh . . . take your time why don't you? I'm sure I don't mind either way,' the driver called back. 'The meter ticks on, whether I'm driving or waiting.'

Another question had niggled at Eileen over these

past few days. 'How did you track us down here? How did you find out when Tony and I would be in Blackpool, and at this hotel? And even the number of days we were booked in for?'

'I know you have always loved this resort, and I desperately needed to talk with you to try and mend bridges between us. I had an idea you might have booked into the hotel we stayed at with you before around this time of year. So I phoned them, and my hunch was right. Then I wrote to Tony and asked to meet up.' She gave a nervous glance to the waiting taxi driver. 'I'm sorry, Eileen, but I really must go or I'll miss my train, and my daughter will be waiting for me at the other end.'

In the face of Eileen's hostility, she gathered her bags and fled without waiting to say goodbye to Tony. Having waited until Marie was hurrying out of the hotel and into her taxi, Tony then made his way down to be with Eileen. He slid a comforting arm about her shoulders, while whispering in her ear, 'My darling, I made one mistake and never a day goes by when I don't regret what happened. It's you I love. It's you I need, always.'

When he looked up, Marie was already out of sight.

Out of their lives.

Maybe forever.

~

'Are you all right, sweetheart?' Tilting his mirror the driver watched as Marie wiped away her tears.

'Yes thank you.' She felt deeply embarrassed at being caught crying in front of a stranger.

'Had a good holiday, have you?' Like all good taxi drivers, he was a bit of a knight in shining armour, determined to cheer his passenger.

'Sort of, yes. Thank you.'

'Going home on the train, are you?'

'Yes, I never did learn to drive, but I enjoy the train ride, so that's all right.'

'Being met at the other end, are you?'

'Yes.' Thinking he was a bit of a chatterbox, Marie gave a whimsical little smile. 'I'm being met by my daughter, Anne, and my granddaughter, Cathy.'

'A granddaughter, eh?' he smiled at her in the rear-view mirror. 'Grandchildren are a special gift. I've got four grandchildren – one girl and three boys – ranging from our Sean, who's just turned three, a right little devil he is. Then there's John and Michael and then our Lily, who's just coming up to her four-teenth birthday.'

He smiled at Marie again through the mirror. 'Lily's the chatterbox. Always talking about how she means to be a nurse when she's old enough. I can certainly see her doing that, 'cos she has the kindest, loveliest nature. Mind you, get her riled up, and she'll show you a temper, and no mistake!'

There followed a moment of silence as he wound

his way in and out of the increasingly heavy holiday traffic. 'I don't get to see my grand-kids as often as I'd like, what with me working all hours, and the kids living some ten miles in different directions from where we are.'

'Oh, that's a shame.' Marie would have preferred a quiet moment, but she didn't want to seem rude by not showing an interest. The conversation with Eileen was still heavy on her mind. Just now, she did not feel comfortable talking about grandchildren . . . especially to a stranger.

'How old is your granddaughter, if you don't mind me asking?'

'Old enough to know her own mind . . . she's independent and opinionated, and she can talk the hind leg off a dog!'

The driver chuckled. 'I know exactly what you mean. When me and Lily get chatting together, it's non-stop like the hens have just been turned out o' their pens!'

Fiddling in his shirt pocket, he handed a photograph to Marie, 'There you go! That's our Sean. He's a right little Tarzan! Swims like a fish, plays football with the big boys, and he can climb trees like a monkey!' He gave a hearty chuckle. 'Born to be a winner, that's our Sean. He's a right little buggeroota, and no mistake!'

Marie admired the little tyke as appropriate, then handed the photo back.

While keeping a wary eye on the heavy traffic, the

driver continued the conversation, 'You didn't say how old your granddaughter was.'

'Oh, well, she's not as young as your Lily.' After her traumatic time in Blackpool, Marie was comforted by the thought of seeing that lovely girl. 'She's eighteen, coming up nineteen. Her name is Cathy. She's sweet-natured, and small-built. She's a kind and caring girl, and animal-mad! In fact, just lately, she's been talking about packing in her job at the shop where she works and training to be a vet.'

'Oh, but that's good . . . isn't it?' He sensed a note of disapproval in Marie's voice.

'Well, yes I suppose. But my daughter, Anne – her mother – has always hoped that Cathy might one day get the qualifications to lead her into a career as a school-teacher. She's very good with the younger children. She used to take them for singing tuition in the village hall. But since she's been working at the shop, she doesn't have much time to plan a different future. But there's time enough yet, I suppose when she's ready.'

Smiling proudly, Marie informed the driver, 'She's torn between the shop and her real ambitions. On the one hand, she loves to be with the children . . . and on the other hand, she used to love helping out at the local vets. She often came home with stray animals. One time she came home clutching a cat in a basket. Both its ears had been torn off – by accident or deliberate, no one knows.'

'Good grief!' the taxi driver was horrified at the idea that someone might have deliberately done such a thing. 'Mind you, there are some nasty people out there!'

'I agree, but we don't know for sure if it was deliberate. The vet had an idea that it could have ripped its ears when climbing under barbed wire, but the damage was so bad, he couldn't really say. He did manage to save enough of both ears for a little wiggle, though. Someone left it on the doorstep of the vets. Maybe they couldn't afford to pay for treatment. Cathy had it sleeping with her on the bed for weeks. She refused to give it up, even when the vet warned her it might have to be put down. Thankfully though, the poor thing survived with at least part of its ears. Cathy called the cat Larry. It followed her everywhere she went, but that was before she went out to earn a wage.'

'It sounds to me like you've got one hell of a lovely granddaughter,' the driver said.

Feeling immensely proud, Marie nodded. 'Thank you! Cathy is indeed a very lovely young woman.'

'Do you see much of her?' Enjoying Marie's company, the driver chatted on. 'I bet you've missed her while you've been here.'

'Yes, I do miss her if I go away. But with this particular trip, I decided to devote some precious time to old friends from years back.'

'Quite right! You can't neglect old friends,' the

driver agreed. 'They're few and far between and the years go so fast, you need to keep in touch. I've found that out myself. I had a really good mate – four years younger than me – he dropped dead with a heart attack. Knocked me sideways, it did. Now I make sure to meet up regular with the old crowd I went to school with.'

What he said touched Marie deeply, what with the sudden death of the friend sounding exactly like Derek's, and the horrible situation with Tony and Eileen. 'You're very wise,' she said. She gave a long, weary sigh. 'These past couple of days, I've really missed Cathy, and my daughter Anne. And of course the rest of the family. My dear son-in-law, Dave . . . he works away a lot. He's a lorry driver.' She smiled to herself, 'Anne says there are times when he comes home after weeks on the road and she doesn't even recognise the man at the door – unshaven, and much thinner than when he left.'

'He sounds like a hard-working man,' the driver said. 'I take my hat off to your son-in-law. I wouldn't want a job now that takes me away for weeks on end. I did that for some months when I was younger, but never again! Driving a huge great wagon into the early hours, and often sleeping over in the cab, down some dark lane or lorry park – not for me, not now I'm older.'

Marie understood. 'The thing is the company's pay really good money for haulage drivers, and Dave is hoping to get enough money together to start his own business.'

'Ah! Well, I can understand that. We all have our dreams. I'm hoping to retire in a few years' time. Or I might buy a few cabs and sit in a comfy office, giving orders!' He gave a hearty chuckle. 'Oh, here we are!' He drew into the station taxi rank. 'Have a safe journey, and I hope your daughter and grand-daughter are there to meet you.' Clambering out of the cab, he carefully placed her case at her feet, then advised her of the amount of fare required, and Marie duly paid it, with a little thank you added on.

After checking he had the right amount, plus a tip, he then dropped the money into his trouser pocket, 'Well . . . thank you very much! Be good now!'

'Goodbye, and thank you, I enjoyed our little chat.' Suddenly feeling empty and lost, she said her goodbye and went into the station.

When the regrets began to overwhelm her, she lingered awhile to look in a jewellery display in a shop window; but she was not at all interested, or even conscious of what was displayed there.

She felt so alone. It was only a matter of seconds before the tears began to fall. Somewhat embar-rassed, she retreated to a discreet corner of the entrance hall where she took out her handkerchief and dabbed the tears away.

How could she have hoped to turn back the years, and take away the bad things? None of us can.

What happened, happened and I took care of my part in it, the best way I could, she thought. If only I had found the courage to confide the truth to Tony and Eileen. Maybe then they might at least have found it in their hearts to forgive me. But maybe too many years have gone by. Maybe this is the way it has to be in order to protect the innocents involved.

Hurrying down to the platform, she fumbled in her handbag for the return ticket home.

She was greatly relieved, as she went through the barrier, to find the train was already waiting . . . with just ten minutes to go before leaving and she clambered on board.

The first carriage was filled to capacity. Marie hurried on through to the next carriage, which was less crowded. Having quickly found a seat by the window, she sat herself down.

Taking in a deep sigh, she felt weary, and so alone.

As the train prepared to leave, she eagerly watched the flow of travellers still hurrying along the platform.

She half hoped that Eileen and Tony might have followed her, but there was no sight of them. Of course, she didn't even know if they'd come by train.

A wave of nostalgia flowed over her for the happy holiday departures of old, as she realised that she may never see those two old friends ever again.

'I'm sorry, madam. Tea or coffee?' The steward's soft voice alarmed Marie.

'Oh . . . tea . . . thank you.' She felt embarrassed at

the possibility that he may have overheard her muttering to herself. 'And a biscuit, please. Any kind will do.'

As the steward handed her the tea and biscuit, took the money and quickly moved on, Marie's thoughts meandered back over the years.

She recalled her shock when she discovered she was pregnant with Tony's child. Right from the very start she had desperately wanted to tell Eileen the truth – all of it – but that might well have caused another kind of anxiety and heartache. When she put it off, she then fretted about it until she had no option than to confide – not in Eileen, but someone who understood, and who had remained by her side through thick and thin. That dear, loving person had shared Marie's worst dilemma, but instead of passing judgement, she had helped her keep her secret, held her hand through the darkest days of her life, and was keeping that secret and holding her hand even now.

Finally, after much heart-searching and consideration, there was practical help when the decision was made. They moved from the old house to a place where no one knew them as a family, just until matters were resolved and there would be no difficult questions.

Everything finally slotted into place, the deed was done and there could be no turning back.

In the years that followed, Marie came to realise that the sacrifice she had made was allowing her to experience an unexpected joy, a sense of peace, and of course, gratitude.

Always, though, at the back of her mind was a small, niggling concern that one day she would have to tell the truth. One thing was certain: these past years she had not really enjoyed her life. It had been a peculiar pattern of guilt and joy, and immense doubt as to the drastic action she had taken.

She had sinned, and now she was paying the price. Being both desperate and ready to make amends, she had gone ahead with the plan even when her every instinct warned her of possible repercussions. These, thankfully, had not yet materialised in damaging terms, but there was no doubt that her estrangement from her former friends was permanent. But even if she never did see Eileen and Tony again, there was another, more important person in Marie's life who must one day be told the whole truth. Would she ever forgive her?

Time alone would tell.

CHAPTER FIVE

'AFTER ALL THESE years, who would have thought it, some coincidence eh?' Folding his arms John gave a warm chuckle.

'It is, yes.' Being a romantic at heart, Danny agreed. 'a really wonderful thing to see her again. And looking as good as the day we last saw her. A smile to knock your socks off when she finally gave me one.'

'I wish I'd been able to see Marie again,' he gave a cheeky wink, 'think I might have chatted her up!'

He now pointed a finger at his friend. 'Hey, are you blushing, Danny Boy! You are, aren't you? Well. That says it all, you fancy her.'

'Maybe . . . Maybe not.' Danny was giving nothing away, focused on rubbing some spots of rust off the corners of the Blue Bench, whistling merrily away.

'See you later, Danny Boy!' John chuckled to himself as he made his way down the Promenade, pushing along the heavy barrow full of tools.

'Not if I see you first.'

Softly now, Danny whispered the name of his old friend to himself, 'Marie,' and couldn't help but smile. The name suited her still, warm and homely and pretty, just like her.

~

Marie woke with a start. 'Oh! Dearie me . . . I must have dozed off!' She had changed trains at Manchester and was now bone weary. Catching the attention of the roving ticket inspector, she asked worriedly, 'Excuse me, but which station are we now approaching?' Heavy with sleep, she sat up straight and peered out of the window, but all she could see were train lines and cows in the neighbouring field.

At first sight she could not recognise any landmarks. 'Oh dear, I do hope I haven't missed my station. I can't seem to recognise where we are.' She started to panic. 'And I've got family waiting for me at the station – they're bound to be worried.'

The inspector looked at her proffered ticket. 'Trust me! You have definitely not missed your stop.' He was a big, lolloping man, with a ruddy face and light brown wispy hair that hung over his forehead like a fluttering veil. Smiling reassuringly, he promised her, 'You've no need to worry, my dear.'

'That's the trouble, I do worry,' Marie said. 'It's no fun waiting on a cold and draughty platform, especially if the loved one you're waiting for doesn't even get off the train.'

The inspector was anxious that she was getting herself into a right old state. 'We're arriving at your station now, so you'd best shake a leg.'

His hearty chuckle was as merry as his twinkling brown eyes. 'Come on, then!' Helping her to organise her handbag and small suitcase, he led her away to the door, chatting as he went.

She felt hugely relieved to be nearing home. 'I hope my daughter and granddaughter will be outside waiting for me. I feel safer with them than with the taxi drivers, who always seem to be tearing about for the next fare.'

'You're right there, m'dear. The trouble is, we all need to do what we must in order to pay the bills. It gets harder and harder as you get older, but we all of us still have to make a living one way or another.'

Shuffling ahead of her, he continued to chat and smile, and when they got to the door, he barred her way with his big frame, until the train stopped, and he helped her off, and lifted out her case.

'Thank you so much.' Marie held out a friendly hand, which he grabbed and shook too long and too hard for her comfort.

'Happen I'll see you again, m'dear.' He had a definite twinkle in his eye, and clearly thought her a good-looking woman.

His eager face smiled down on her. 'I must say,

you don't look half as tired as you did when you came on board. Been burning the candle at both ends, have you? Some wild party or other was it? Am I right?'

Marie recalled the sadness and anger that had tainted her reunion with Tony and Eileen. 'No, you are not right! Sadly, you could not be more wrong if you tried!'

The flirtatious inspector looked taken aback. 'Well . . . I'm sorry . . . I didn't mean to upset you. It's just me being stupid, as ever! But you did look just a little worn out, like you might have been dancing all night. You've been in the Land of Nod ever since you got on the train.' He gave a cheeky wink. 'I kept an eye on you though . . . ' He was disappointed when she moved away from him. 'Hang on . . . please don't go just yet.' Now, at the corner of his eye, he saw approaching up the platform a wobbly old gentleman who appeared to be in some distress. Apologising to Marie, he approached the old man. 'I'll be back in a minute, dear,' he called to her over his shoulder, 'Don't be in such a hurry to get away from me, will you?' The minute he had the inspector in his sight, the old man launched into a most vociferous complaint regarding the sorry state of the toilets on board the train. Marie smiled to herself as she walked away to find Anne and Cathy. Let the over-friendly man give his attention to someone who needed it, she was back with her family now.

But as the train pulled away, she thought what a waste of time her trip to Blackpool had been. It had solved nothing. Instead, she had lost any chance she might have had to make up to Eileen for what she had done. Nothing had changed, nothing was mended, and her friendship with Eileen was still damaged beyond repair. Alone on the chilly platform, Marie could hear the drone of the engine some way along the track behind her. She gave a quiet smile. If I had a choice, I would get on that train and go wherever it takes me. Just go, and never come back, she thought.

Shaking her head in anger, she reminded herself that she had family at home: Cathy, a beautiful and loving girl, and Cathy's loving parents, Anne and Dave – all of them good and decent people, and every one much loved by Marie.

Anne and Dave had been the saving of her, when she was struggling to find an answer, and she would be grateful to them for the rest of her life.

In this dark and telling moment, however, Marie could only decide two things with some measure of accuracy.

There was no way on earth she could ever change the past.

And there was no way of knowing what the future might hold.

'I am truly thankful to have such a loving family,' she thought. That much at least she could rely on.

The thought of seeing her loved ones brought a smile to her face. 'If I didn't have them . . . I don't even know how I might have coped,' she murmured.

She would never forget how they had helped her at the lowest, most worrying time in her entire life.

She still felt guilty, and so very undeserving of their love.

In her own home, all those years ago, she had been so lost and lonely following Derek's demise. But the family rescued her. They gave her a home with them. They afforded her a purpose, and not once did they ever question her failings. Instead, they took her as she was. And they gave her a second chance, to be herself and to live in the arms of their love.

For all her life, she would never be able to thank them enough for the support they had given her when she needed them most.

But where were they now? Growing frantic, Marie looked up and down the platform, hoping to see familiar faces. She needed her family around her. She had to put the bad things behind her, although she knew, in reality, that she never could.

Even in that warm and welcoming place she called home, the burden of guilt never left her. Instead, it weighed heavily on her mind.

She worried about the loved ones who had gone to great lengths to help her when no one else could. Although in taking care of Marie – in the only way they possibly could – they too had been rewarded over the years, with such joy as they had never known before.

While what had transpired back then had given her the lifeline she so desperately needed, it had by its very nature also created a ticking time bomb. Marie's greatest fear was that the innocent party in all this would never forgive her if she was to learn the truth. And surely the time was drawing near when she would have to be made aware of her shameful beginnings.

And so, in the years gone by, it was agreed by family, that for now at least, it might be wiser to let sleeping dragons lie, for all their sakes. Marie feared she would keep the secret until the day she died.

Living with the lies and pretence created over the years, Marie had never found peace. She always carried the deep nagging worry, and at times she felt such despair and bitter regret.

Through every waking moment, she dreaded the day when the truth might be discovered . . . when the lies and shocking deception would surely catch up with her. Mostly, she feared for the innocent, who had no idea of the sordid but well-meant decision that was taken all those years ago.

While the innocent was kept unaware, Marie, along with her caring conspirators, could only hope and pray that they had done the right thing. Sometimes she prayed that the secret would never out so everyone was kept protected, other times it was her deepest, sweetest wish that she could shout the truth from the top of Blackpool Tower.

Thankfully, the secret had remained safe within the family for so long, that it was almost as though there had been no conspiracy at all. No lies. No deception. And so far, no punishment. Life just went on, for both Marie, and also her family. But what if difficult questions were asked and answers demanded?

Each of the conspirators was increasingly dreading the inevitable day the secret must come out, bringing with it a river of heartache to all concerned.

CHAPTER SIX

D AVE GAVE ANNE and Cathy a lift to the station
to meet Marie. Anne assured him they would
get a taxi home; the train might be running late or
Marie might have missed her connection at Manchester
so there could be a long wait. They were far too early
for the train, but he knew Anne was anxious about
her mother and whether she'd at last plucked up the
resolve to tell her former friends Tony and Eileen
about Cathy. He hoped so. Anne was patient and
encouraging in the face of Marie's wavering sense of
purpose and he would have liked Marie not to have
to bear the burden of her secret – of their shared
secret – for much longer. Dave was a simple man
and believed that now Cathy was a young woman it
was only fair to tell her the truth, no matter how
hurtful.

It was a beautiful day and having done a few quick
jobs, Dave was between trips for the haulage company

so he decided to have a little stroll to the newsagent's to get his newspaper, then maybe sit out with a nice cup of tea while he read it.

He was just turning back into the street where he lived when he heard raised voices, and saw a flat-bed truck was parked before the house next door, the semi-detached property with which his own shared a wall. A very heated altercation was starting up right there on the pavement. As he drew nearer, slowing his step to make sure he missed nothing, while making himself as inconspicuous as possible in case he should become subject to the fall-out, Dave was amazed to see that the argument was about a 'To Let' board. Several of these were in the back of the truck, and the driver had evidently managed to hammer one into the ground beside the pavement in front of the house before Dave's neighbour, Bob, confronted him.

'What the hell are you doing putting that thing up here?' he shouted. 'You can just take it down again right now because there is no way this house is to let.'

'I've instructions from the landlord,' said the sign man.

'What instructions?' spat Bob. 'I've not heard anything about this house being to let. I'm the tenant here and the landlord hasn't said anything to me. So you can take that ruddy sign down now.'

'I have my instructions . . .' the man started, but Bob, who had a short temper, a loud voice and plenty of practice with a noisy family over whom he had to assert himself, just raised his voice and yelled over him.

'I told you, this house is not to let. It's got tenants already – *I'm* the tenant – and you can get that there sign down now. And I mean now! No, don't you turn your back on me! I'm the tenant here and I'm not leaving this house until the landlord tells me I am. And this isn't telling. This is sneaky! This is dishonest! I've got a wife and children to keep and obligations to other folk – how are we going to manage without a roof over our heads? Answer me that! Eh? Eh?'

The sign man had started to edge away, but as Bob grew angrier, and his language grew more colourful and his shouting grew ever louder, the poor man gave up trying to reason with him, turned tail and legged it back to his truck.

'No you don't!' bawled Bob. 'Don't you dare go off and leave that sign there. Don't you dare, do you hear me?'

As he proceeded to tell the man exactly where he'd like to put the sign, the terrified sign man started the engine and the truck pulled away. It quickly picked up speed but Bob was not one to give up and he gave chase, thundering down the street and threatening hell and damnation if the man didn't clear the sign off his property immediately.

The truck soon disappeared round the corner, and Bob was left cursing and swearing in the middle of the road, with other neighbours beside Dave taking an interest by now.

Dave wisely decided the matter was not his business – that is, he wanted no active part in it, though he was blessed if he wasn't going to find out what he could – and he slipped indoors while Bob was shaking his fist in the direction the truck had gone, and took up a good position to hear and see what happened when Bob returned to his side of the property.

First of all Bob gave the sign a good kicking, but when it didn't budge he strode indoors with a very dark expression. Soon Dave heard a row erupting, and he decided to follow his original plan and take a cup of tea and his newspaper outside at the back, where he could hear without being seen. Cathy's boyfriend, Ronnie, lodged with Bob and Peggy's bois- terous family as their tenant, so Dave felt it was his duty to find out as much as he could. Ronnie was a nice lad, hard-working and polite, and Dave didn't like to think he'd be made homeless along with his feckless landlord.

Soon the accusations were flying and Bob and Peggy did not hold back.

'What do you mean, you didn't pay the rent? How could you not pay it? Answer me that.'

'How could I pay it when you stole the money I'd put by and spent it in the pub?'

'Stole? You accuse me of stealing and it was my money all along!'

'It was for the *rent*, Bob.' Peggy's tone grew sarcastic, as if she was explaining to an idiot. 'You know, the rent, the money we have to pay the landlord in order to keep a roof over our heads.'

'So what? You've always managed to pay it before . . . haven't you?'

'You stupid man, how do you think I pay it when you keep stealing it and drinking it away? I haven't paid the rent for weeks.'

For a moment there was silence, but Dave guessed that the argument was just getting going after that revelation. Sure enough Bob's temper erupted once again in a frenzy of swearing, and Peggy was giving as good as she got.

'. . . And if it's not bad enough there've been complaints,' Peggy shouted. 'Folks round here have been snitching on us to the landlord about the kids.'

'Who?'

'I don't know, Bob. He'd hardly tell me, would he? Just sent a letter saying the kids were making too much noise too late at night. A warning, he said.'

'Well, that's your fault, that is. It's your job to discipline the children and you're so lazy you can't even manage that. You've got no control over those kids and you've brought them up to be ruffians with no respect for anyone else.'

'Who says it's my job? You're their father, you tell them!'

'Tell them what, that their mother can't keep them

in order? Whenever I chastise them you complain so they take no notice of me whatsoever. Tell them that you're a born liar who gets a letter from the landlord and doesn't tell me – me, the man of the house – and then gets behind with the rent and doesn't tell me that either?'

'I'm telling you now, aren't I?'

'Too ruddy late now, you daft woman, when we're about to be homeless. You created this mess, now you deal with it . . .'

And so it went on, each blaming the other and neither doing anything to help the situation. Their voices rose and there was a sound that Dave thought might have been a plate smashing.

'I'll be round there giving that landlord a piece of my mind. He can't go throwing us out without formal notice,' Bob yelled. 'It's not legal.'

'You'll be in trouble if you do, Bob, 'cos he has given us notice.'

'When? Answer me that. When did he give us notice?'

'I don't know! It was a while ago, some weeks. Some snooty letter asking us to leave. I was that angry I threw it in the bin.'

'You did *what?*'

'You heard!'

'I don't believe you were so stupid. What in hell's name did you think would happen? Did you think it would just all go away – that he'd forget about it? Well, did you?'

'Ah, shut up, Bob. I've had it up to here with you, *and* the landlord.'

'No, you shut up. You just shut up and listen . . .' The shouting continued, the language becoming quite shocking, and Dave retreated indoors, having got more than the gist of the situation.

He hadn't been inside long before there was a knock at the back door. When he answered it Ronnie, Cathy's boyfriend, was standing there, a knapsack at his side.

'Come in, Ronnie,' Dave said. 'I know about next door.'

Ronnie gave an ironic smile as he stepped inside. 'Yeah, I reckon there aren't many who haven't heard,' he said. Bob and Peggy's raised voices were audible even now and the two men stood listening for a few seconds.

'Thing is, Dave, I'm going to have to find myself a new place. No use waiting a minute longer when it's this plain which way things are going. So I'm off. Is your Cathy in? I wouldn't go without saying goodbye.'

'But what about your job, Ronnie? What about Cathy? I know you and our girl have got really close these last few months, and it'd break her heart if you left.'

'I wouldn't hurt Cathy for the world, Dave. Of course I wouldn't. She means everything to me. But they've just laid me off at the garage as there's not enough work to go around, and with what's happening next door it's time to move on. I mean to find something that pays enough for me to save up, make a future for Cathy and me. I shan't let her down, but I do need to look around, see what's on offer, and I know already that there's nothing here for me. It won't be long before I'm settled and then I'll be able to make some plans with Cathy and our future in mind.'

'I'm sorry you're having to get away to look for a new job, Ronnie, and Cathy will be that upset when she hears. Thing is, she isn't here now. She's gone to meet her nan at the station. She's been there a while but I don't know how much longer she'll be.'

Ronnie looked stricken at this news, but then he had an idea. 'I'll go there and see if I can find her. But in case I miss her I'd better leave her a note. I need to find somewhere to stay tonight and I've got to see Beth, too, so I best be getting on.'

'Of course,' Dave approved. Ronnie was a good lad who cared deeply for his sister, the only family he had. Dave couldn't think of a nicer man for Cathy, though she was very young to be thinking of a permanent relationship. 'Here, I'll just get you some paper. I think there's another cup in that teapot if you can squeeze it.'

Ronnie laughed and poured himself a cup of the, by now, very strong but not very hot tea while Dave disappeared briefly and returned with a writing pad, a ballpoint pen and an envelope.

Ronnie dashed off a few sentences in a spikey scrawl

while Dave loitered at a polite distance and the muffled sounds of smashing pots and swearing came from next door.

'Reckon you're well out of that, lad,' said Dave as Ronnie folded the paper and sealed it in the envelope.

He wrote 'Cathy' on the front and gave it an unself-conscious kiss before handing it to Dave. Then he drank down his lukewarm tea and shook Dave firmly by the hand.

'Thanks, Dave. I'll see you soon, I hope. Tell Cathy . . . well, tell her I'll be in touch. She knows . . .' He nodded at the envelope, which Dave had propped behind the toaster.

'If you hurry you may yet see her at the station,' Dave said, showing Ronnie to the door. 'Take care, young fella. And best of luck.'

'Thanks, Dave.'

'And we'll see you again before long.'

'Sure will. Goodbye.' Ronnie shouldered his heavy bag and, with a smile and a wave, set off down the path to the front of the house, where, next door, the fight had erupted into the garden and Bob and Peggy were yelling obscenities at each other and hurling flower pots.

Dave hoped the young man would meet up with Cathy to say goodbye in person. She'd be devastated to have missed him.

CHAPTER SEVEN

MARIE, STILL IMPATIENTLY waiting at the station, placed her case on the bench and took to pacing along the platform, back and forth, until she felt bone weary. After a while, she settled on the bench, content enough to watch another train disgorging its passengers. Feeling weary, she closed her eyes and, leaning back into the cold, iron bench, she mentally took stock of her predicament once again.

Drifting into sleep, she felt the shiver of a breeze, and in that most private moment her heart leaped, on hearing a beloved and familiar voice calling to her from the far end of the platform.

'Mum, there you are!'

Marie looked up, smiling happily as her two dear ones, Cathy and Anne, headed straight for her . . . And now they were running, with wide smiles and arms open for a hug.

After the damaging and fraught exchange between herself and her two former friends in Blackpool, Marie felt happy, and also hugely tearful on seeing her family.

With an uplifted heart, she hurried towards them. 'Oh, look at you!' she called. 'How lovely to see you both! I was worried I'd got it wrong, and you might not come and meet me, and here you are!' Her voice shook with emotion as she continued, 'You have no idea how I missed you!'

Feeling somewhat weary, she stopped to drop her little suitcase to the ground, and thanked the Good Lord for the family she cherished. Then again, she hurried towards them, arms opened for a hug, she felt incredibly fortunate to have these two wonderful people in her life.

As they neared and came into sharper focus, Marie took stock of them. Anne was a young-looking thirty-nine-year-old, a slim and attractive woman with short bobbed fair hair, light green eyes, and a ready smile that would brighten any rainy day. She was kind and loving, and her loyalty to family was fierce. She had a whole-hearted, noisy laugh that Marie loved to hear because it never failed to lift her spirits.

Hurrying along holding Anne's hand, Cathy was a pretty, lovely-natured girl, with chocolate-brown eyes, and long, thick brown hair, presently tied back in a blue ribbon. Cathy ran ahead now, calling, 'I'm so glad you're home, Nan! Mum wasn't sure which platform you might be on, so we came early and asked at the desk. Then, of course, we decided to have a drink and next thing, you're here before we are.'

After hugging Marie hard, Anne apologised. 'I know you told me which platform you should be on, but I lost the slip of paper that I wrote all the details on.' She was relieved to see her mum safe and sound. 'We've been here for ages. There's that little drinks bar on one of the other platforms. When there was no sign of you, we began to think you might have got on the wrong train.'

'What! You cheeky pair!'

Laughing, Marie hugged the both of them to her again. 'As if I would be stupid enough to get on the wrong train. Hmm! I might be knocking on the wrong side of sixty, but thankfully I've still got all my marbles.'

She suddenly grew tearful. 'I've missed you both so much.' Cradling Anne's face in her two hands, she admitted softly, 'It's so lovely to see you, it really is.' Reaching out she now took the girl into the curve of her arms. 'You look tired, Cathy. It seems to me that maybe you've had too many late nights?'

Anne smiled knowingly. 'Well, I must say, you've been getting a bit pally with that family next door, and that has meant a few late nights. Twice I've had to come and get you, or have you forgotten?

'But at least you were out in the garden where I could see you all.'

Rolling her eyes, Cathy informed Marie, 'Mum treats me like a child, and I'm not a child! I'm eighteen now, and I'm sensible. We were just playing music, having a good time, that's all. They're nice people. We weren't doing anything wrong.'

'I'm sure you weren't! It's just that it's a mother's place to worry. And besides I'm sure your mother trusts you. So stop fretting, and leave it there, all right?'

Cathy readily agreed. 'Yes, all right, I won't say any more.'

'No, don't go that far,' Marie told her with a cheeky little grin. 'You see, I'm nosy, and I might want to know more. I might need to know what music you were playing, and what they gave you to eat, and what the house is like inside, and everything there is to know. Warts and all, if you don't mind.'

'I don't mind at all.' It didn't take much to make Cathy happy when she had one arm linked with her mum's, and the other arm wrapped about her nan's slim waist.

The three of them went out of the station and into a taxi, catching up with the local gossip and having a giggle as they squeezed into the back seat and the driver stowed Marie's case in the boot.

However, when Marie began passing on news of the two workmen who tended the Promenade, Cathy teased her, 'Which one do you like best, Nan, the Irishman, or the big Scot? Who would you like to be your beau if he asked you?' Cathy had met them both, when spending a weekend in Blackpool some time back, with both her parents and nan.

'Well, I like them both.' Marie had never thought about the two men in a romantic way before. 'I must admit, it was lovely to see Danny after all this time. He always makes me laugh out loud, while if I'm honest, John used to make me feel just a little nervous, what with his great size and deep, booming voice – not to mention all that thick, dark hair.' She gave a quiet smile. 'They're both good men, though, most polite and kind. I like them a lot, but not in any romantic way. Don't go getting silly ideas like that. I didn't even see John this time, only Danny. And besides, I'm sure neither would be the slightest bit interested in me. From the tales that both used to tell, they always had more than enough women chasing after them. It just reminded me of the old days, that's all. Some happy memories.'

'All right then, so – not in a romantic way – but which one do you just like the best as a friend?' Cathy was most insistent. 'I'm sure you must like one of them more than the other, so go on, which one is it?'

Marie was amused. 'As a friend? Well, just let me think . . . ' She recalled the cheeky, meaningful wink the little Irishman had given her as they parted yesterday morning. 'To tell the truth, I reckon Danny Boy might be more fun to go out with, and if he was to get some funny ideas about me fancying him, I'm about his size, so I could fend him off. But if it was John, I'd have to run a mile.'

Both Cathy and Anne laughed out loud, while Anne wagged a finger at Marie. 'We said you had a fancy for the little Irishman, and we were right!'

Marie blushed bright pink. 'Give over, you two. And anyway, I'm not in the market for a man – not any man, not taxi drivers or ticket inspectors, or any other man who thinks he's God's gift. I'm well past all that silly business. In my experience men are trouble and I'm better off on my own.'

She had to smile, though, when the other two exchanged looks that said they did not believe her.

'Oh, Nan.' Cathy hugged Marie close in the taxi. 'I'm really happy that you're back. Next time you go away, can I come with you? I do miss you when you're not here.'

'Well, I missed you as well, sweetheart, all of you.' Marie gave a little groan. ' . . . I even missed your father's scary snoring in the early hours of morning.'

They all laughed at that and Cathy agreed that his loud, invasive snores were enough to wake the dead.

~

The traffic was always heavy at that time of day, and today was no exception. The family were tired and ready for a cuppa, and after the long journey Marie in particular longed to put her weary feet up.

Everyone gave a sigh of relief when the taxi reached the quieter, more familiar streets, and finally pulled up outside their house.

'Oh, thank goodness, home at last!'

'I need a nice, fresh cup of tea, and ten minutes or so to soak my poor old feet.' Marie gave a long, weary groan. 'Right now it's like they're on fire! My bones are aching, and it seems like I've been away for months, instead of just a couple of days!

'It's all right, Anne. I'll settle with the driver,' Marie quietly instructed her daughter, who was dipping into her handbag for the fare. She took her purse out ready. 'Meantime, can the two of you get my case?'

'Yes, Mum. We're fine, and look, you don't have to do that.' Anne gestured to Marie's open purse. 'I'll deal with the driver.'

'No you won't!' Marie protested. 'You've done enough already.'

'But Mum, Dave's given me the money for the taxi.'

The taxi driver chuckled heartily. 'It don't bother me, ladies! I'm sure I don't care who pays me so long as I get paid. I wish all my customers were that eager to put their hands in their pockets or purses, as the case may be.'

Anne thanked her mother and then handed her the money she had been given by Dave. 'If you see to the driver, Mum, Cathy and I will sort out your case.'

While Cathy and Anne went to get the case from

the boot, Marie paid the driver with Dave's money, silently thanking her lucky stars that she was home again. The taxi driver thanked Marie. 'You've got a lovely family there, m'dear,' he told her. 'Three generations of good-looking women.' Marie smiled her thanks and waved him off. In some ways it had become so easy to keep the secret. People saw and they just assumed.

As everyone bundled towards the front door, Cathy suddenly stopped in her tracks. 'Look there,' she said, and pointed towards the neighbours' house and the massive board that was fixed to a wooden pole by the path.

Marie could hardly believe what she was seeing. 'It says next door's house is to let! But it can't be! How can it be to let when there are people living in it? What about Ronnie and the others? They can't throw them out, can they?'

'Oh, Nan!' With tears flowing down her face, Cathy turned to Marie. Anne and Marie were every bit as surprised as Cathy, especially Anne. There had been no sign up when they left and there hadn't been a word about moving out from Peggy or Bob. 'It can't be right, can it, Nan? What does it mean?'

When her father came to the front door, she ran to him. 'Daddy! What's going on? The house next door can't be to let. It must be a mistake. What about Ronnie? Is the landlord throwing Bob and Peggy and the boys out? He can't turn them out, can he?' She was getting herself in a fret. 'Why does it say the house is to let when it can't be?'

'Hey!' Marie took hold of her hand. 'Calm down, sweetheart. Like you say, it must be a mistake. I'm sure someone will be back to collect the board, and put it up at another house where it should have gone in the first place.'

Marie took her inside the house, while Dave relieved Anne of Marie's case, then hesitated to let them go ahead.

'What's happening next door? It must be a mistake,' Anne said to her husband. 'The family have only been in the house for, what, a few months and they seemed intent on staying there.'

'There's definitely no mistake,' Dave said darkly.

Anne lowered her voice. 'Are they still inside?' she asked Dave.

'For the moment, yes, but Ronnie's gone. He came round to say goodbye. He was sorry to miss Cathy and said he'd try to catch her at the station.'

'Oh no!' Anne was disappointed. 'We didn't see him. Cathy's going to be terribly upset.'

'Of course she is, poor lass. She thinks a great deal of Ronnie.'

Dave and Anne went inside, where Marie had already got the kettle on. She told them Cathy had gone up to her room and that she was just going to take her up a cup of tea. Dave took Marie's case up and then came down to find the tea poured and

Anne putting a plate of biscuits on a tray for Marie to take up to Cathy.

When Marie had gone up, Anne sat at the kitchen table in eager anticipation. 'Tell all!' she said.

Dave told Anne all about the drama she had missed earlier, about the sign going up and the argument between Bob and Peggy. 'You could hear the pair of them shouting and arguing, accusing each other of Lord knows what. It was like World War Three in there!'

He went on to explain, 'Things were being thrown across the room . . . I could hear a lot of what they were saying . . . I should think the whole street heard them. Yelling and screaming at the top of their voices. It was like Bedlam in there.'

He shook his head in disgust, 'I don't mind telling you . . . I really thought the pair of them had completely lost it. They obviously didn't get official notice that the board was going up . . . or maybe they did and they decided they were not having it, because when he caught sight of that poor fellow out there . . . Bob was on him like a shot . . . threatening him, and demanding to know what the hell was going on. Like a maniac he was.'

'Well I for one will be happy to see the back of them. I mean, Ronnie was never any trouble, in fact he was out working most of the time. And, on the whole, whenever I've asked the young ones to turn the music down, they have.'

'They are a noisy lot, aren't they?'

'Well, yes, if I'm honest, it can get a bit noisy, and they do fill the garden to capacity. They don't kick up a riot or anything like that, but last Saturday when the record-player went on, it did get a bit loud and intrusive until I went out and gave them a ticking off. Mind you . . . on the whole they all seemed well-behaved, sometimes you have to give people the benefit of the doubt.'

He shook his head in disbelief, 'Honestly though, Anne . . . you should have heard the two of them going at each other. Both of them were convinced that it must have been the neighbours who complained, and then he was threatening to find out who it was that complained to the landlord, because he would be sure to teach them a lesson. Whatever that might be, I dread to think!'

Afraid they might be overheard, Anne lowered her voice. 'I must admit, I'm convinced it had to be a neighbour who complained. But can you blame whoever it was? I mean . . . I'm sure you agree, we wouldn't have chosen them as neighbours.'

Meanwhile, upstairs in Marie's room, Cathy was explaining to Marie how worried she was about Ronnie. 'What's going to happen to him? He doesn't have anywhere else to go. He can't go to Beth's house because he doesn't get on with her horrible husband.' Now the tears began to flow.

Marie slid a comforting arm about Cathy's shoulders.

'Aw, now, don't go getting yourself all upset. I know it's a bit of a shock, but I reckon we should stay calm until we've had time to talk about it properly. I've no doubt Ronnie will tell you all about his plans in the light of what's happened next door. But, I promise, if you haven't heard from him by the end of the day, I will have a word with her next door.'

Cathy was not convinced. 'She probably won't want to talk with you, Nan, after what's happened. She'll be upset herself.'

Marie had the very same thought, but she put on a smile. 'Let's be patient, eh? I imagine Ronnie doesn't even know that we're home yet. Either way, I don't want you worrying, because I believe that either Ronnie will be round to see you, or he'll call to let you know what his plans are. If he loves you – and I'm sure he does – he'll be in touch, you'll see.'

'I hope so, Nan.' Cathy sniffed. 'I told you, didn't I, Nan, how when his parents died – they were old, much older than you are, and not very well – he and his sister lived in the house but when his sister got married, he came to lodge next door because he didn't want to live in his parents' house by himself.'

'Yes, you told me all of that.' Marie continued to unpack her case. 'I still believe he will contact you so you can stop your worrying.'

Cathy was not so confident. 'If they're evicted, he won't have anywhere to go, and I'm really worried about him. Where is he, Nan? Where could he have gone?'

Marie shook her head. 'I'm sorry, sweetheart. Like you, I have no idea. There is a chance that he might not even have seen the board yet, if he's been at work today. Think back, was it there when you and Mum left the house?'

'No, Nan. I would have noticed it.'

'Well, there you are then! Maybe he left for work before the board was put up, and if that was the case he might not even realise what's happened. All we can do, is be patient and see what transpires. I'm sure he'll be in touch. Either way, you must be patient and see what turns up.'

'Oh, Nan! It's so unfair. It really suited Ronnie to live at Bob and Peggy's because it's near his work at the garage, and also he said he wanted to be near me.' Remembering that lovely moment when he'd told her this, she blushed a tender shade of pink.

'I never told anyone else, Nan, but Ronnie said he was saving up for a deposit on a little rented place of his own. He said he was looking to the future and wanted us to be together.'

'Really? Well, I never! And you didn't even say a word to anyone.'

It seemed as though Cathy was truly in love. That they were planning a little nest together meant that she and Ronnie were more serious than Marie had thought.

She realised that the time to tell the truth was not all that far away.

Maybe her relationship with Cathy would be damaged as her darling girl's trust was undermined by the lies.

The clock was ticking fast now, bringing the dreaded moment ever closer.

For now though, Marie forced herself to put away her own fears, and concentrate on Cathy and the young man it seemed she loved and possibly intended to spend the rest of her life with.

'Mum, Cathy, what are you doing up there?' Anne's raised voice resonated through the house. 'You must be hungry. Come down, I've made us some more tea and some sandwiches.'

Having been duly summoned, Marie and Cathy quickly arrived and were seated at the table in the cosy kitchen.

'There you are!' Anne proudly indicated the late lunch she had set out. There was a large home-made chocolate cake, baked that very morning, set along-side a plate piled high with sandwiches, and right in the centre of the table sat the big old china teapot hot and ready for another round of tea.

While everyone was tucking in, the conversation continued about next door, Dave filling Marie and Cathy in on the drama, and what might happen to the family, although Cathy was more concerned for just one special person. 'Daddy?'

'Yes, Cathy?' Dave glanced up. 'What is it?'

'Well . . . it's just that I'm worried about Ronnie. Did you hear if he was caught up in the rowing and such?'

'Well, no. It was just the two of them, Bob and Peggy, going at each other . . . like two maniacs they were!' Dave's imagination had been much exercised by what he'd heard of the row, and he couldn't stop talking about it.

'But I'm afraid love, Ronnie has gone up North for a while, to find some work and sort himself out a bit. He couldn't go on living with that pair now could he?'

While the others talked of the neighbours, Cathy's thoughts, as ever, were with the young man she had given her heart to. Now, though, doubts were creeping in, and she began to believe that maybe, just maybe, he did not feel about her the same way she felt about him. Maybe he had not been sincere when he told her that he loved her.

The cruel possibility that he might have been stringing her along made her deeply unhappy.

And she was feeling quietly troubled, even if she had no real reason to be. It was just the little things that made her unsettled, to do with the family. Maybe it was her own vivid imagination that made her uneasy. In fact, Nan was always telling her how she had too vivid an imagination.

And maybe her nan was right. But things hadn't

been quite the same ever since her nan had booked her holiday to Blackpool. Because one time, when she'd walked into a room and her nan and mum had been quietly talking, she'd noticed how the conversation had suddenly stopped when they saw her. She recalled how she was made to feel oddly uncomfortable. It was almost as though they had been talking about her, and were afraid she might have overheard the conversation . . . which might have been something she was not to know.

Whatever it was . . . there was no doubt whatsoever in Cathy's mind that her unexpected entrance had startled them into an uncomfortable silence.

But for whatever reason, she still felt there was something not quite right with her life. There was always some little thing niggling at her peace of mind. And when she'd mentioned it to Ronnie, he assured her that she mustn't worry, because he also had doubts and worries. Mainly his thoughts were for their future, and the hope that nothing would go wrong to interfere with their plans, to be together and stay together, for the rest of their lives.

'I'm sure everyone has doubts and worries,' he told her now, 'it's the way of life, I suppose. It seems that there is always someone worrying about something.'

When he gently gathered Cathy into his arms, she told him softly, 'I think you're right. So! We shall have to stop worrying and start believing, won't we?'

With Ronnie by her side, she felt as though she

could face anything that fate had to throw at her, and all of a sudden, she felt immensely grateful for what she had. He was the love of her life and with him by her side she felt strong and safe. She ached for the moment he was back here with her. What would she do without him?

'And now he's gone? Left without a goodbye?' Cathy said sombrely. 'I just know I won't see him again.'

Dave had reached a point in his narrative where Ronnie had come round hoping to see Cathy. Suddenly, he leaped to his feet. 'Dammit! With all the noise and chaos next door, I almost forgot!' He grabbed an envelope from beside the toaster and handed it to Cathy. 'I'm so sorry, love, it went out of my head until just now.'

She turned the envelope over and over in her hands. 'I'm almost afraid to open it,' she admitted. 'I worry about what he might have said, what plans he might have. I was thinking he'd gone away without even letting me know. I should have realised he would never do that.'

Cathy instantly recognised Ronnie's haphazard and swirly handwriting. She was pleased and greatly relieved that he had thought of her especially when he must have had so many worrying matters playing on his mind.

'On the contrary, as I was just about to say, Ronnie came round to see you.'

'Came here? When? How long ago? If I go now will I catch up with him?'

'No, I'm sorry, love, I think you really have missed him,' said Dave. He told the women how Ronnie had appeared in the hope of seeing Cathy, what he'd said about finding a new job and then had left for the station.

'We didn't see him there,' said Cathy, looking tearful again. 'He must have got there after we had set out in the taxi home.'

Anne put her arm around Cathy's shoulders. 'Don't worry, sweetheart. I'm sure he tried and it was just bad luck.'

'I know he tried,' said Dave. 'There's no doubt that the young fella is mad about you. He's off to seek his fortune and it's all with your future together in mind. He'll be in touch, right enough, when he's settled. And in the meantime he left that note for you. Why don't you open it and read what he has to say? I'm sure he's explained it all much better than I can.'

As Marie watched Cathy unfold Ronnie's letter she saw the joy on that lovely girl's face and her eyes brimmed with tears which she quickly and carefully brushed away, so that Cathy and the others would not see.

A moment later, Cathy was out of the chair and heading for the stairs. 'I'll finish reading it up in my room,' she said. 'Oh! And he sends his love to everyone!'

As she ran up the stairs, Anne called out to her, 'While you're up there, you can tidy that bedroom. It's disgraceful. Oh, and put your shoes in the wardrobe, there's a love! And in future hang your clothes up instead of draping them on the backs of the chairs. It's like a rag-and-bone shop in there at times!' Chuckling quietly, she added, 'Read your letter first, though. You can tell us all about it later.'

While Cathy lay on her bed, reading Ronnie's loving words, the three of them downstairs quietly discussed where Ronnie might be now, and whether he had had any success in finding a place to stay.

'This upset with the landlord was bound to have made Ronnie think of his own, unstable situation,' Anne said. 'It can't have been a picnic living there, what with the shocking rows, to say nothing of the lack of discipline with the sons, and all the other yobs coming round for late-night parties, causing chaos and uproar in the early hours. I'm sure neighbours have complained time and again – I'm ashamed to say I've been tempted once or twice.'

Being that much older and wiser, Marie had seen this kind of thing before, 'Yes, you're right, and it looks like they've gone too far this time or the landlord would never have put up that board.'

Dave added his own opinion, 'I'm not sure if they've had a warning before like they did this time, but they would have probably ignored him if they did. If you ask me, what with one thing and another, the poor landlord must be fed up to his eyes with the pair of them.'

Anne recalled one particular incident, 'Oh . . . yes, what about that time when they insisted the landlord should replace the back door. They told him it happened during the night and they had no idea who had done it. They never did tell the truth . . . as to how it was the husband who kicked it down, after she locked him out following a huge row between the two of them. The poor landlord still believes that it was done by some angry drunkard. He never did find out that it was the husband himself who did the damage.'

'They really are a shameful pair, aren't they? I know I shouldn't gossip but she swears like an old soldier, sometimes I hear her let rip from the kitchen window. Father O'Malley must think hellfire's been let loose on us.' But after saying that, Marie was not altogether without feelings for the family. 'To be honest though, and even after they've been noisy and offensive to us and the other neighbours, you never know the circumstances, do you? I've had some long chats with her over the fence when we've been hanging the washing out, we've talked about the kids mostly. I can't help but feel a measure of sympathy for them . . . or for anyone else who is threatened with losing their home.'

'Ah, but that's because you have a soft heart and you always look for the best in everyone, Mum.' In truth though, Anne had also felt a pang of regret for their rowdy, troublesome neighbours.

Marie was relieved that they might shortly have newer, quieter neighbours. 'I don't imagine for one minute that Ronnie would want to stay any longer in that madhouse. Of course, the entire family will be heading off any day now unless they somehow wriggle out of their current troubles and manage to make peace with the landlord.'

Anne added quietly, 'From what you tell me, Dave, I really think they've gone too far this time. We know the landlord has threatened them before, but as far as I can tell they've taken no notice of him whatsoever. This time, though, it looks serious.'

'Maybe Ronnie's sister can put him up,' Dave suggested worriedly. 'If he's got a sound base to work from, he'll soon find employment, I'm sure.'

'Well, I hope she can.' Families, she thought – who'd have them!

Anne was ever optimistic, but she did have her doubts. She knew Beth's husband was a difficult man and there was no love lost between him and Ronnie.

CHAPTER EIGHT

Now that Marie was fortified with sandwiches and the delicious chocolate cake, and Cathy was occupied upstairs with Ronnie's letter, Anne wanted to hear all about Marie's trip to Blackpool. Dave offered to tidy away the tea things and do the washing up while Anne and Marie took themselves into the sitting room and sat close together on the sofa so that they could converse quietly.

Marie was glad to unburden herself of the unpleasantness of her encounters with Eileen and she had to confess that she had failed in what she had set out to do.

'I thought in that cheerful place, with the holiday atmosphere and all the wonderful memories of the good times we had, that they would forgive me,' she said sorrowfully, 'but it was not to be. I think Tony might have done, but Eileen didn't give him a chance to get a word in. She's very bitter towards me still.

Had it gone better, I might have ventured to tell them the truth about Cathy but I don't think they're ready for that now, if ever.'

'How awful that must have been,' said Anne. 'You were obviously made uncomfortable just being with them, weren't you?'

'Yes, I admit there were moments when I was sorely tempted to make my way home. I desperately needed to tell them the truth, but then I would imagine their reaction, and I couldn't do it. Like I said, Eileen still believes that I ended the pregnancy. And Tony knows nothing.'

Anne was greatly relieved that the secret had not got out somehow. 'To be honest, Mum, I'm always nervous that one way or another they might find out. I don't mind admitting, I still have nightmares about that.'

She lowered her voice further. 'Oh, dear Lord, if the truth ever did come out, and it wasn't us that revealed it, it would be the end of love and trust as far as Cathy is concerned. She would be absolutely devastated. It doesn't even bear thinking about. She would never forgive us – never in a million years – and I for one would not blame her.'

Marie was stricken with guilt all over again. 'For pity's sake, Anne, do you think I don't know all that? I fall asleep at night to that thought rampaging about my head, and I wake up in a nightmare that's never ending. And when I look at her and remember the truth of what we did, I don't know what to do, or even to think, knowing that it was me who actually caused all this deception. I should never have turned to you. It was incredibly selfish of me to put you and Dave in that situation, but I had nowhere else to turn.'

She admitted tearfully, 'I often wonder if it might be best if I was to confess everything now, to throw myself at Cathy's mercy and hope she might find it in her heart to forgive us.'

Thinking of Cathy now – the look on her face when she'd seen Ronnie's letter – Marie's heart grew warm. There had been many times over these past fretful years when she had asked herself if it would have been better if Cathy had never been born. And each time the answer was a resounding no. Of course Cathy was meant to live, and love, and experience the joys of being in a world that held such beauty and promise. Cathy was a lovely-natured young woman with a heart of gold and a way of making friends wherever she went.

So often Marie asked herself how she could ever have given birth to such a darling girl, a girl who was born out of badness and deceit, but who had grown into a beautiful woman. She had a way of caring about people so that they instinctively returned the love back to her.

Feeling threatened by her own imaginings, Marie leaned closer to Anne. 'It frightens me, the fact that one day everything will be out in the open. I know it's the right thing but it scares the living daylights out of me. For all these years, the truth of what happened has been such a heavy cross to bear, but it's only what I deserve. If I could change the past, I would in an instant, but I can't. I often think how my life might have been if I truly had terminated the pregnancy. Lord knows I meant to. I found out where to go, which was difficult, as I didn't want anyone I knew to hear that I'd been asking, but I could not bring myself to do it and at the last moment, I ran away. I could not end an innocent child's life, not even if it ruined my own. I always knew in my heart that I could never go through with it.'

She reached out to take hold of her daughter's hand. 'I'm so sorry to have brought you and Dave the problem, that was unfair of me. I should never have done that to you, my daughter.'

'You didn't bring us into the problem,' Anne told her mother softly. 'It was the two of us who convinced you that we could help. How could we let you do that terrible thing? If you'd been found out you'd have gone to prison. And do you know what, Mum? Neither of us has ever regretted helping you. Somehow, at some time, like you, I know the truth must come out. But when it does, we'll be there with you, me and Dave, together. Like we've always brought Cathy up – as a family. Until then, you must stop punishing yourself. What will be will be.'

She lovingly squeezed her mother's hand. 'I've

thought about what might happen when we tell Cathy the truth. Many times I've been dangerously close to confessing the circumstances surrounding her birth, but I lose my courage and I wouldn't tell Cathy until you felt ready, too. In my heart and soul, I know there will be a day when it feels right to tell her, and I have a feeling it won't be too long before we sit her down and explain what we did.'

Leaning in to Marie, she kissed her on the cheek. 'Try not to worry, please, Mum. I promise we will do what's right, from there on. We will explain what we did, and why. It will be a terrible shock to her, but if we're honest and able to explain the way it was, then I hope she will understand.'

Marie nodded tearfully. 'After all I've done, and the shocking things I've allowed to happen, I don't deserve any of you.'

'Don't torture yourself, Mum.' As always, Anne was concerned for her mother. 'We did what we thought was for the best. In a situation like the one you found yourself in, we all had to pull together because the alternative was too awful to contemplate. We have Cathy now, and she could not be more loved. I pray she will always be with us, and able to forgive us in spite of the inevitable upset to come.'

She paused to control her emotions a moment before going on. 'I only hope that when the time comes for Cathy to know the truth she won't think too badly of us. All three of us did what we thought was right, and I still believe that it was the only possible decision.'

'I hope you're right, Anne. I admit, I've often wondered if she might have been better off being adopted. At least it would have all been legal and out in the open, without dark and sinful secrets waiting to shame her.'

Anne believed that her mother had suffered enough over these past years, and she hoped that at some point it would somehow all come right, although there were times when, in her deepest heart, she felt it never would.

And now her mother's friends had upset her all over again. 'I know how you feel about Tony and Eileen, and I know you deeply regret what happened,' Anne said to her mother. 'But Dave and I would never have turned you away. We're family, and families look after each other always.'

Anne recalled the night when she found Marie crying on her doorstep. 'Yes, it was wrong what you did, but we're a family and we've always been there for each other. Dave is right, you've been punished for what you did and even now, you're still suffering, haunted by the truth and how it may affect Cathy's future.'

Marie shrugged. 'I deserve to suffer, but not Cathy. She is the innocent in all this. She will find it difficult to accept, but like all of us, she will have no option but to live with what happened. Oh, Anne, I'm so ashamed of myself, and I'm truly afraid for Cathy. But there is nothing that can be done, except to let her down as gently as possible when the time comes. I have agonised about that, but there is no other way. She has to be told, and it must be the truth – however difficult that might be for all of us.'

'After almost twenty years, we've come to that crossroads. There is no way of going back, no way of making it easier,' Anne said, wrapping her arm about her mother's shoulders.

Marie agreed. 'All we can do is hope that she can find it in her heart to forgive us, to understand, and know how much we cherish her.'

'Oh, Mum, she must know that already.'

Hugely grateful for her daughter's reassuring words, Marie thanked her with a loving kiss on the cheek. 'I'm a fortunate woman to have such a caring family around me.'

The truth still weighed heavily on her mind. Marie whispered, 'One day, maybe sooner rather than later, Cathy is bound to meet some fine young man she hopes to marry. She may even have met him already in Ronnie. They may want to start a family. And what then? How do we explain our long silence? Which way do we turn? Do we wait until then to tell her the truth, or do we tell her some time soon? So many questions, sweetheart, and I don't have the answers.' Marie felt broken. 'All I know is that we must tell her. She deserves that much at least.'

'You're right! And whatever happens after that, we must all be there for her.'

'If she still wants us,' Marie replied softly.

The silence that followed said it all.

'For all these years, I've fretted over it – waking or sleeping, it has never given me any peace – yet even now, when we have finally decided that Cathy has to know sooner rather than later, I don't know if I can do it. What will she think of me, sleeping with my best friend's husband and then, when I find I'm pregnant, bringing my troubles to you? Yes, I was at my wits' end, but involving you and Dave was a selfish, cowardly thing to do. Yet you helped me through it and you never once condemned me.'

'You would have done the very same if it had been the other way round, if I had been pregnant with another man's child,' Anne assured her. 'You were absolutely distraught, almost suicidal. We wanted to help, whatever it took. Now, after all these years, we find ourselves with a terrible dilemma, and the prospect of heartache for Cathy, but we will get through it, one way or another.'

With a heavy heart, Marie hugged her daughter. 'I've caused such mayhem, and I'm so afraid. What if Cathy turns away from us when we tell her the truth? What if she leaves and we never see her again?'

'Nothing will come of you constantly punishing yourself. You'll make yourself ill. And what you and Tony did, well, I've always believed you were totally lost after Dad died so suddenly. It rocked your world, and for a long time you were out of reach, devastated and alone. Dad was everything to you. If he hadn't died, you never would have done what you did.'

Marie could not find words to explain how strange and lonely life had been without her beloved husband. She discreetly brushed away her tears, which always rose when she thought of the wonderful man she had loved and lost.

'That's very true,' she said softly. 'But it doesn't justify what I did. Instead it makes me feel as though I had sullied his memory. Oh, I know Tony and me – it meant nothing to either of us. It just happened in a moment of loneliness. And now, until the day I follow your dad to the grave, I will be forever ashamed.'

'You were in a dark place,' Anne reminded her kindly. 'After Dad died, we were so worried for you. I remember you crying all the time, going without sleep, not eating, and walking for hours on the common.' She gave a little smile. 'With me sneaking along behind you to make sure you were all right. Dave and I could do little to help, except to have you with us, to love and protect you. Somehow you had to get through it, and what you did, I'm convinced, was out of inconsolable grief because you were confused and lost. For a long time, you were not thinking straight.'

When Marie's eyes again filled with tears, Anne

reached out to draw her closer. 'Please, don't upset yourself, Mum.'

'But I do, Anne,' Marie cried, 'because hand on heart, I don't know if I could reveal the identity to Cathy of her true father.'

'But, Mum, I thought we agreed to be truthful to her when the time came? Lord knows, I'm not looking forward to explaining that the father she's loved all these years is not truly her father.'

Marie nodded, worrying now about those the truth coming out would affect who weren't part of her family. 'Tony's wife is also an innocent casualty in all of this, and I've already damaged their marriage. I saw that clearly for myself in a look, or a word. The total trust they once had has gone, and I did that to them. I can hardly imagine the damage it would cause if I were to reveal that Tony is Cathy's father. As far as Tony and Eileen are concerned, I haven't yet decided which way to go. I need to think.'

Anne was very patient, but she didn't want her mother to lose all sense of purpose when she seemed to have decided to act at last. 'But you have agreed that Cathy should be told the truth, and you've said you're nearly ready to confess everything to her. If she insists on knowing the name of her real father, you must tell that too. Are you ready to do that, Mum? Because a half-truth won't do. So think long and hard, Mum, because there will be no going back.'

'I know, and how hard this is for you and Dave.

We have always known that this day would come, but it's for me alone to explain. You do understand that, don't you, sweetheart?' Marie took a long, hard breath, before nervously assuring her, 'I won't shirk my duty, however uncomfortable, but it's going to break all our hearts, especially poor Cathy's.' A sob trembled in her voice. 'Oh, Anne, I fear she will want to know the name of her real father, but whatever happens, I will answer whatever questions she puts to me.' She shook her head in despair. 'Though when the truth is out, so many good people are going to be hurt.' Her voice fell to a whisper. 'Oh, Anne! Will Cathy ever forgive me? Eileen hasn't and I can't blame her. She doesn't even know everything.'

'I honestly don't know. But whatever happens, you must tell her the truth. The older she gets, the harder it feels.'

'And I will tell her!' Marie's voice fell to the softest whisper. 'It's time.'

In that pensive moment, Marie cast her mind back to the day she had lain with Tony, and even now after all these years, her guilt was like a lead weight about her neck. The worry when she found herself to be pregnant with his child with Derek not even cold in his grave. She felt wicked. It all came flooding back – all the disgust and shame when she first discovered she was pregnant, then the unbearable ordeal of having to turn to her family with the shameful truth. She had involved them in a shocking deception, and for that she would never forgive herself. And Marie was crippled by guilt that she had deceived Eileen into believing that she had aborted Tony's child. If she were to tell Cathy that Tony was her birth father, two more lives could be ruined. It was a step too far for Marie's conscience. Her old friend had believed her when – out of panic – she had told her that the pregnancy had been terminated, but because of that, she was able to come to terms with Marie's liaison with Tony and at least find a semblance of peace with him in their later years.

Marie had just mopped away her tears when the sitting room door opened and Cathy's smiling face peeped in. 'What are you two chatting about? You've been ages in here!' She came over and joined them on the sofa.

'Oh, it was just something and nothing.' Marie gave Cathy a cuddle. 'Sorry, but we got talking about the holiday. You know what it's like – your mum wanted every little detail.'

Marie's heart skipped a beat when Cathy wagged a finger at them. 'Don't tell lies, you two, because I know what you were talking about, you can't fool me!'

CHAPTER NINE

Fᴏʀ ᴀ ᴍᴏᴍᴇɴᴛ, both Anne and Marie were para-
lysed with shock at Cathy's remarks, but then
greatly relieved when she innocently explained, 'I'm
guessing you were talking about my birthday, I bet
you've already started to make plans. So, am I right
or am I wrong?' She laughed. 'Got you! You might
as well own up. You know I don't like surprises, so
come on, give me all the details.'

Marie rallied and gave a nervous smile. 'We're
saying nothing. You'll just have to wait and see.'

Cathy sensed that something wasn't right, and her
heart sank. She often felt that they were keeping
something from her and it worried her. But she kept
up the pretence. Cathy groaned and argued about
her birthday but the women would have none of her
bullying. 'Oh, all right then.' Cathy kissed them both.
'I knew it, you really were planning my party. I knew
I was right!'

'No more questions, Cathy.' Anne was laughing with relief. 'Just leave it to Nan and me, and I promise you'll not be disappointed.' She got up and went to see what Dave was doing.

'When you plan my party, can we have a huge cake and candles and lots of music? And will I be allowed to invite all my friends and colleagues from the shop? Is that all right, Nan?' Cathy asked, shifting across the sofa.

'Yes, you can invite whoever you want,' Marie smiled. 'And speaking of the shop, why aren't you there today?'

'It's my day off,' said Cathy. 'But don't let's talk about work when there's a party to plan.'

Marie gave Cathy a hug. 'I have no doubt you'll have us worn out before the day arrives. It's still a few weeks away, so there'll be plenty of time for us all to finalise the arrangements. For now, just try and calm down. You're like a little whirlwind.' She shook her head and tutted. 'It sounds to me like you want a wild, rowdy party that will send the neighbours running for the hills. I can see it all now. None of us will get any peace until your party plans are up and running. I should have stayed at the seaside for another week or so, at least it's quieter there.'

'That's not fair! And anyway, I don't think you should go there on your own again. I vote we all come with you. We can keep you in check, and keep an eye on that Danny Magee you're so friendly with.

I suspect you've taken a fancy to him.' She gave a cheeky little wink.

'No! I have no wish to link up with any man! Oh, I'm not saying Danny Boy isn't a decent fellow, or that I don't enjoy his company, because I do. I've spent many an amusing hour listening to him and John. They always make me smile.'

She laughed now, as she described some of the antics the two men had got up to in the years that she was a regular in Blackpool. 'Oh, but I do love to hear their crazy tales about the many tricks they've played on the boss, or when they got in a tiff with some feisty woman. But best of all, I've been amazed at the wild plans they seemed to be forever hatching. It was always something big and bold, which was bound to make them rich gentlemen of leisure, but which, in the end, never came to fruition.' She laughed, remembering times past. 'Mad as hatters they are, the pair of them!' Thinking about John and Danny, and how unhappy this latest trip to Blackpool had been made her feel a little sad. She actually felt a pang in her heart at having met up with Danny when she was all alone, and finding him aged but yet unchanged. 'Genuine fellows, that's what they are,' she told Cathy. 'What you see is what you get. They don't care who knows what they've been up to. Flirting with the ladies, gambling at the betting shops, or doing dodgy deals with anyone who has something valuable to sell – it all comes out eventually. But I tell you what, the place would not be the same without them.'

Cathy remembered them, but from a young girl's point of view. They'd seemed quite old to her. 'What do you think they would do if they retired and they didn't have to work any more?'

Marie did not have to think too hard about that, 'I really can't say exactly what they might do, sweetheart, but I would imagine it would probably be something a little devious, maybe involving dodging and diving on the wrong side of the law.' She chuckled merrily. 'I've a feeling they might enjoy that.'

'I hope it won't be too long before we can all see John and Danny again,' Cathy remarked. 'It would be awful if we went there on holiday and they had already gone.'

'It would be awful, as you say,' said Marie. 'The thing is, though, they're almost part of the furniture, if you know what I mean, causing mayhem and being their naughty selves. I'm convinced they will be there for many years, so long as their health keeps up. They belong there, an integral part of the Promenade, even of Blackpool itself. They're like the Blue Bench and the Victorian railings, the candyfloss and the Punch and Judy Show on the beach.'

Marie tried to picture Blackpool without John and Danny at the heart of it all. 'If they were not there any more, with their hearty laughter and loud arguments, and their utmost dedication to keeping the

Promenade beautiful – well, I know for sure they would be sorely missed by everyone, especially the children.'

Cathy was intrigued. 'Why the children, Nan?' she said, kicking her shoes off and kneeling up on the sofa.

'Well, because they love them! Danny once told me that he had not been fortunate enough to be married and have children. Too busy playing the field, I suspect. It's such a shame, because from what I've seen, the children love him, and he loves them. He always has a bag of sweets in his jacket pocket, or he might have a magic trick up his sleeve. If they're lost and upset, he turns their tears into laughter until a parent or relative comes to collect them.'

'Oh, yes Nan, I remember what parents tell their children they must do if they ever get separated from family: find their way to the Blue Bench and wait for their parents to collect them.'

Marie explained, 'You can see the Blue Bench from anywhere on the beach, and that's when children mostly get lost, running about on the beach.'

'I think that's a really good idea, Nan. So when I have children and we go on holiday to Blackpool, I'll know what to tell them, won't I?'

Momentarily pulled up by Cathy's innocent comment, Marie merely smiled, but her heart was torn, as always, when thinking of the awful truth that was sure to be revealed in the not-too-distant future.

Marie always loved her talks with Cathy, they could talk about anything and everything for hours on end. But the family secret was always lurking like a dark ghost.

'Nan?' Cathy's voice interrupted Marie's troubled thoughts. 'You didn't finish telling me about Danny. Why do he and Big John argue so much?'

'Because they can't help it, that's why. They're a right pair. One minute they're arguing the toss, then in the next they're off at a run, hiding from the boss and giggling like a pair of schoolkids. But on the whole they're good people, and nobody, not even their boss, could accuse them of being lazy. They work their socks off, they really do. So yes, I like Danny, as an occasional friend. He's a bit like the Blue Bench, sturdy and handsome in a boyish kind of way, but with a hint of eccentricity and glamour. Oh, and he's always there when you need him. And yes, I'll admit, he's a bit of a flirt. In fact I suspect he thinks all women fancy him, but then he's a man, isn't he?'

'Does he ever flirt with you, Nan?'

'Of course he does. He flirts with all the women, he just can't help himself. But I always manage to put him in his place.'

'And do you flirt with him sometimes?'

'Absolutely not! I haven't seen him in years and back then it was your granddad Derek and our friends that used to while away the hours talking to those two old pals. But with Danny I believe that if you gave him an inch, he would take a yard!' she added with a little smile. 'But I have to admit that his is good company.'

'How old is he, Nan?'

'What? How am I supposed to know that?'

'Well, if you don't know, make a good guess.' Cathy was insistent.

Marie had no idea as to Danny's age, and neither did she want to know. 'Let me see . . . I heard him and John arguing years ago as to how they were heading towards the retirement door any time soon. I recall John saying how fortunate they both were to still be in full-time work. Danny reminded him that they were hard workers, and that was probably why they were still gainfully employed. He was willing to bet the last shilling in his pocket that the powers that be would never find a couple of younger blokes who would be willing to work the long hours and still keep a pride in their work.'

'And that's the truth, Nan?' Cathy asked. 'Do they really work all hours?'

'Absolutely! Last night when I'd left the bench to head back to the hotel for my dinner, it was way past six o'clock, and the pair of them were still working away, painting the railings. Yes indeed sweetheart, I do believe that they must be way past their sixties now, and still working like a couple of young lads.'

'So do you think the bosses will let them carry on working?'

'Why all these questions, young lady? I wasn't up there up to no good!'

'Oh, I'm sorry, Nan, I was just being nosy, that's all.'

Cathy had an idea of how lonely her nan had been ever since Granddad Derek had died, even before she herself was born. And she often felt truly sad that she had never known him, because she knew he had been a lovely man from what everyone said about him. Whenever she looked through the family photograph album, his kindly face made her smile.

Cathy still thought that maybe the little Irishman did have a little fancy for her nan. And if he did, maybe it wouldn't be a bad thing if the two of them did get together some time. As far as she could tell, there was nothing wrong in that, although if he were the rascal her nan had described him to be, Cathy did wonder whether he might even be married.

Her thoughts were interrupted when Marie picked up on the very subject. 'If I'm honest, I have to admit that Danny is really good company,' she told Cathy. 'But he's a storyteller, and a dreamer. It wouldn't surprise me if he doesn't add a few untruths to his supposedly true stories to make them more exciting, and make him seem more like the man every woman wants.' She laughed. 'To tell the truth, he really is a scallywag! In fact, I wouldn't be at all surprised if he's got a couple of wives tucked away somewhere.'

'But you do like him, don't you, Nan?'

'It's hard not to like him! In the main, he's a good and kind man. In the old days, when I was a regular in Blackpool, it was almost like he knew when I was tired or weary. Often, when the sun was burning overhead and I stopped to rest on the bench, he would turn up with an ice cream for me, or a bottle of pop, and if it got too hot in the sunshine, he would always let me sit in the tool-shed where it was nice and cool. One time he even trusted me with the keys.' She laughed at the memory. 'That is until the boss found out and threatened him with the sack right there on the Promenade, with everyone listening. I don't mind telling you, it was embarrassing.'

She hoped it would not be too long before she was back there again, settling on the Blue Bench with an ice cream and the warm sun shining down on her. And Danny Boy spinning his beautiful yarns, like he actually believed them.

Now, though, she thought it only right to let Cathy know that she was not the slightest bit interested in any man. 'Danny is a good and kind fellow, and I'm sure he would make a suitable husband for some lonely woman, but not for me, sweetheart. First of all, I'm not really lonely, especially when I have my wonderful family about me. And besides, I had a truly fine and good man in your granddad, bless his heart and soul, so why would I want a relationship with any other man? No, I am not interested in any man,' she gave a dreamy kind of smile, 'and I never will be.'

'I tell you what, Nan!' said Cathy, cuddling up. 'Why don't we all of us go to Blackpool next time – the whole family, I mean? Why don't we all come with you to the seaside and sit on the Blue Bench and watch the sun set, just like we sometimes used to do?'

Cathy grew increasingly excited at the idea. 'Oh, and would it be all right if we took Ronnie? I know he likes Blackpool because they used to go as a family when he was a little boy, and he and Beth haven't been for a long time.'

'We'll have to wait and see what the others think. Let's leave it for a while, eh?' Marie gave a knowing smile. 'You really like Ronnie, don't you? I mean, you've been good friends for a year now?'

'A bit longer than that, Nan.' Cathy blushed. 'It's more than "like". I think it's getting really serious.'

'I suspected so from what you said earlier. But at your age you don't want to go diving head first into a serious relationship.'

When Cathy blushed and simply nodded, Marie suspected that she might have been too stern, and so she made an effort to put it right. 'I must admit, he does seem like a nice young man, always polite, not too rowdy like the others next door. And he's good-looking, too.'

'If I tell you a secret, Nan, will you keep it to yourself?'

'Woah!' Marie did not like the sound of that. 'So, you're hiding a secret, are you?' Both the past and the future rushed in to make her feel guilty. 'What kind of secret is it?'

'It's all right, Nan, and please don't laugh, but, well . . .' she blushed crimson.

'Go on then, tell me!' Marie encouraged her.

'Well, I think . . .' Cathy blushed even pinker, 'I might be in love with him, Nan.'

Marie was taken aback, and felt an urge to protect this lovely young girl. 'Cathy, sweetheart, are you sure you don't just like him a lot, because – well now – I hope you know that "love" and "like" are two sides of the same coin.'

Cathy was confused. 'What does that mean, exactly?'

'Well, "loving" someone is a truly huge commitment. It's a much bigger, more powerful emotion than when you just "like" someone. Love abides much deeper in the heart, whereas liking is a gentler, more disciplined feeling, like the feelings you have for a friend, maybe.'

'But how can you tell which is which, Nan?'

'Well, like I said, with a friend, if you could not see them for maybe a few weeks, it would be all right and you wouldn't worry too much. Whereas if you love someone, you would probably miss them every minute. You might have such powerful, even painful feelings that you would want to be with that person all the time, you can hardly bear to be apart from them because you miss them too much. And it truly hurts. Do you see what I mean, Cathy?'

'Yes, Nan. I think I do.'

'So is it love, or like that you feel for Ronnie?'

Cathy's answer was both swift and decisive. 'It's love, Nan. When we're apart, I feel so terribly lonely. I just want to see him and hold him and hear him laugh. I want him to hold me, and never let me go. I just want to be with him all the time!'

'Shh, it's all right, you'll get him back. Ronnie will never abandon you. It's obvious that he loves you too much for that.' Marie slid an arm about Cathy's shoulders. When she thought of her beloved husband, now gone, Marie understood Cathy's anxiety that Ronnie had had to leave, and her eyes filled with tears. She could see Derek in her mind's eye, and as always she thought if she could only turn back the years and have him here again, she would in an instant.

'Listen to me, sweetheart,' she urged Cathy. 'Just now, when you described how you feel when you and Ronnie are apart, well, that's exactly how I felt with your granddad.' As the memories flooded back, she paused to compose herself.

Superimposed on the memories was the shameful thought of how she had disgraced herself in having created a child with a man she had no real feelings for, which only made the deed more sordid and unforgiveable. And yet, whenever she looked at that lovely girl, she had to ask herself, if she could turn back the clock and wipe out what happened, could she? Would she? Would she trade Cathy's existence in return for a salve to her conscience? Whenever she asked herself that painful question, she always reached the same conclusion. Cathy was so very precious, how could she ever wipe out her very existence?

Unaware of Marie's deeper thoughts but seeing sadness in her face, Cathy apologised. 'I'm sorry, Nan, I didn't mean to upset you.'

It was obvious to Cathy that her nan was still thinking of her much-loved husband, and she said as much.

Marie shrugged off the old memories. 'You haven't upset me, sweetheart. I was thinking of you and Ronnie actually, and the way you feel about him.' She paused momentarily. 'Will you do something for me, sweetheart?'

'Of course I will, Nan.'

'I just want you to promise me that you won't rush into anything, You're not yet nineteen, and Ronnie is in his early twenties, so you and Ronnie have time on your side to get to know each other much better before you actually start thinking of marrying.'

Cathy must definitely be told who her real parents were before she offered herself in marriage.

'Nan!' Cathy was concerned that her nan appeared to have wandered off in deep thought. 'What's wrong?'

Marie brought her thoughts back to reality. 'What do you mean?'

'Well, you went all silent. I was talking to you, but it was like you had gone into a trance or something,

Were you thinking I'm far too young to be talking of getting married?'

'I suppose so. I mean, I don't think you should *not* get married – I like Ronnie, he's a good sort and he adores you – but a wedding will cost a small fortune and, to be honest, I can't understand what all the rush is about.' A dreadful thought occurred to her. 'Oh my Lord, you're not pregnant, are you?'

'No!' Cathy giggled. 'Oh, Nan, is that what you thought?'

Marie smiled. 'Not really, I imagine you and Ronnie are both far too sensible to get yourselves in a pickle of that sort.'

'I won't rush into anything, Nan, hand on heart. I haven't even told Mum how I really feel about Ronnie.'

'Wise girl not to be in a hurry.' Marie approved of that. 'It's always best to wait and be sure than to make mistakes and be sorry afterwards.'

Anne popped her head around the door.

'What are you two plotting?' she asked. 'You've been in here ages.'

'Just chatting,' said Marie.

'We've got a lot to talk about,' Cathy added.

'We have, that,' Marie replied, and she and Anne exchanged knowing looks.

Cathy couldn't shake the sense that something was wrong, and asked her mum what they had been chatting about when she'd burst in to the sitting room. She was told that her nan had got herself into a sorry state of anxiety, about something and nothing.

Beyond that curious explanation, her mother would not discuss the incident, in any way, shape or form. Instead, she also made good her escape, and left Cathy wondering if she had done anything to trigger their 'odd' behaviour.

In truth, she wasn't sure they had been discussing her birthday at all, they seemed too much on edge. But she did still feel that they might have been discussing her. But if that was the case, what could have been so important or private that would make them want to hush up like that?

After a while though, Cathy told herself she was just being paranoid, and so dismissed the incident from her mind.

Instead, she focused on Ronnie . . . the love of her life.

She was so immensely relieved that he was now fully committed to her, in heart and mind, as she was to him.

She had a loving family, and she had Ronnie, and she was immensely grateful for all of that. And when Ronnie said those reassuring things to ease her questioning mind, all her doubts would fade away, and so she silently chastised herself for being too anxious about nothing in particular.

Thankfully, she was blissfully happy with her life. Indeed, she realised just what a fortunate girl she was, to have a strong, supportive family, and she considered herself especially fortunate to have Ronnie . . . a decent and loving person.

Sadly though and through no fault of his own, Ronnie was not with her just now, and she felt oddly lonely, and a little afraid.

He was the love of her life, and always would be. With him by her side, she felt strong, and safe and she ached for the moment when he was back here, with her.

PART TWO

Where There Is A Will There Is A Way

CHAPTER TEN

Ronnie had been trudging along for almost an hour.

He had chosen to walk across the fields, because the journey was much shorter, albeit rougher, and mostly uphill. Eventually, he rejoined the town and cut through the narrow walkways between the houses to speed his progress to his sister's house.

He felt both worn and hungry, after setting off without a bite to eat. His feet ached like merry hell, and the weight of his knapsack seemed to increase with every step.

Maybe I should have caught the bus, he thought. But then again, I needed to get out in the fresh air after the noise and chaos of Bob and Peggy's house . . . it helps me think. And I need to save every penny I can until I find work.

The thought of finding a new job, and earning a wage lifted his spirits.

As he walked along, he wondered if Cathy had got his letter by now. He also wondered if she was missing him like he was missing her. He hoped she realised that he truly meant what he said in the letter: that he loved her, and that one day in the future, he wanted to marry her and be with her for the rest of their lives.

More than anything, he hoped she understood why he had to leave.

He had walked to the station in happy anticipation of finding her waiting there with Anne for Marie's train, but when he neared the station building he saw the place was quiet and there were no taxis drawn up outside. Sure enough, the Manchester train had been and gone, the passengers had dispersed and Cathy was surely heading for home in a taxi. He had missed her.

He loved her so much, and he wanted to give her the world, but things were not right for him at the moment. It was as though he was stuck in a dead end and he felt miserable, especially as he was now without work or a place to lay his head.

As he walked from the station, and turned into Beth's road his troublesome thoughts were suddenly interrupted by a familiar voice. 'Ronnie!'

His sister, Beth, was running down the street towards him, and the sight of her filled his heart with love.

'Oh Ronnie!' she called out excitedly, 'I wasn't altogether sure it was you at first. But how lovely to see you!'

When she threw her arms about his neck he almost toppled over with the weight of the bag hanging over his shoulders. 'What are you doing here? Have you come to see me at long last? I was wondering if you'd ever call by again after the frosty reception Mike gave you last time. I am really sorry about that.'

'Don't be,' Ronnie assured her. 'It's all forgotten, so don't worry, eh?' They walked to the house arm in arm.

'Come on in and I'll make you a cuppa,' Beth said.

Some four years older than Ronnie, Beth was a shy and gentle woman, with a slim figure and a smile that lit up her small, pale face. Her light brown hair was long and flowing, and she had the brightest brown eyes, which were shining as she led her brother into the house.

Ronnie was so very happy to see her, even though it had been only a week or so since he and Cathy had met up with his sister at a little café.

He made a point of keeping in touch with his only sibling, especially since their parents had died, Beth had married Mike and the family house had been sold. Ronnie had made a vow that he would always keep an eye on his sister. He thought she had made a huge mistake in marrying Mike, the man she adored, and since his last visit here his suspicions were confirmed. Since then he'd made a point of meeting up with her elsewhere.

As they entered the kitchen, the questions came

thick and fast from Beth. 'What's happening? Why are you here? It isn't that I don't want you to be here, but I'm a little worried.'

She glanced at the big, heavy knapsack on his shoulder. 'You haven't fallen out with the lovely Cathy, have you? She's the loveliest person – the best girl-friend you've ever had – and I know you think the world of each other. Oh, Ronnie, please . . . don't tell me you two have fallen out?'

'Hey! No! Look, I'll explain if I can only get a word in. Cathy and I have not fallen out. I still love her, every little piece of her. And, unbelievably, I think she loves me.' He hesitated, feeling somewhat nervous. The last time he had been to Beth's, her husband had not been the most helpful man in the world. He worried deeply about his sister and knew he wouldn't be welcomed under their roof by Mike – he'd asked once and got short shrift.

'So, what's happened? Are you all right, Ronnie? Out with it. What's going on?'

'Nothing is "going on". Everything is fine. But I need to talk with you and Mike if that's all right. Now, don't take offence, but is everything okay between you and Mike?' He recalled how, some months back, Beth had confessed that she and Mike were suffering a sticky patch in their relationship. He didn't want to come barging in now if things were awkward between them.

Beth put him right. 'Everything is absolutely fine,

thanks for asking. And I sincerely apologise for the last time you came to see us. Mike was not very welcoming. But he had been feeling a little under the weather, and his workload was impossible at the time. And you know what he's like when he can't get his paperwork done and delivered to his clients.'

Ronnie nodded in agreement, although he knew his brother-in-law to be a nasty sort if he took a mind to be. 'But you're all right, are you, Beth?'

Because of the greeting he'd got last time from that miserable brother-in-law of his, Ronnie was beginning to feel guilty at having come here today. 'Look, sis, if my being here is going to cause bad blood and tempers flying, I can turn around right now and walk away. It's not a problem, really.'

'No!' She wrapped an arm about him. 'You're here now, and I want you to stay awhile. Besides, where are you off to . . . with that heavy knapsack over your shoulder?'

'Come on, sis! You didn't answer my question. Are you all right? Have things been okay between you and the man of the house?'

'Absolutely! We're very happy. So, will you stop whittling, and sit down.' She added somewhat nervously, 'About the last time you were here . . . Mike was really sorry for being like that after you'd gone.'

'It's all right, really. Please, Beth, let's just forget about it now. I do absolutely understand why Mike was unable to let me stay. He has a responsible job and I know he works at home a great deal of the time, so it's only right that he should have his quiet space without me padding about all over the place. Water under the bridge, as they say. So, where's that cuppa? I'm absolutely parched.'

As Beth turned away to put the kettle on to boil again, Ronnie could not help but wonder whether she was altogether telling him the truth with regards to her husband and herself being 'very happy'.

Since the first time he'd met his brother-in-law, Ronnie believed that his sister had chosen a man who was self-centred and miserly, and with a nasty temper to boot. Ronnie had sensed Mike's dark nature, and he vowed to keep a wary eye on this pompous man, who had carefully chosen the placid Beth as his doting wife.

So far, Ronnie had found no real cause to intervene to protect Beth in any way whatsoever, but that was not to say he was happy about his gentle sister being married to this arrogant man.

To Ronnie's mind, it was like putting a young chicken and a fox together: one was timid and afraid, the other capable of tearing it apart before devouring it.

Ronnie's sister appeared content most of the time, although over the years of her marriage she had often suffered with bad nerves.

Whenever Ronnie attempted to talk with her about the reasons for these attacks of nerves, she would simply brush him away with excuses: 'I'm just over-tired, that's all.' 'A few good nights of sleep and I'll be right as rain.' Thankfully, however, she did appear to get herself through these attacks.

Ronnie had no choice than to go along with what she said, although his deeper suspicions about her husband had never gone away. He had managed to extract a promise from Beth that if ever she felt the need to confide in him, or ask for his help for what-ever reason, she would, without hesitation. But she had insisted there was no need for him to worry about her in any way because she loved Mike and was content with him.

'So, Ronnie, what's going on in your world then?' Beth asked, pouring water into the teapot. She thought to mention it now, by way of an apology on her husband's behalf. 'I'm sorry we let you down the last time you were here,' she whispered nervously. 'Mike was really sorry about turning you away, but please, don't judge him too harshly, will you?'

Ronnie appreciated her trying to build bridges between himself and her husband, but the very idea of being friendly with that man was abhorrent to him. 'Please, Beth . . . let's leave it alone now, eh? There is no harm done . . . honestly. As far as I'm concerned, it's all water under the bridge.'

He put on a smile. 'I've got plans, and I need to find work and a place to stay temporarily until I get myself properly settled. That's why I'm here, to tell you of my plans, and to say cheerio. And to tell you not to worry about me, because I'll be fine, although I might not be able to call you for the next few days.'

Beth looked relieved at his positive tone, but, even so, he sensed her nervousness. 'Well, I'm very glad you came round to explain what's happening. I'm sure Mike will be pleased to see you too, he should be home any minute.'

Ronnie explained that the house next door to Cathy's, where he had been lodging, was now being let out, and the present tenants had been ordered to move on. 'So when I saw the way things were going there, I went back and grabbed my things. I was laid off at the garage a few weeks back, so I'm making a new start.'

'I know you'll find work, and a home, even if it is only temporary. At least it will carry you through until you decide to put down roots with Cathy.'

Ronnie agreed. 'I love her so much,' he confessed. 'I mean to do her proud. Whatever it takes, I want to marry her, to give her a home where we can raise our children. I'll miss her terribly while I'm away, but I hope it won't be too long before I fulfil my ambitions for the two of us.' He smiled shyly. 'Cathy is the only one I have ever wanted, and I mean to do my best for her.'

'And you will, I have no doubts about that. I'm sure Cathy will be waiting for the day you get back. But . . . you must keep in touch with her – and with me – in the meantime. Do you promise?'

'Of course! You don't even need to ask.'

'Good!' She gave him a fond hug, to seal the promise.

~

While Beth was setting out the tea things, Ronnie noticed that the garden underneath the back window was becoming overgrown. Before Beth had realised, he was out there weeding and clearing up for all he was worth to save Beth the job.

Suddenly her voice startled him. 'No! Please, Ronnie, don't be doing that,' she called anxiously from the kitchen door. 'That's Mike's job, and for whatever reason, he likes to work on that area himself. I think it's probably because he's always sitting at a desk, and never gets much exercise.'

'Oh dear, I'm sorry. I should have asked before diving in, only I thought that maybe you were the one who tended it,' Ronnie replied. 'I'm really sorry, sis. I should have asked.'

'It's all right, don't worry.' Sounding somewhat nervous, but with a bright smile, she called, 'Come back inside. I've got a slice of walnut cake with your name on it.'

After returning to the kitchen and washing his hands, Ronnie sat with Beth at the table.

The two of them were sharing cake and a precious moment of laughter about something that had happened when they were children when the door was flung open and Mike stood there, eyes wide and legs straddled, looking startled to see his brother-in-law.

'Well, if it isn't Ronnie! Hmm! Welcome to our humble abode. All right, are you?' Whipping his coat off, he flung it over the back of the chair. 'And what, might I ask, brings you here?'

'Well, first of all, thank you, yes, I'm fine. And, I hope you don't mind, but I just popped in to see you both and to tell you my news, that's all.'

'Really? And what "news" might that be?'

Before Ronnie could reply, Mike gave a twitchy little smile as he caught sight of Ronnie's bag. 'Ah, by the look of it, you're on your way somewhere, so I take it you'll be off any minute now, will you?'

'Well, yes, that's the plan.' Clearly Ronnie's brother-in-law could not get rid of him soon enough.

'Oh well, that's all right then. I was thinking there for a minute that you might be looking to stay awhile. But I'm afraid the answer would be exactly the same as last time: no can do.'

Ronnie was disappointed but not altogether surprised at Mike's caustic comments, and he thought he should make tracks sooner rather than later.

'I'd best be off and away, before it gets dark.' Ronnie pushed his chair back and stood up. Then he pushed the chair back in, and after tidying his plate and cup away he picked up his knapsack.

'Thanks for the cake, sis.' He gave Beth a long hug. 'You always were a good cook.'

Mike nodded. 'It looks like we understand each other. You see . . . I've taken on a bit of extra work at the accountants, and I'm still using that little boxroom as an office. Sorry, mate! We would put you up if we could, but no can do, I'm afraid.' He ended the sentence with a sharp click of the tongue, almost as though applauding himself.

Going across the room, Mike put his arm about his wife in a possessive way and gave her a sound kiss on the cheek. 'Sorry, sweetheart, you haven't already promised to put him up, have you? Maybe the next time your brother needs somewhere to lay his head we might be in a position to give him a helping hand, but not this time, I'm afraid.'

Ronnie fully understood, but to avoid upsetting Beth, he was determined not to reveal his dislike of this arrogant man.

Going over to Beth, he took her hands in his. 'Look after yourself, sis. If you need me – for whatever reason – write or call Cathy.' He looked into Beth's eyes and knew she understood exactly what he was implying. 'I haven't got an address just yet, but I'll be in touch with her, so don't fret, I'll be fine . . . soon as I've tracked down a job . . . which I am determined to do.'

'Oh, I see . . .' Mike had a curious little grin on his face. 'So you're unemployed, are you? Well, I'm sorry to hear that. What's your plan, then?' He added with sarcasm, 'I do so hope you and Cathy are not having difficulties?'

'No, Cathy and I are as strong as ever. We love each other, and as soon as we can, we'll be planning to get married.'

'Really? Hmm!' Mike gave a grudging smile. 'Well, I hope she knows what she'll be getting herself into.' He chuckled. 'Sorry. That was just a tease. No offence meant.'

Ronnie felt the urge to punch him, but then he thought of his sister and held back his anger. He didn't want her to suffer after he was gone.

'Well, I'd best be off . . .' He wrapped his arms about Beth. 'I need to find a place to stay, a base of sorts so I can look about for work. There doesn't seem to be much work going in these parts at the minute, not that I've heard of anyway.'

'You'll find work, don't worry,' Beth assured him, 'Someone is always looking out for good workers, and I'm sure they won't get better than you.'

'Thanks, sis, for that boost of confidence. I'll let you know how I get on.'

'Good! And just make sure you do!' Beth reached up and cupped Ronnie's face in the palms of her hands. 'I'll be thinking of you.'

A moment later, the two of them hugged goodbye, and then Ronnie picked up his knapsack and slung it over his shoulder. He was going out the door when Mike called him back.

'Hey! What kind of work are you looking for?'

'Well . . . I'm not all that fussy, and I'm not afraid of hard work. I'll be up for anything that can earn me good money. Like I said, Cathy and I have plans, and I am determined to come back with money in my pocket so I can make her my wife sooner rather than later.'

'Well, let's hope you get fixed up then, eh?' Mike was ever so slightly jealous. 'You should remember, though, never to promise more than you can deliver or you'll have both Cathy and her family on your back, not to mention my wife!'

His snide comment was quickly overridden by Beth. 'If Ronnie says he'll do a thing, I'm sure he will, because he's always been a person of his word, even as a boy.'

'Oh, really?' Mike had a dark scowl on his face. 'You know that for certain, do you?'

'Of course I do.'

'Well, then! He should have no trouble charming himself into a job of sorts, and good luck to him.' He turned to Ronnie, 'Yes, good luck, mate. I expect you'll let your sister know what happens, will you?' Beneath the smile his dislike was palpable.

As Ronnie went out the front door, Mike followed him. 'Look, if you're not afraid of hard work, as you say, you might do well to contact the council office. They've always got work going on. If you're prepared to work down the sewers and pick up all the uncomfortable jobs that others would never touch you might just be lucky and get taken on. It's worth a try, don't you think, unless of course, you would rather not get your hands dirty?'

Realising that the other man was deliberately goading him, Ronnie gave a little smile. 'Oh, don't worry, Mike. And thanks for the tip anyway, but I'm used to getting my hands dirty. The thing is, we can't all have cushy numbers in a warm, spick-and-span office, can we, eh?'

When he caught the little warning grimace on his sister's face, he realised he should not have goaded her husband like that. He hoped she wouldn't have to pay for his annoying Mike.

Now he tried to make amends, for Beth's sake. 'What I mean is, Mike, if I had your ability with figures and such I would not be so eager to shovel muck. The trouble is, I never did much learning. Instead I used to skip school at every opportunity. I was always off somewhere messing about with muck and rubbish, and wasting my time sailing silly paper boats down the canal.'

'Well, there you go, eh? You reap what you sow – isn't that what they say?'

'Yes, and it's true! I became a bit of a wanderer after I left school. Mum and Dad had died and I didn't want to live in the house all alone. I wanted excitement and adventure, but I soon learned that there was no future in that.'

Satisfied that he had diffused the atmosphere and played up to the other man's bloated ego, he again said his goodbyes. 'I'll be in touch, and make sure the two of you are looking after each other, eh?'

As he shook hands with Mike, he gave as genuine a smile as he could manage. 'Thanks, Mike. I apologise for having interrupted your day. I know you would have put me up if you had the room.'

He had learned over the years that his sister's husband was a proud and peevish man, who loved a bit of flattery.

'Oh! Think nothing of it, Ronnie, we do what we can, but at the moment, I'm afraid our space is limited.

'Best of luck then!' Mike lost no time in closing the door.

Outside on the pavement, Ronnie felt the need to say some final words, a proper cheerio to his sister, so he tapped on the parlour window, where he could see Mike talking sternly to her. Beth rushed outside to him. 'Oh, Ronnie, I'm sorry we weren't able to help you . . . again.' Obviously upset, she flung her arms about his neck. 'Please look after yourself, and stay well,' she murmured. 'Promise me that you will keep in touch. I'll be worrying until I know you're all right.'

'Don't fret.' He hugged her hard in return. 'You know I can take care of myself if I have to. It's you I'm worried about.'

'I shall be all right,' Beth said quietly, and her tacit acknowledgement that there was cause for worry rent Ronnie's heart. This was his big sister, who had been so protective of him when he was very little and she wasn't much bigger. Now it was she who seemed small and vulnerable.

Suddenly a reckless idea flew into Ronnie's head and he found himself saying it aloud without thinking it through.

'Come with me, Beth. Leave Mike and let's go make our fortunes together. He's not good for you and I hate to see you so . . . so cowed by his temper and his bullying.'

'No . . . no, I can't . . . we're fine.'

'We could go right away from here, find a place that will take us both on, somewhere you will feel safe and happy. 'Cos I think you feel neither safe nor happy with Mike, do you? You're brilliant at baking – that walnut cake was the best I've ever eaten – someone would pay good money to employ you to bake like that for them. There's a whole world of possibilities, of people who would recognise your talents out there, Beth, and I don't want you to . . . well, to throw your life away because you've made a mistake and married the wrong man.'

'I can't, Ronnie,' Beth said in anguish. 'I can't just go. I married him, I promised to love, honour and, yes, obey him. I can't just walk out when things get tough.'

'But they shouldn't *be* tough,' Ronnie reasoned. 'They should be loving and kind and fun. That's what marriage should be; that's what I want to give Cathy.'

'And it's what Cathy deserves. She'll be a lucky girl the day she becomes your wife, but we all have a free choice and I have made mine. I can't just walk away now without trying as hard as I can to make it work.'

'Beth, please—'

'I'm sorry, Ronnie, but that's the way it has to be.'

'Then there's nothing else I can say.'

'I think we've both said enough,' Beth replied with a sad little smile.

In return he hugged her again, and now he was heading away.

At the corner of the street, he turned to wave a farewell, calling out, 'Look after yourself, Beth, love you! I'll let you know how I get on.' And then, he was gone.

Left behind, Beth felt incredibly lonely and abandoned.

For what seemed an age, she remained there, standing very still, gazing at the spot where her brother had lingered. But he was gone now, and she was truly sorry.

After a while, she turned away, and, glancing towards the house, she felt a sudden urge to run from there, as far and as fast as she possibly could. She wished now that she had been strong enough to tell Ronnie how deeply unhappy she was in her marriage. He had guessed, but she should have had the courage to admit it, and maybe gone with him.

But that would not have been fair to him, especially when he had no work and no place to live. She would have been a burden to him.

In that lonely moment, the driving urge to go after Ronnie was very strong in her. She so needed to confess her soul to him, about the truth of her marriage. But she was so afraid of what might happen if she did.

Without a doubt Ronnie would confront her husband, and Mike would no doubt retaliate violently, as he always did when rattled, which was often.

And so, for that reason alone she must keep her silence for at least a while longer.

Her voice trembled, as she chided herself, 'Oh, Ronnie . . . I am such a coward! I wish I had the strength to tell you the truth . . . to ask for your help and find a way to escape this prison of a house, and get far away as fast as I can, from the monster I fool-ishly married!'

With a deep sigh, she turned around, when in that crazy moment she told herself that she should be running after her brother . . . pleading with him to take her along, to wherever he might be going.

Now she had no choice but to hurry back inside, before Mike came out, ranting and raving. She took a deep breath, and turned away from the street, while holding in her heart the image of her brother's loving smile as he waved to her.

On entering the house, she softly closed the door behind her, and made her way along the corridor to the sitting room, where Mike was knocking back a generous glass of whisky.

From the dark scowl on his face Beth realised with a sinking heart that he was not in the best of moods. 'Oh, you're back, are you?' he snapped at her. 'I can see now that you'd rather spend time with your brother than be with your husband. Well, I don't want him in my house ever again, d'you hear?'

When she was slow to answer, he began pacing back and forth, faster and faster, muttering under his breath. 'That cocky brother of yours has got a damned cheek coming here again expecting us to put him up. I've told you before, I have no time for the likes of him.' He stopped pacing to glower at her. 'Did you hear what I said?'

'Yes.'

'And what were the two of you whispering about outside, eh? I hope you weren't talking about me behind my back, were you?'

'No!'

'I'm about to ask you and you had best give me a truthful answer because I won't like it if you lie to me. No, I won't like it at all!' Beth did not reply because she did not know what he wanted from her. For what seemed an age she waited for him to ask his question, but he remained silent, which unnerved her especially as she could see from the bottle that he had drunk a lot of whisky. He was angry, and when he was both drunk and angry he was like a madman.

Fearing his temper, she gave a small, nervous smile. 'Please, don't drink any more whisky, sweetheart,' she pleaded with him.

'Don't tell me what to do! So, what were you and that brother of yours talking about just now outside?'

'We were just saying goodbye, that's all.'

'You had better be telling me the truth!'

When he now took a menacing step forward, Beth recognised he was in one of his dark moods, and she instinctively inched away.

Enraged at her silence, Mike began ranting. 'Huh! Took you long enough to say goodbye, didn't it? Forgot your husband was waiting inside, did you? Rather be with your precious brother instead of spending time with your husband – the man who clothes and feeds you, and puts a roof over your head – something that your precious brother would probably never be able to do!'

His rampage made her nervous.

'So, tell me then! Why did you linger outside with him instead of getting back in here to spend time with me, your husband, who by the way, is not impressed at your behaviour. Not impressed at all!'

He sauntered unsteadily towards her. Recognising

the look in his eye as he approached, Beth felt threatened. As always, he went straight for her. Grabbing handfuls of her long thick hair with his strong hands. He ignored her cries and forced her up the stairs and onto the bed, where he climbed on top of her.

As always, he also ignored her pitiful pleas for him to let her go.

He loved her, and he hated her at the same time. To the sound of her cries for him to stop, he took her when and how he wanted. He was never gentle, nor loving, and not once did he think of her fear or pain.

To Beth at such moments, he was the devil in disguise, a monster gone mad. And when it was over, he simply walked away, satisfied and smiling wickedly.

She was too afraid and too weak to fight him, and she would never dare betray him, or reject him.

She knew him well enough to fear the consequences if she did.

CHAPTER ELEVEN

Ronnie was fast losing hope. It was two days later and he'd had no success in finding a job. The problem at first was that he was on foot and so his options were limited. He'd found a very cheap bed-and-breakfast place to stay but he soon exhausted all the possibilities of employment as far as he could go in every direction.

He risked a bus fare and went further afield, towards Manchester. Sometimes he spoke to the boss, sometimes he met workers coming off shift, but at every place he was told there was nothing for him.

There was one office job at a print works, but Ronnie had no skills for that and was turned down flat when the manager enquired as to his education. At another place, a clothing factory, he thought there was a real chance of some work, but he hung around for over two hours and then was told that the job had gone to someone already known to the boss.

His hopes were raised at a canning factory, where there was a vacancy on the production line, but as he waited outside the office above the factory floor to see if he was to be taken on, he overheard an argument between a shop steward and the manager, and it was plain that the factory was a hotbed of dissent and strikes were commonplace. Ronnie knew he would never be able to save up for a home for Cathy if his pay was continually docked because he'd been called out on strike so he upped and left without being interviewed.

There was nothing for it but to move on and keep trying. Shouldering his bag again, he set off on foot. The scenery grew more rural as he traipsed further north. He held out hope of maybe finding a job on a farm, inexperienced though he was at that kind of work.

Feeling bone weary, he decided to take a quick break to catch his breath and think things through before making any rash decision, but he needed to get away from the main road where there was no footpath on which to stop safely. He glanced about and was relieved when he spied a turning not too far away. It seemed to be a lane of sorts, cutting away from the major road, and partially hidden amongst a chaotic mess of what looked like a natural growth of bracken and trees.

He made for that, hoping that maybe, just maybe, he would find a mobile snack bar, or a café. His throat felt parched and his whole body was aching from tip to toe.

After only a few steps into the narrow lane, he was relieved to find a rickety snack-wagon, a shack of a café, tucked away in a sheltered spot, yet set forward just enough to catch the eye. The trees either side had been stripped of their branches where the passing traffic had squeezed by, trimming and slicing the overhanging boughs and creating a kind of archway and a clear path for incoming and outgoing vehicles.

Eventually over time, the volume of traffic had created a deep, wide area in which to park. Ronnie saw that there were four parked vehicles: two cars, a big white van, and a lorry loaded with huge wooden crates.

Ronnie found himself a small, level corner beside the parked van to put down his knapsack. Thankfully, the area was clean underfoot.

For the first time in many a long hour, he began to unwind. Lazily stretching his weary arms above his head he felt a surge of contentment and, as always, he took a moment to think of Cathy. He missed her like crazy. When trekking his way along the highways and byways, he had felt so lonely without her.

Behind him, the constant drone of traffic noise along the main road could still be heard, but the heavy overhanging tree branches and wild growth all around reduced the noise

He gave a great, weary sigh. Here, at least, he would

be able to think straight. He had to get himself together, rework his plans, and consider what to do now.

The thought of trudging along that road again was a troubling one. 'Like it or not, I have to push on,' he mumbled. 'The thing is, do I carry on in the same direction, or do I call defeat and find my way back to Cathy?' That particular option had its appeal, but also made him feel like a failure.

Either way, he reminded himself, there was no time to waste. The dark would be closing in soon and he hadn't arranged anywhere to stay yet.

He decided to continue on his chosen journey north. He thought it wiser to see it through, whatever the consequences. If he had not found work within a few days, he would still have the option to turn around and make his way back south to his beloved Cathy.

Thinking of her, he decided to find a phone box and call her up the minute he got the chance. He would ask her opinion as to whether to head back south as soon as possible . . . or to persevere up north, at least for a week or so.

After all, he had only ever embarked on this journey to secure a life for the two of them together. The very thought of living a life with Cathy by his side, building a family and making a home together was all he had wanted, from the moment he had first set eyes on her.

Ronnie ached in every bone of his body. His shoulders had gone numb from the weight of the heavy knapsack, and his feet were hot and sore, as was the inside of his throat. The man at the food-van appeared to be packing up, so Ronnie decided he'd better get over there to see if there was any chance of a drink and maybe a sandwich.

'Hey, young man!'

Ronnie was just fumbling in his knapsack for some money when he heard someone calling.

'Hey! Are you deaf or what?' The person shouting was a mountainous lump of a man, but with a kindly face beneath a mess of thick, black hair, which was tied in a raggedy pigtail with a piece of bright pink twisted cord.

He sauntered over to Ronnie, who belatedly realised that the man was talking to him.

'I'm sorry . . . I didn't realise you were calling to me,' said Ronnie, standing up.

'That's all right.' The man towered over Ronnie, his great, tattooed arms folded like two massive sausages across his chest. 'I've brought you a message from Charlie, the van man over there.' He gestured impatiently to the skinny fellow at the food wagon. 'He's about to shut shop and bugger off and he asked me to tell you that if you want a sandwich or a drink you'd best get it now, or what you'll get is nowt at all! And that's what he asked me to say to you!'

His message delivered, he turned about and strode off without another word.

Ronnie began to panic, unsure if he'd find his

money in time. 'Thanks a lot! I'll just find some money. Could you please tell him yes, I'll have a cold drink and a bacon sandwich?' Grabbing his knapsack, he began turning out the contents.

'You cheeky little sod! I'm not your servant. You can tell him yourself,' the big fellow shouted gruffly. He sauntered off to the little blue hut down the lane, which was the lay-by lavatory.

Meantime, Ronnie hurriedly rifled through the jumbled mess from his knapsack, and, thankfully, his little swag of change fell out.

The waifish snack-wagon man was now yelling at Ronnie, 'What the hell are you doing, lad? Shift yourself. I've got your order ready, and now I need to be away! You might not have a home to go to but I have, and I've got a wife who takes no prisoners. So get yourself over here now.'

Without further ado, Ronnie went at the run to collect his snack, which turned out to be a thick, heavily buttered cheese sandwich, and a cracked cup filled to the brim with lukewarm tea, as strong and thick as Ronnie had ever tasted.

'I'm sorry, but I asked for a bacon butty,' he meekly informed the sour-faced man.

'Oh, did you now?' The man was not best pleased. 'Well, hard luck, 'cos I ain't got no bacon left. It's a cheese sandwich or nothing! Make up your mind, lad! Come on, drink the tea. I need the cup, then I'll be on my way!' He held out his hand. 'That'll be two and six. Come on! Like I said, I'm in a hurry to get away.'

Ronnie was disappointed because he had really been looking forward to a bacon sandwich. But at the same time, he had to smile at how down-to-earth and straight-talking these Northerners could be.

He quickly swigged his drink, paid his scant bill, and returned the cracked cup. 'Thanks a lot.' He felt better for the drink, despite it not being very hot. 'I really needed that.'

'Ah, lad, don't even mention it! You're very welcome, I'm sure! Although I'm sorry that all the bacon was quickly gone this morning.' The man continued tidying away. 'You look absolutely clapped out, lad!' He noted the dust-covered boots, and the tired lines on Ronnie's face. 'Been travelling long, have you?'

Ronnie nodded. 'You could say that, yes.'

'Where are you off to then?'

'I'm headed north, have been walking and hitching for miles, looking for work and a place to stay. To tell you the truth, I'm beginning to wonder if I've made a mistake coming this far. Maybe I should turn round and head back home. The thing is, though, I've not had any luck back there either and, to be honest, I'm getting a bit desperate.'

'Oh aye, we all get like that at times. There's nobody but yourself who can make such an important decision. But it seems a shame for you to have come all this way for nowt. If it were my choice, I'd carry on in the same direction. It sounds to me like you've got nothing to lose. What is it they say – nothing ventured, nothing gained?'

He had more fatherly advice for Ronnie. 'Give it your best shot, lad. Do whatever your heart tells you to. If it doesn't work out, then you can still turn round and head back to where you came from, but if it were me, I'd carry on. You're already here now, so keep going, persevere, and you never know, you might find what you're looking for.'

'You might well be right.' Ronnie thought the older man spoke sense, and being tired and worn from his journey, he was glad of the sound advice.

'I am right, lad! I've lived a bit longer than you, young fella, and I reckon I know what I'm talking about. If you look hard enough, there's always work about.'

Returning from the blue hut, and having caught the end of the conversation, the big man also offered an opinion. In Ronnie, he recognised a decent young man trying to make his way in the world. 'He's right, son. If you want my own advice, you'll forget about turning back and stick to the route you're on. You've come too far to turn round now. It would be a waste of energy and valuable time.'

The snack-wagon owner now chipped in again. 'That's good advice, lad, from two men who've been about a bit.' He carried on packing up and when he had finished hooking the wagon to the back of his van, he bade the other two a good day and a safe journey. The big man bade him cheerio.

'I should have been long gone by now,' the little fellow grumbled, manoeuvring the van forward. 'Good luck, young'un!' He waved a cheerio to Ronnie and then was off, down the lane and away.

The big fellow turned his attention on Ronnie. 'So! I heard you talking to matey there, and from what I understand, you're looking for work and not afraid of getting your hands dirty, is that right, lad?'

'Yes. That's true,' Ronnie answered.

The big man gave Ronnie the once-over. 'I must say you seem well put together. I mean, you certainly don't look like a lazy lad to me, so why was it that you couldn't find work in your own area?'

Ronnie hunched his shoulders. 'That's exactly what I've been asking myself. I think it's bad luck as well as the economy. There just doesn't seem to be anything for me, though I've tried loads of places.'

'Try not to get too down-hearted, son.' The big fellow again looked Ronnie up and down, watching him wolf down his cheese sandwich as if he hadn't eaten in days. It reminded him of himself in harder times. 'Like I said . . . you appear to be a strong and able lad. And unlike a lot o' lads your age, you seem to have a brain in that head of yours. I reckon you've done well having got as far as here on Shanks' pony. Moreover you seem to have the appetite, the build and the heart to tackle any kind of work.'

Ronnie thanked him. 'Well, yes, you're right. I'm fit and I'm willing, and what I don't know I'm always ready to learn. I'll take whatever work I can get. Any sort of work – dirty work, heavy work – it won't bother me, as long as I get paid.' He thought of Cathy and, in that moment, his loneliness was overwhelming.

'Hmm!' The big man sensed Ronnie was unhappy. 'Tell me the truth, lad, are you in trouble of any kind? Is that why you're running away?'

'No!' Ronnie was shocked. 'I'm not running away. I've left people behind who love me – family and friends, and my Cathy. She's the reason I'm doing this. You see, I want us to get married as soon as we have enough money. We'll need a place of our own. And that's why I want the work.'

'I see.' The big man applauded the fact that Ronnie had tackled a long and hard journey. 'So, you've left your girl behind in order to earn enough money to go back and get married? Well, I never! She must be someone very special.'

Ronnie gave a sorry little smile. 'Yes, she is.'

The big man took further stock of this determined young fellow. 'Right then . . .' He began walking away. 'You'd best pick up your bits and pieces, 'cos I'll be off any minute, once I've checked the ropes to make sure they're still tight. I've a lot of good stuff under that tarpaulin, it's worth a bob or two and a bit more besides if I can squeeze it out of that tight-fisted bugger I have to deal with.'

Ronnie felt sad to see him walk away. 'Thanks for your advice,' he called out with a wave. 'It was nice to meet you.' In that desolate moment, he felt incredibly lonely.

'Hey!' The big man stopped in his stride. 'What the devil's wrong with you, lad? Move yourself. Get your bony arse in the wagon or I might be tempted to go without you.'

'What?' Ronnie was shocked and so excited he dropped his knapsack twice as he ran to the lorry. Then he dropped it again as he climbed up the high step.

'For pity's sake, lad! What the devil are you playing at? I'm beginning to wonder if you might be a liability. There's me thinking you're capable of anything, and here you are, tripping and falling up the steps, like you've spent a few hours in the boozer. Just calm down and shut the damned door or I'll put my foot on the throttle and leave you where you fall.'

A minute later, the cab door was shut and secured, but still the big man continued to moan and mutter, though he was smiling to himself. 'I can't believe you did all that travelling on them busy roads and you didn't manage to get yourself killed when you can't even climb into the cab of a wagon. All right are you, lad?'

'Yes, thanks.' Ronnie had taken a real liking to the big fellow.

He poked Ronnie in the ribs, 'Whatever else you

might do, just don't let anyone know that you're a real liability,' he chuckled. 'Not if you want to get a responsible job.'

As the lorry pulled on to the road north, Ronnie and the big man began to chat openly and honestly. 'Have you never properly trained in any sort of work at all?' asked the lorry driver, who introduced himself as Jake Martin.

'Not really, no, but I wouldn't mind doing an apprenticeship, only now I think I might be too old.'

'How old are you then?'

'In my early twenties.'

'I see. But there are now more and more employers looking to train young folk up to scratch, including lads of your age.'

'Like I said, I can turn my hand to anything and everything, and I'm a quick learner,' Ronnie reminded him.

Jake chuckled. 'You're a feisty little sod, I'll give you that.'

He had taken a fatherly interest in Ronnie, and he thought him worthy of a helping hand.

When Ronnie lapsed into a thoughtful silence, the big man offered another piece of well-meant advice.

'You'll need lodgings, and you obviously want big wages if you're planning a wedding. When a woman wants a wedding, it has to be special, and that costs money.' He gave a little groan. 'I know, 'cos I've been there twice!' He paused before adding seriously,

'You'll need to find lodgings as soon as possible. And you'll need to get your skates on and find work.'

'That's right, yes, I do need big wages, but I'm ready to earn them! If somebody takes me on, I'll make sure they don't regret it.'

'Good on you.' Jake gave a wink. 'So, let's see what we can do, eh?'

Ronnie thanked him. 'I really do appreciate your help and advice.'

Jake smiled. 'I have an idea who might be able to put you in touch with someone who could help you find work, although don't hold me to that. It's just a thought, that's all.'

After an hour of pleasant chat and getting to know each other, both men lapsed into thought as the journey progressed.

'Where are we headed?' Ronnie suddenly realised he had no idea where Jake was taking him, or what he might find when he got there. With the miles quickly rolling away, he was beginning to grow concerned.

Numerous lorries and cars had already turned off the highway, and the traffic was thinning out. 'Well, first of all I need to offload this wagon at the depot,' his companion explained. 'After that, I'll take you to meet my sister and her husband. They're always in the know, and they just might be able to point you in the right direction. You see, in their line of business, they keep their ears to the ground. That way they know what's going on from one week to the next.'

'So what do your sister and her husband do then?'

'You'll soon see, 'cos we're less than five miles away from where they live. And I promise you if there is anyone looking for reliable workers, they'll know to point you in the right direction.'

Ronnie felt more confident by the minute. He sensed a simple honesty about this big, kindly man. After a few more miles, Ronnie was relieved to find that they were now turning off the highway, and Jake carefully wound his way along the narrower roads towards the coast.

'Wow! Look at that!' Laughing out loud, Ronnie peered down the streets leading to the Blackpool seafront. Lights flashed and glittered, and although it was dark the streets were thronging with happy-looking people enjoying an evening out.

Suddenly Jake cut away from the seafront. 'We're not allowed to go there,' he informed Ronnie, 'not with a lorry this size. There are numerous horses and carriages up and down the front every day and into the night. Then there are the trams that constantly ferry people up and down the miles of Promenade. And as you can see, there are hordes of pedestrians. You can see for yourself why a lorry of this size is forbidden along the front.'

He turned the wagon into a wide road to the right. 'This is the best route for us, round the back and away from the seafront. The haulage company I work for has a massive depot about half a mile from here. They bought it some years back, for the purpose of parking and servicing the lorries. We have a warehouse there and a fleet of small vans, which we call runners. They carry the goods to the final destination.'

Jake nodded knowingly. 'The man who set up the business was a far-sighted man. He established his haulage business many years ago, when land was cheap and plentiful. His son took it over some five years back, a chip off the old block he is, and he treats his men well.'

Ronnie was both impressed and hopeful. 'I haven't got a licence for driving heavy goods vehicles, but I can turn my hand to anything else. Do you think your boss might have work for me?'

'I'm not sure, but it's definitely worth asking. Although he did set two blokes on only a fortnight back, and as far as I recall, all vacancies are now filled. But if there are no vacancies at the minute, don't worry too much, it's not the end of the world. Like I said, my sister might well have heard that some other outfit is on the lookout for good workers.'

Ronnie thanked his companion.

'I'll keep my fingers crossed,' he said. 'My sister picks up all the gossip. Keeps her ear to the ground, she does. If there's a company looking for good workers, Sally is sure to know about it.'

'Well, thanks. That's really good to know. I'm beginning to feel hopeful that I just might get fixed up.' Ronnie was feeling much better. 'It's years since I've been to Blackpool. I've almost forgotten it. My Cathy's been here several times, though. It's a favourite haunt of her nan's. In fact, she's not long come back from a short holiday here.'

Ronnie took note of everything, the hordes of visitors, the kids happily eating candyfloss, and the heightened sense of excitement all around. 'I can't believe it's so busy! The best time of day is mostly gone, and it looks as if everyone is still having a whale of a time.' He particularly admired the proud horses trotting along, each one looking magnificent as it held its head high and pulled a brightly painted landau. Some of the horses even had plumes of bright feathers attached to the halter about their necks and heads, and all seemed to have their muscular bodies looking magnificent, all handsomely bedecked in highly polished brass-ware and thick, shiny leather strapping.

Jake was delighted to see Ronnie's reaction. 'I'm telling you no lie when I say you'll be hard pressed to find scenes like Blackpool seafront anywhere else in the world.'

'It's certainly a sight for sore eyes, that's for sure,' Ronnie agreed. 'No wonder my Cathy and her nan love it here. I reckon her nan in particular would live here in Blackpool, given the chance.'

He spoke proudly of Marie. 'She's the real heart of the family. No doubt she would probably miss them all too much to leave them behind. I do appreciate you bringing me here, Jake, because I understand now why Cathy gets excited about coming here.'

'That's all right, son. Maybe, when you're able to, you should take the time to have a lazy walk about. Get to know the area better. Get down on the beach. There is always plenty to do and see. My sister would never want to live anywhere else . . . and why would she when this resort, with all its facilities and natural features, is one of the finest in the land? And I've seen a good few in my time, I can tell you.'

He continued to urge Ronnie on. 'You really must go and see inside the Tower. Even if you went when you were little you'll appreciate its scale now you're grown up. Oh, and maybe you've forgotten that there's a fantastic set-up at the other end of the beach. It's a massive fun fair covering a huge area, with so many rides and stalls hellbent on making you want to stay that little bit longer. There's a big wheel, and bumper cars, and great swings that carry you up to the heavens.'

He grew excited. 'Oh, and carousels of every shape and form, and you really must try the ride that takes you up to a great height, before dropping at one hell of a speed down into a seemingly bottomless, dark hole that turns your stomach inside out.'

He giggled like a child. 'You'll hear the screams of terror before you ever get near the ride.'

He continued to describe so many different rides, some that would have you twisting and writhing, and others that would make you scream for mercy while turning you upside down, until you began to think you would never recover from the fear and horror of it all.

'Or there's the magical helter-skelter,' he went on. 'And the myriad colourful stalls, every one offering different and exciting fun, like the coconut shies and the shooting range. I promise you will not want to come out, not until you've tried everything there is to try.'

But the one ride Jake recommended above all others was the big wheel. 'You won't be able to get off until it stops and by then, you'll be off your head and screaming like a good'un!'

Ronnie was not too sure about all that. 'I've never been good at things that swing you about and turn you upside down,' he sheepishly confessed.

Jake chuckled. 'You don't know what you're missing, that's all I can say. Ask your girl – I bet she's been on every ride there is. Once you're hooked, there's no getting out of there. Trust me, I know!'

He did however assure Ronnie, 'When you get the chance, give yourself time to explore and experience everything you can while you're here. I promise, hand on heart, you will not regret it!'

In spite of his horror of crazy rides and things that dropped you into a big black hole before whizzing you back at ferocious speed, Ronnie nodded.

'I'm hoping I'll be too busy,' he muttered. 'My first

priority is to look for a place to stay, and then I need to find work. But I'm thankful for your help. And I'm glad I took your advice, about not going back on my tracks. I can't tell you how much better I feel now that I'm here in Blackpool,' Ronnie said, caught up in Jake's excitement. 'I don't know why, but I've got a good feeling about it. Oh, but Cathy will be so jealous, when I tell her where I am.'

He smiled mischievously, 'Maybe I won't tell her until I manage to find work because if I don't get fixed up I'll need to be moving on again.'

He felt hopeful, though, with this kindly man helping to guide him in the right direction and eager to search out a job in this fascinating place. 'I can't wait to get searching for work and lodgings,' he told Jake. 'It would be so wonderful if I was able to call Cathy with some good news.'

He could see her in his mind's eye, her cheeky smile, and her pretty, bright eyes.

He missed her so much it was like a physical pain inside him.

Noticing Ronnie's silence, Jake felt for him. 'Come on, lad! Don't be down-hearted.' He gave Ronnie a little wink.

In truth, he had been thinking hard, about how best to help this troubled and sincere young man. He reminded him of his younger days, times were tough then. Jake hoped he had come up with an idea that worked but he decided to keep his thoughts to himself just in case they did not materialise. Ronnie noticed that his companion had gone quiet.

'Are you all right?' he asked him worriedly.

'I'm fine, Ronnie. I was just thinking, that's all. Let's see whether or not we can get you sorted out.'

'That would be wonderful!' Ronnie's smile stretched across his face. 'You don't know what it would mean for me to find work and earn good money so I can tell my Cathy that I'm doing well for her.'

'We'll do our best,' Jake assured him again.

His kindly words lifted Ronnie's lonely heart.

PART THREE

Secrets Revealed

CHAPTER TWELVE

Tony and Eileen had settled back into their normal post-holiday routines, Eileen out playing skittles or bridge or shopping, Tony pottering around, mostly getting underfoot. He liked a long walk to get his morning paper, and next door was his favourite greengrocer's shop. It was a nice traditional place, not in the part of town where he and Eileen lived, but a good walk on a fine day.

He'd often half-noticed the pretty young woman who worked there on previous visits. She wasn't always behind the counter, but she was there often enough for him to have come to recognise her. Over time he saw the young woman in the shop and at other times she wasn't working. Tony eventually worked out when she was there and his walks to that part of town became more regular on those days.

One particular morning, soon after he'd returned from Blackpool, it was she who packed his paper bag and added up the bill. Tony smiled and wished her a 'Good morning' as he prepared to leave. The strange thing was that when she smiled back he felt he had met her before – not just here, but that he actually *knew* her from somewhere else. He racked his brain to think where that might have been, but concluded he must have imagined it. Where on earth would an old buffer like him have met a vivacious and pretty young woman like that?

Then, the next time he went in, the same girl was there again, and again he had a curious feeling that they had once known each other well.

The feeling would not leave him and he started thinking of this young woman often and spending every idle moment trying hard to remember where they had met. The memory seemed just out of reach but the need to know grew in Tony until he felt it like an itch that needed to be scratched. For some reason that he couldn't quite explain to himself, though, he didn't mention any of this to Eileen.

A few days later, he returned from his walk to the greengrocer's with a bag of salad to find that Eileen had been going through the desk in the drawing room with a view to clearing out one or two of the over-stuffed drawers and had unearthed some old photograph albums from the bottom drawer, then put them aside to have a proper look at while she put her feet up later. However, she hadn't been able to resist a quick flip through, drawn by the carefully posed, sepia-tinted family groups with their half-familiar features and their elaborate old-fashioned clothes, and it was then that Tony came in and found her kneeling on the floor, an album in her lap.

'Look at these wonderful old photos, Tony. I'd forgotten what was in this album and I think you'll want to keep these. They're pictures of your family from way back. This one must be your grandmother – am I right? Heavens, what a tiny waist she has in that corset! And what about that hat, eh? And there's your mother; I recognise her, of course. My, she was pretty when she was young, wasn't she? She must be eighteen or nineteen in this photo, do you think?'

Tony looked over her shoulder into the smiling eyes of his mother in her youth and knew in that moment – knew with absolute certainty – why he thought he recognised the young woman in the greengrocer's. She was an exact copy of his mother. She could even be his mother's granddaughter, with those same merry eyes and that winsome smile.

He murmured something noncommittal to Eileen and quickly retreated to his shed, where he could think through the idea that had struck his mind with the clarity and suddenness of a lightning bolt.

He sat down on the mower box and took a few deep breaths as he tried to think through logically what he knew in his heart to be the truth.

The young woman at the greengrocer's was about nineteen years old. That was the exact age his child would have been had Marie been pregnant after their one-night stand. He had never slept with any other woman except of course Eileen, and there was no way Eileen could have given birth and he not know. Indeed, it was a sadness to them both that they had not had any children. Yet the idea of his being a father and not knowing it seemed ludicrously far-fetched. Surely Marie would have told him if she'd had his baby? But then she was a widow, and the scandal of an illegitimate child would have blighted her life. Could it be possible that she had given birth and somehow kept it a secret? There was the young woman, living in this town where he knew Marie still lived, the spitting image of his own mother – what other explanation could there be? Perhaps that's why Marie had come up to Blackpool after all these years?

Over the next few days, Tony wondered frequently whether to make further enquiries. It would be easy enough to ask the greengrocer something about the girl one day when she wasn't in, and then that could lead to his being able to make further enquiries until he found out the truth. But what good would that do? It would only cause heartache for Eileen, and he felt he had disappointed her enough. Oh, yes, she was a good wife to him, and had put the Marie incident behind her, but he knew that their marriage was a little stale, that they lacked excitement in their lives, and that it was his fault. He'd let himself go, he was becoming boring and old and fat, whereas she was fashionable and lively, always smart and a credit to him. She had a wide circle of friends and was often out with them, whereas the highlights of his week were taking a walk to the greengrocer's and mowing the lawn.

Better to let the truth lie buried. It didn't matter, and it was Eileen who would be hurt. It was too late for Tony to play a part in his daughter's life now, and anyway, she may not want him. She looked self-assured, with the kind of confidence that came from being part of a loving family.

He decided never to mention what he had concluded. He should treasure what he had, not be worrying about what was never meant to be. Eileen should be his only concern now they were getting old and had no other family but each other. Tony made a vow to himself to try to become more like the man she had married all those years ago, when he had been handsome and strong and full of idealism. He could not change the past but he could aim to be once more the man Eileen had fallen in love with.

Tony decided to stop going to that greengrocer's altogether. It seemed better not to meet up with his daughter at all. He didn't know her really, and to have her in his life in even a small way felt like deceit, as if he were betraying Eileen all over again, and also as if he were somehow spying on the girl. Better to try to put her right out of his mind.

It seemed that fate was playing a hand, then, when only a couple of weeks later Tony saw the unmistakable sight of the pretty girl with his and Eileen's friend, Beth, shopping in town.

All his resolve about turning his back on her disappeared and the next time he saw Beth he found himself mentioning that he had noticed her shopping with a friend – a nice-looking girl with long brown hair.

Beth smiled widely, knowing to whom Tony was referring straight away.

'That's Ronnie's girlfriend, Cathy,' she explained. 'She works at a greengrocer's. She's been seeing Ronnie for some time now and I'm hoping they'll settle down eventually. She's such a lovely girl and Ronnie is absolutely mad about her. Though he's had to head north to find work, I know he plans to come back and marry her one day.'

'Cathy, eh?' said Tony, composing his features into an expression of mild social interest. 'Pretty name, pretty girl.'

'Yes, she's a real looker,' said Beth. 'Nice personality, too.'

'Mmm . . .' said Tony. 'I think I might have seen her in the greengrocer's.' He couldn't help it, he just had to find out more. 'It's not nearby here, though.'

'No, the other side of town,' Beth volunteered, 'nearer where her parents live.'

'Oh? Have you met her parents at all?' asked Tony,

pushing himself towards the brink. His heart was beating so fast he was sure Beth must be able to hear it.

'Yes, although her dad's often away. He's a lorry driver.'

'And her mum . . .?' *Stop it, Tony,* he told himself, but he just had to find out.

'Oh, Anne's a housewife. Cathy's gran lives with them, too. I'm particularly friendly with her. Marie, she's called.'

Marie. Of course. It was only what Tony had started to guess, but in a flash he saw exactly what Marie had done to cover up her pregnancy.

He made an excuse to part quickly from Beth and walked home, his head buzzing. There was no doubt at all now that Cathy was his daughter.

Eileen was at her bridge club when he got home so Tony had a chance to think very carefully about what he had learned for certain, and the conclusion he reached for the second time was that Eileen must never know. He owed it to that poor woman, who had forgiven him for his betrayal. In his heart, he would have loved to have had a child and it pained him that fate could be so cruel. But he owed Eileen, he had devoted everything to making up for hurting her. He would never speak a word of the secret Marie had kept all these years.

CHAPTER THIRTEEN

IT WAS LATE afternoon and Cathy came home
from her part-time job at the shop, kicked off her
shoes, dumped her handbag on the floor and threw
herself down on the sofa with a heartfelt sigh. She
was feeling increasingly despondent and weary these
days, but it was nothing to do with her job at the
greengrocer's, which was hardly demanding. What
was bringing her down was that Ronnie seemed to
have disappeared from her life. Not only had he
upped and disappeared – to find a job and make his
fortune, he'd said, having pledged his love for her
– but now, weeks later, he still had not been in touch.
She had trusted him when he whispered words of
love and said he was determined to make good for
her, but now doubts were beginning to creep into
her mind.

Cathy had, of course, kept the precious note
Ronnie had written to her on her own parents'

kitchen table all those weeks ago. It was lodged at the top of the jewellery box her mum had given her for her tenth birthday and she'd read it so many times it was now a little grubby, the fold along the centre a deep crease, and the envelope sagging and dog-eared.

If Ronnie could write such sweet words then, how come he hadn't written even one single word to her since?

Cathy thought of him all the time – literally *all* the time – which left little time to concentrate on anything else. Today she'd given the wrong change to a customer, who'd complained loudly and embarrassingly, and another day she'd heaped a whole lot of potatoes into the basket where the lettuces usually went, and then had them all to move, and the loose soil that had fallen off them to clean away. Often she added up the bill wrong if a customer had bought several items, and her employer had undoubtedly noticed. Cathy half feared he might be going to 'have a little word' shortly, but another part of her didn't care; didn't care for anything except that Ronnie had not got in touch.

Anne put her head around the sitting-room door, smiling, and Cathy wondered meanly what she had to look so cheerful about.

'What, no "hello" for me and your nan?'

'Sorry. Hello, Mum. I'll come and give Nan a hug in a minute. I'm just feeling a bit . . . Oh, Mum, if

I don't hear from Ronnie in the next few days I think I'm going to explode.'

Anne beamed wider, stepped into the room with an exaggerated pantomime stride and – 'Ta-dah!' – produced a picture postcard from behind her back.

'What! What!' Cathy almost snatched the postcard out of her mother's extended hand and turned it to the writing side to see Ronnie's familiar spikey scrawl. She scanned the words quickly – oh, thank goodness he was okay – then read them again slowly, absorbing his news, thinking all the time that Ronnie's hand had touched this postcard right where she was holding it now.

'He says he's fine, that he's had a hard time finding permanent work but he's been doing a series of seasonal jobs and he mentions the name of a pub where he's working. It sounds as though he's been on a right adventure. He's moved lodgings a few times, too, so he hasn't got a permanent address. He says he thought he'd be more settled by now, and he's been waiting for that to get in touch. Oh, Mum, he says that he's not asking for the moon, just a place to stay and work, in order to make money for his girl's future. That's why he hasn't written before now, he wanted to tell me he'd got a real job and a place to live, and I think maybe he's been a bit ashamed to admit otherwise. As if I mind! As if I wasn't waiting every day to hear from him, whether he was sweeping streets or he'd become a millionaire.'

'He must have a lot on his mind right now, but that doesn't mean he's not thinking of you. It's a shame his sister didn't take him in really but I get the sense there's trouble there. But Ronnie is a sensible young man and he's doing what he thinks is right by you both . . . Seeing that board up when he got home must have been a shock. Try and be patient, love. He's been in touch the first moment he's had a minute to breathe.'

Anne had of course sneaked a peek at the postcard when it arrived in that morning's post, and so she and Dave had had time to discuss it. They'd been all too aware of Cathy's low mood and absent-mindedness these last few weeks, and had felt indignant that Ronnie had built up her hopes on his departure and then done nothing since. It seemed to them that he had rather let her down and they had been wondering if they'd been mistaken in him and he wasn't as reliable and true to Cathy as they had thought.

Marie, however, had kept her faith in Ronnie and had constantly tried to reassure Cathy and bolster her hopes. Marie had even guessed at the true situation, as Cathy remembered now.

'Nan said it would be something like this. I knew she was right. I didn't ever give up hope of hearing from Ronnie, Mum.'

'Well, Nan can be very astute. Now, I'll get on with making your tea and you get changed and come and set the table.'

'But, Mum, I've got plans to make.'

She turned the card over and studied the slightly garish photograph on the front: Blackpool, in all its glamour. It was a picture of the Promenade, the Central Pier poking out to sea in the distance, the golden sand stretching towards it, and the Tower in the foreground. The sky was bluer than an English sky had ever been, and the sea matched it perfectly.

'If I get some things together, can Dad take me to the station?' Cathy asked. 'I'm sure there'll be a train to Manchester at this hour and then I can change and be in Blackpool tonight.' She got to her feet and straightened her short skirt. 'I've not a moment to lose.'

'Now just hold on one minute, love,' said Anne. 'Think this through. You can't just go off to Blackpool with nowhere to stay arranged, and all by yourself. It's lovely that Ronnie's written to you, but you can't drop everything and go rushing off like that on the strength of one postcard.'

'But, Mum—'

'I won't let you.'

Cathy had suspected deep down that her entire family felt nervous about her feelings for Ronnie, they probably all had the same outlook that they should wait until they were somewhat older, and had saved enough money that might set them up for married life. But Cathy loved him dearly and hoped that it would be sooner rather than later that she would be his wife. And then perhaps a mother to his children.

'But, *Mum*—'

'I said no, Cathy. You cannot go to Blackpool alone.'

'Ah,' said Marie, coming in through the open door, 'but she can go with me.' Marie took hold of Cathy's hand. 'This lad is special to Cathy, so if she's going then so am I.'

Cathy had always known she could ask her nan everything and she'd always have the answer. They had the same temperament and could talk about anything. It made Cathy's day that her nan would be at her side on her trip to see her Ronnie.

But just then her father's voice broke into her thoughts, clearly having heard the row from the hall. 'Hang on a minute, you two, I'm not sure anyone should be haring off to Blackpool in the middle of the night! Now I know Ronnie is a decent bloke. He has a level head on his shoulders and worships the ground you walk on. And I'll admit he's proved himself to be a responsible young man, unlike the rest of the lot next door. And then we can help out as much as we can. We'll have to wait and see. But I'll not have you two getting lost in Blackpool on the strength of a bleeding postcard.' For once Dave put his foot down, leaving Cathy and Marie speechless.

～

Dave was at a loss as to how he might come to a decision that would please everyone. For the life of him, he could not see it happening. 'The thing is, I have a bad feeling about letting the two of them go off on their own. And yes, I do realise that Cathy is sensible, and that Marie is a strong and competent woman who would protect Cathy with her life, but I have to be honest, I am not easy with the thought of the two of them taking off like that. Anyway, it's too late now, because I imagine the trains have stopped running.'

Anne, however, was torn in two directions. 'I agree that travelling so late is not such a good idea. But Mum is not best pleased with either of us – and you in particular – because of your determined efforts to scupper the plans she's made with Cathy.'

'Yes, I know,' Dave admitted. 'But there's no need to go racing off in a mad hurry. Surely there's time enough for Cathy to catch up with Ronnie, without tearing off in the late hours.'

Anne was not so sure now. 'I don't know about that. I have never heard her so angry and upset. And to tell you the truth, I think we may have made a mistake in trying to stop her from going. After all, she's nearly a grown woman, and Mum is more than capable. There's probably no need for us to be poking our noses in.'

When Dave started to say something, Anne waved a hand to stop him. 'No! We should never have interfered in their plans. We should have sent them off with our blessing, or better still, even travelled up there with them. We should have supported Cathy all the way – you know what she's been like these last weeks – but we didn't and I for one am ashamed that we let her and Mum down. You know how she frets about Cathy. And that is all I have to say in the matter!'

Marie and Cathy were sitting on Marie's bed while Marie continued the tirade she'd started three hours previously, in the hope that her son-in-law might see how he was being too protective in not allowing her and Cathy to make the trip, although she now feared the last train was already gone.

'It's disgraceful! Here I am, a woman in my older years, but a sensible and capable woman all the same, but do they trust me to look after my cherished Cathy? No! They do not! Instead, they forbid me to take you. Forbid me indeed! I am a sensible and very capable woman, and yet here we are – you and me, Cathy – forbidden to catch a train and go on a particular and very important mission, to track down your Ronnie and let you see him again . . . an errand that needs to be dealt with, sooner rather than later!'

She ranted on with sincerity . . . but mainly it was play-acting for the two downstairs. 'Neither of us will sleep a wink tonight, wondering if Ronnie is waiting for you to turn up, and you here with your heart nearly broken . . .'

Marie made sure Anne and Dave would be able to hear as she rambled on for their sake, 'I think I'll call the station. There might still be time enough to catch a train!'

She turned to wink mischievously at Cathy and projected her voice once more. 'I think it's downright shameful to realise that my daughter and her husband are not able to trust me to take care of you. I mean, I'm a grown woman, for pity's sake!'

She continued to rant. 'I've been independent all these years, and I have had to get on with life, and yet here we are – the two of us – being treated like irresponsible, rebellious children!'

The more she grumbled, the more het up she got. 'I have learned over the years, to look after myself. And anyway, what's wrong with the two of us arranging an overnight trip to Blackpool on our own? We are both sensible and capable enough to take care of ourselves, and I would have thought they might know as much, but oh no! Instead, they seem to think we'll get lost or be set on by some rascal in a dark alley!'

While Marie continued, Cathy was struggling not to laugh out loud. 'You're right, Nan,' she answered sombrely. 'It's shameful, that's what it is! Like you said, we're not children, and we're not irresponsible either. We are sensible people, aren't we, Nan? We know what we're doing, and we're old enough to take care of ourselves. So, why can't Mum and Dad see that?'

Although Cathy was herself deeply disappointed, she could understand her parents being anxious for the safety of both herself and her beloved nan. And now she told Marie as much. 'I suppose it's because they love us, and they need to be sure that we'll be safe.'

'Well, yes, sweetheart, that's exactly right!' Marie was sad for Cathy, who was aching to see the young man she had decided to spend the rest of her life with. 'I suppose I can understand their anxiety but, having said that, they should be able to trust me to keep you safe.'

Downstairs, Anne and Dave listened, shaking their heads and smiling as they heard Marie and Cathy deliberately airing their many grievances at the tops of their voices.

'If I was in Mum's shoes I reckon I would be angry too,' Anne quietly confessed to Dave. 'If I was forbidden to go somewhere, when I knew I would be fully capable of handling it, hell and high water would not deter me.'

Dave stifled a chuckle. 'That's because you are every bit as stubborn as your mother! To tell the truth, sweetheart, I kind of see how your mother has got herself all riled up, and she's right in what she says,' he confessed. 'Both Cathy and your mother are well able to take care of themselves, and each other if need be. It was just the idea of rushing off up there with no preparation and no proper planning. But I think there may be time to make a few plans, don't you?'

Upstairs, Cathy and Marie were done putting on an argument for the benefit of the two listeners downstairs. 'Right, Cathy, time for bed. In the morning, we'll make enquiries as to when the train departs. But for now there is little we can do except leave the bags packed. Try and get a good night's sleep.' She slid her arm about Cathy's shoulders.

'You're right, Nan.' Cathy was disappointed, but still hopeful.'Let's see if we can sort it all out in the morning, eh?'

The two of them were startled when a determined knock on the door halted their conversation. 'See who it is, will you, Cathy?' Marie had now kicked off her shoes and was on her hands and knees, searching under the bed for her slippers.

Going to the door, Cathy called out, 'Who's there?'

'It's me,' Dave answered. 'Ask your nan if I can come in for a minute.'

'Won't it wait until tomorrow?' Still searching on her knees for her elusive slippers, Marie deliberately put on a stern voice. 'We were just about to turn in for the night.'

'Oh, I'm sorry, but I need to talk to the both of you, if you wouldn't mind?'

'Hmm!' Cathy was thinking that maybe Marie's loud grumbling might have touched the consciences of her parents. 'All right then, you'd best come in.'

She opened the door to let Dave in. 'What is it, Daddy? We were just going to bed.'

'That's all right, love, because I'll only take a minute to tell you.'

'Tell us what?' Marie got up and stepped forward.

Dave felt decidedly uncomfortable in having doubted these two determined and confident women. 'I'm here to say I'm sorry. We heard Marie's grievances, and it made us realise that maybe we're being selfish, and also a little too cautious in not wanting the two of you travelling all that way on your own and we're sorry.'

'Oh, really?' Marie happily chipped in. 'Well now, we are very glad to hear that, aren't we, Cathy?'

'Yes, Nan,' Cathy agreed emphatically. 'From the way Mum and Dad were arguing against us going, anyone would think we were incapable of travelling on our own.'

Dave shook his head. 'Not so! And I'm sorry if you got that impression. But we would much prefer that we went as a family together. Not because you're not capable, but because then it would be like a little break for all of us, a belated family holiday, and that's the truth. I've got a few days off anyway, and Cathy's not at the shop again until next week, so it works out perfectly.'

Dave was keen to assure them, 'We really are sorry if we've upset either of you in any way. Of course, we're well aware that the two of you are perfectly responsible and able to plan a journey without us whittling and worrying. The thing is, it was all too quickly decided, and I have to admit we did kind of panic.'

'Well, Cathy and I have been thinking too, and you may be right.' Marie was eager to settle things one way or another. 'If there's a train going that way tomorrow, Cathy and I will want to be on it. So, does that suit both Anne and yourself, and can we now go ahead and make the arrangements first thing in the morning?'

'But you don't mind if we come to Blackpool with you?'

'No, of course not.'

'Right! So you had best set your clock for an early hour, and be sharp about it, because Anne and I will be packed and ready to leave, and if you're not ready, we'll just go without you. We've made the arrangements and we intend setting off at six a.m. sharp – and I want no arguments from you two, all right! So I'll leave you now because I need to get a good night's sleep. I've got a long drive in front of me in the morning.'

'Oh, my word!' Marie was excited, though half wondering if Dave was just teasing. 'Do my ears deceive me or what? Are the two of you really coming with us, or are you just aggravating me and Cathy?'

Dave smiled from one to the other as they waited for the truth. 'Yes! If it's what you want, we really are off to Blackpool. I've been thinking, it's high time we had a family holiday at the seaside, and what does it matter if it rains or the wind blows hard? We will at least be together, and I won't be back here worrying.'

The ensuing shrieks of excitement echoed through the house. 'Oh, Dave!' Marie was close to tears. 'Thank you so much. I promise you won't regret it.'

'Oh, thank you so much, Daddy. I'm really glad you're going as well,' Cathy joined in, and she gave him a huge hug to show how grateful she was. 'I'm so happy you've decided to come with me and Nan.' She could hardly speak for laughing and crying at the same time.

'Right then!' Dave was thankful that he had made the right decision. 'So, we all need to be ready early. I expect the two of us will be up and about before the two of you, but I don't intend hanging about too long for you. So be warned! I want you ready no later than six, packed, with your backsides parked in the car and your overnight bags waiting to be loaded alongside the two of ours. If you are not waiting there then I'll take that as a change of plan on your part, and myself and my good woman will simply take off without you!'

Leaving them both open-mouthed and shell-shocked, he turned about and hurried away, and his merry whistling could be heard all over the house.

'Anne, you were undoubtedly right when you

decided that your mother really was putting on a show for our sake, no doubt to make us feel guilty. They're a pair of devious devils, that's what they are!' he said, having joined her again in the kitchen.

Anne laughed. 'That's very true, and yet we still love them, don't we?'

'But of course. How could anyone *not* love them?' He blew her a kiss. 'In fact, I reckon that we are all truly lucky, to have each other.'

He thought of the many trials and difficult times they had endured over the years, and how they had actually managed to get through them, so far. Sadly, he was well aware, the worst was still to come with the prospect of revealing to Cathy the truth surrounding her birth, and her real position within this close-knit family.

The thought of hurting Cathy made his heart sink. But there was no way around it. She surely must know – and very soon – now that she had found Ronnie, the love of her life.

With love and trust, they had carried Cathy and Marie through every step of the difficult journey so far, and after all the worry, all the lies and the deep heartache, there was little else they could do except confess to Cathy the true story of her beginnings and hope that the love of her family would see her through.

But how would she ever deal with such a crippling revelation?

'What's wrong, love?' Anne asked, seeing he had sunk into a deep and worrying silence.

Dave shrugged. 'It's nothing. Don't worry.'

Anne understood and went to him on the pretext of giving him a kiss. She lowered her voice to the slightest whisper. 'You're thinking what I've been thinking a lot lately. It's almost time now, isn't it? But she'll be all right. We'll help her to come to terms with it all. We'll be here for her, just as we've always been here for her. All of us together, we'll carry her through it. No untruths, no fancy words, just the plain, honest truth, given with love and a huge measure of joy and reassurance.'

Dave looked up and found a precious strength in this woman he adored. 'I've thought of it over and over, and I am so afraid of losing her. It's a terrible secret for her to be confronted with. What if it completely crushes her?'

'We won't let that happen. We'll be there for her, all of us.'

Dave nervously looked about to make sure the others could not hear what they were saying. 'That's all very well, but what if she rejects us, as anyone might after learning such a shocking truth?'

Anne could feel his pain and concern, for it was hers also. 'Listen to me, sweetheart. I have every faith that we can carry her through it, with love and a strong belief in her own inner strength. She's a deter-mined character. You know that, don't you?'

'Yes, of course I know that, but will it be enough? I'm afraid she might turn on us. She's our lovely girl – what if she blames us for not telling her sooner, as we should have done? And now, after all these years, the shock will be much harder for her to deal with!'

It was a formidable and terrifying thought.

CHAPTER FOURTEEN

CATHY THOUGHT SHE was the first one to wake. Excited, she ran onto the landing in her pyjamas, where the hallway clock was already merrily chiming the start of a new and, she hoped, a very special day. It seemed Marie was already up, though, as Cathy could see her applying foundation to her face through the half-open door.

'Come on, you lazy pair!' she called outside Anne and Dave's room. 'It's already five o'clock. I'm about to get washed and dressed, and Nan is putting on her make-up, so come on you two lazy bones!' When there came no reply, Cathy raised her voice and called out again, 'Mum! Dad! You had best answer me or I'll keep yelling until I know you're both up and getting ready!'

She glanced out of the hallway window, where the hazy light from a new day was already creeping through the house. It made her feel wide awake, and impatient to be on the road.

The thought of being with Ronnie lifted her young heart and she yelled all the louder: 'Come on, Dad! Get up! You said for us to be up early. It's already gone five.'

Then she heard a door being opened downstairs, and her father's familiar, grumpy voice calling up to her, 'Cathy, for goodness' sake! Stop that yelling and bawling! Your mother and I have been up for over an hour already. And for your information, young lady, both our overnight bags are packed and waiting at the door.' He raised the volume. 'So you had best go and tell Marie that you have just fifteen minutes before the pair of you need to be outside and waiting, ready to set off. And if you're not there, we'll go without you. Or we might even decide to abort the journey altogether. Have you got that?'

'For goodness' sakes, will you two stop all the yelling and screaming, or we'll have the neighbours at the door!'

That was Anne, who had just run out of the sitting room. 'Like your dad said, we'll be ready to leave any time now, so just move yourselves, will you? We need to be off so just go and shout your nan, will you please? Dad and I need you both down here, with your bag and baggage!'

'All right! I'm going.' Cathy took off along to the

other end of the landing, where she burst into Marie's bedroom.

'Cathy, love, I'll be just a few minutes now,' Marie assured her. 'I've packed my case, and checked yours as well. If you discover that I've missed something we'll just have to get it at the other end. So, go on, move yourself, before they have a chance to change their minds about taking us!'

'Oh, Nan, I'm so excited,' Cathy said, dancing on the spot. 'I can't wait to be with Ronnie.'

'I can see that,' Marie replied with a groan. 'And, I have to admit, I'm hoping to see that little Irish rascal Danny Magee. He's a friend now, after all these years, and I want to keep in touch with him.' Marie could see Danny in her mind's eye and she had to smile. She remembered a story he used to tell her years before, how he'd been out walking in the countryside and stumbled into a flight of fairies, dancing in the breeze. She closed her eyes and just for a moment she could see his dancing eyes, he could tell just fanciful lies that one, you could almost believe him. Her heart warmed. It must be the excitement getting to her!

By the time they reached the front door, Anne and Dave were already putting the bags into the car.

'Come on, you two. Leave your bags and get into the car, I'll stash them away,' said Dave. Without further ado, he grabbed the two overnight bags and in two seconds had them stashed in the boot alongside the others.

'Right! At long last we're ready for the off. Now, are you sure you haven't left anything behind, because I'm not coming back for it?' He looked from one to the other.

'We're ready to go, if you are,' Cathy said. 'Are you okay, Nan? Have you got enough room, because I can easily slide along?'

'I'm fine, love, and have you got enough room for comfort?'

'More than enough, thanks, Nan.'

'Right, you two!' Dave called back to them from the driver's seat. 'If you're quite ready I'll set off – and I intend to keep going.'

Marie and Cathy assured him again that they were satisfied that they had not left anything behind.

Marie, though, had a question. 'Are we stopping along the route?'

'I haven't decided, but why do you ask?'

'No reason.' Marie shrugged. 'It doesn't matter anyway.'

At the end of the street, Dave checked for oncoming traffic while asking Marie, 'If it doesn't matter whether we stop or not, why did you bother to ask?'

Anne answered him. 'Well, for starters, none of us had time for any breakfast to speak of, and we might need to stop to pop into the toilets, or even to just get out of the car and stretch our legs.'

Dave groaned. 'If we can do without stopping then

we'll just keep going, and we might be in Blackpool that much earlier.'

Anne heartily agreed, but: 'If anyone does need to stop, then we'd be best to go where we've stopped before, and besides, it's the nearest café off the main road. Also, as I recall, the breakfast they served up was well cooked, and piping hot.'

'Yes, that's right, and the whole place was spotlessly clean. You could eat your breakfast off the floor.' Marie recalled that very café.

'Oh, for goodness' sakes, you lot!' Dave grumbled. 'We've only just set off, and already you're talking about stopping. If you had got up earlier, you might have had time to cook breakfast – and there would be no need for us to stop on the way then, would there?'

Dave laid it out for them. 'All right, if we do need to stop, it will be a quick in and out, no rummaging through the sales counter, looking through maga-zines for ages before you make your minds up which ones to buy! And as for you, Cathy, no hanging about in the loos dolling yourself up. We have no time for half an hour fussing about and doing your hair, or putting on your lipstick, d'you hear?'

'All right, husband!' Anne lovingly patted the back of his neck. 'We hear you. In and out, and down the road again. Point taken.'

Dave concentrated on the road, while Anne softly sang a little ditty that showed she was in good spirits, until Dave asked her not to sing out loud because she could not sing anyway, and besides, it spoiled his concentration.

Cathy remained silent, lapsing into a kind of dreamy state when she cast her mind on Ronnie and the knowledge that every moment carried her nearer to her beloved man.

'Cathy?' That was Dave again.

'Yes, Daddy?'

'Well, nothing really. Except, what's with the smile, eh?' He grinned at her in the driver's mirror. 'Or do I even need to ask?'

'Hey!' Leaning forward in her seat, Marie playfully clipped him across the shoulder. 'Stop taunting her. She has things on her mind, that's all.'

'Really? Well, I never would have guessed!' Dave again gave Cathy a cheeky little smile through his rear-view mirror. 'You miss him, don't you, your precious Ronnie?'

Embarrassed and becoming rather tearful, Cathy simply nodded.

'Not to worry, eh?' Dave had not forgotten what young love was like. 'Before you know it, we'll be there, and you'll have him all to yourself for a couple of days.'

Glancing again in the mirror, he lifted one hand from the wheel and carefully reached back to tap Cathy on the arm. 'I'm so glad we were able to make this trip. I reckon we could all benefit from it, eh?'

Having seen him stretch his hand out to Cathy, Anne gave him a gentle, little slap across his knee. 'Get your two hands back on the wheel! Are you trying to kill us all or what?' Anne was ever the nervous passenger.

Cathy looked up to smile at Dave in the mirror, and he sheepishly smiled back. Then all was quiet once again with Dave concentrating on the minor roads, which were growing busier by the minute as early workers set out to go to work.

Meanwhile, Marie looked ready to take a little nap, while Anne sat up straight and watched the road with Dave.

Cathy could only think of Ronnie – her dearest love, her best mate and confidant – and she felt she could not wait to be with him.

Marie sensed Cathy's deep yearning to be with Ronnie, but she wisely remained silent, just reaching out to wrap a loving arm about young Cathy's shoulder. 'Try and get a little nap, sweetheart,' she told Cathy, but Cathy assured her that she was too excited to sleep.

'How long will it be before we're there, Daddy?' she asked Dave.

As always, Dave was philosophical. 'Oh, well . . . I suppose it will all depend on the volume of traffic, but thankfully we were early starting. So, with a bit of luck, we might just miss the worst of it. All we can do is take it as it comes.'

A few minutes later, feeling somewhat reassured,

Marie again wrapped a loving arm about Cathy's shoulders, and soon the two of them fell asleep, Marie lightly snoring, and Cathy somewhat restless, lolling against her.

However, Cathy's dreamy thoughts of meeting up with Ronnie were soon broken when Marie patted the back of Cathy's hand.

'Don't fold your legs underneath you like that, sweetheart,' she whispered in Cathy's ear. 'It's not safe. If we should need to stop quickly for whatever reason, you could very easily get flung about.'

Dave approved of Marie's warning. 'Your nan's quite right, love. And besides, you're sitting higher on your haunches, and blocking my view through the back window.'

When he gave Cathy a wide smile in his mirror, Cathy promptly slithered down into her seat. 'Sorry, Dad. Is that better now?'

'Yes, sweetheart. And are you comfortable enough?'

'Yes, thank you.' After Cathy assured him that she was perfectly comfortable, order was returned, at least for the moment.

They were now leaving the familiar, narrow urban streets. Soon they would turn onto the main highway and the major roads that would carry them north.

As they passed through the last of the residential streets, Marie watched with interest as the workers tumbled out of their neat little houses to set off for work. 'Here we are, heading for a lovely short break, while these good people are rushing off to a hard day's work,' she commented thoughtfully. 'No doubt they would rather be fast asleep and tucked up in their warm beds.'

She gave a deep-down, weary sigh. 'I know exactly how it feels to drag yourself out of bed and trudge off to work, when you don't really want to.' She gave a wistful little smile. 'I don't mind telling you that I am very thankful to have left all that behind me.'

As Marie glanced along the street she was surprised to see a familiar face. 'Well, I never! If I'm not mistaken, that looks like Beth – Ronnie's sister.'

She gestured to the young woman, who appeared to be hiding in the doorway of the little terraced house where she lived with her bad-tempered husband. 'What on earth is she doing standing outside in the cold air with no hat or coat on? Good Lord, she'll catch her death!'

'Oh, my word, it really is Beth, and at this hour of the morning.' Anne could hardly believe her eyes. 'Why in heaven's name is she lurking outside like that, and on such a cold morning? She looks absolutely perished.'

From comments Ronnie had made in the past, Anne suspected that Beth's quick-tempered husband might easily lord it over the shy, homely little woman. She hoped all was well with Beth, who was a sweet and amiable young woman, without a bad bone in her entire body.

She glanced back to see if Beth was still in the doorway, but there was no sight of her. 'Well, thank goodness, she's gone now. She must have felt a bit chilly and gone back inside.'

'Good!' Marie was relieved to know that. 'Maybe she just popped out to get the milk in. Or maybe she was calling the cat in for its breakfast.' But she had an uneasy feeling.

After much thought though, Marie had convinced herself that Beth would be okay. And God willing, she was right. She would be there for anyone really, but Beth was a special lady.

And yet, after seeing Beth today, standing outside the house, in the cold, at that time of the morning . . . without a coat or hat on, Marie's fears for Ronnie's sister couldn't be quietened. Marie knew she was a worrier by nature but still, the very idea of Ronnie's sister living in fear of her quick-tempered husband, made Marie fear for quiet, amiable Beth.

Remaining uneasy, Marie drifted into a reflective mood . . . Marie knew Ronnie to be a sensible young man. He would never barge into Beth's home, all guns blazing . . . that was not his nature. Instead, he would probably talk it through with Beth first, and hopefully she might trust him. She wondered if she should talk to Ronnie when she saw him, put her mind at rest?

'Well! I'm glad that's all sorted out.' Dave gave a long groan. 'Honestly, you women! Why must you always make a drama out of nothing? Always thinking the worst. Beth was out there for some reason or another, and now she's back in the warm. So can we please relax and stop making such a fuss over what was probably nothing at all?'

And having said his piece, he returned his concentration to the traffic. Marie, however, could not help but worry about Ronnie's sister. She had her suspicions and she was sorely tempted to have a little word in Ronnie's ear with regard to Beth's wellbeing.

The wisest thing to do, she thought, would be to confide in Ronnie . . . or then again, maybe not. If he learned of even the slightest suggestion that Beth was in danger, Ronnie might well seriously be down here taking Mike to task, and who knew what damage might ensue? She was well aware that there was no love lost between the two men in Beth's life. They were like chalk and cheese and had nothing in common, except for Beth, whom each valued, in his own way. There was never a jot of hope that these two men might ever form any kind of friendship. At best, they merely tolerated each other.

From the scant details of her husband's failings, which Beth had reluctantly confided to her in the recent past, Marie had captured a clear enough picture of his selfish nature and his bad temper.

The last time Beth had confided in Marie, however, was almost a year ago. Lately, Beth was always reluctant to speak of her husband, except to promise Marie that the two of them were now getting on better. She told Marie that he had controlled his anger and had cut down hard on the boozing. He hardly ever came home drunk, and that on the odd occasion when he had drunk more than he should have, he was never spiteful, nor angry with her. 'Of late he is more like the man I fell in love with,' she had said.

Marie had to wonder whether Beth was either fooling herself, though, or even if she was actually telling the truth at all, but being reluctant to upset Beth by asking further questions, she had let it go, hoping that Beth really was safe and content now.

Nonetheless, she had said to Beth the last time they talked, 'I'm glad he's trying to mend his ways, sweetheart. But please remember if you ever need to talk to me – about anything – I'm here for you. If you need advice on any matter whatsoever, or if you just need to talk, or simply to go out for a bit of lunch, or a walk in the park, come and find me. I promise that in future I will not make any judgements, all right?'

Beth had heartily thanked her, and each of them went her way, with differing thoughts playing on her mind.

Now Marie said, 'I think I might go and visit Beth when we get back from Blackpool . . . see if she's all right.'

'Try not to worry about Beth, Mum, I'm sure she's fine,' said Anne, although she wasn't sure.

'Yes, love, you're probably right.' Marie was still wondering if she should mention to Ronnie about Beth being out on the doorstep at this time of the morning, without a coat. But then she decided not to say anything, because it would only worry him.

She hoped with all her heart that Beth had truly and honestly found a measure of happiness with the man she appeared to love, but she intended to keep a wary eye on her when they got back home.

Marie had learned just a few scant details of Beth's husband. Beth confessed that he would often come home from the pub drunk and moody and ready for an argument. As men do, she'd said. She wouldn't call him over. But beyond that, she would say no more.

In truth, Marie could sense that the marriage was over, and Beth felt no affection towards him. He had killed off her love and respect during the many times he had upset her for no good reason.

She seemed to dread him coming home, after many hours at the pub with his rowdy friends and admirers. But whatever he said or did, she was now far too nervous to say anything, because he had a quick and nasty temper.

It must have taken so much strength for Beth to have confided in her but she strongly believed that Beth had viewed it as a weakness.

She had made her decision to stay and had thanked Marie for her valuable help and for being such a good and special friend when she desperately needed one, but that everything was all right now, and she and her husband were getting on much better.

She had gone on to say, that from that day on, she did not want to talk about the fights and rows between herself and her husband any more. 'I really need to put it all behind me, especially now, when the two of us are getting on really well.'

Marie told her that of course she would abide with whatever Beth thought was the right thing to do.

And since that day, Beth had never again raised the issue with Marie . . . which had given Marie hope, that the troubles between Beth and her husband were now behind them.

Feeling hopeful but not absolutely sure that Beth's troubles were at an end, she had decided to trust Beth at her word. 'I'm happy for you, sweetheart . . . but please . . . will you promise me, that if you ever feel threatened in any way in the future, you will call me, won't you?'

Beth had readily agreed, along with imparting the news, that, 'I truly am much happier now, Marie.'

And so, Marie had taken Beth at her word, and prayed that there would be no more troubles for Beth to deal with in the future.

Though somewhere in the back of her mind, she remained somewhat uneasy about Beth's reassurances. She had her own troubles and secrets and knew to keep her nose out of others' lives. And, much to her relief, Marie had truly lately seen a great improvement in Beth . . . But even so, she thought it her duty as a friend, to always keep a wary eye on her.

All she could do, as Beth's close friend and confidante, was to promise that she would be there for her through thick and thin, wherever and whenever she was needed. For Marie, that would never change. It was Beth's choice to make. Women always seemed to have the hardest choices.

CHAPTER FIFTEEN

MARIE, ANNE AND Cathy laughed out loud on leaving the services building with their purchases. 'Will you just look at him?' Marie was not altogether surprised to see Dave leaning nonchalantly against the car door, wearing a little smug smile.

'Daddy thinks he's the cat's whiskers, because he beat us back to the car!' Cathy said.

Anne was shaking her head and grinning like the Cheshire cat. 'So, he did get back first, eh? Mark my words, we will never hear the last of this.'

'He'll be impossible now!' Cathy chuckled. 'Boasting and grinning all the way to Blackpool!'

'My word!' said Dave as they approached. 'I thought you might have got lost in the make-up counter, and here you are, all shopped out and ready to go. Well, I never!' With a grin, he opened the car doors to let them climb in and settle down. 'Right then, we'd best get back on the road. To be honest, I'm quite staggered that you three women got back so quickly.'

'Well thank you, kind sir,' said Anne. 'I bet you tore round the place like a madman just so you would get back to the car before us am I right?'

When Dave simply smiled and shook his head, the women knew for certain that Anne was right.

Marie could not help but smile. 'Well, I must say, Dave . . . I never took you for a show-off.'

Turning out of the services and onto the slip road, Dave checked for any oncoming traffic before easing into the flow, pleased that the traffic was not half as bad as he had feared. 'As long as we can keep going along at a steady pace, I reckon we should be in Blackpool within the next couple of hours, depending on whether or not you women want to stop yet again . . . and whether or not I might agree.'

'Cheeky monkey!' That was Anne. 'And what if it's *you* who wants to stop?'

'Well, I would rather not until we get to Blackpool.'

'That's fine by me!' Marie's thoughts turned to Danny, and she realised how much she was looking forward to seeing him. The very thought of his cheeky smile brought a warm glow to her lonely heart. Seeing him there weeks ago had brought back so many happy memories, in those moments her troubles had felt lighter. She'd been so lonely for so many years, caught up in the problems of the past, she couldn't look to her own future.

As Dave's beige Ford Anglia neared Blackpool, Anne started wondering if she'd brought the details of the guesthouse she had booked the previous evening, on the phone. She'd written it down in her little notebook but now she couldn't remember putting it in her bag.

Trying not to panic unnecessarily, she rifled through the capacious handbag, pulling out a hair-brush, a make-up bag, a powder compact, her purse, a can of hairspray, some rather sticky humbugs, and eventually drew out her little notebook. 'Oh, here it is. Thank goodness for that!'

She gave a sigh of relief. 'It's fortunate that I didn't leave the address and details at home. It's a wonder though, with everyone tearing about to get out of the house and away.' She quickly scanned what she had written. 'That's it! Two double rooms overlooking the seafront. Brilliant! Two nights, with bed and breakfast, and the guesthouse is right behind the Promenade. Beach View – that's the name.'

Marie actually clapped her hands with excitement. 'Oh, I do believe I know the place. If I'm right, it's the pretty, blue-painted guesthouse opposite the floral clock.'

'It sounds all right to me,' Dave chirped in on the conversation. 'I hope the food is good, Anne, espe-cially when you mentioned that the wife cooked all the meals.' He gave a disapproving little grunt. 'I often wonder if using the wife as cook is simply a cost-cutting exercise.'

'Oh, really? So what's with the condescending attitude to the wife being the cook, might I ask?'

When he was lost for words, Marie gave him a little dig on the shoulder. 'If you want my opinion, I'm of the mind that a woman is always better at cooking than a man. Women just have a natural talent for it. Well, I think so, anyway.'

Anne tutted and rolled her eyes. 'Honestly . . . you two are like a pair of juveniles, arguing about something and nothing. As far as I'm concerned, I don't care one jot who does the cooking, as long as it's nicely presented and tastes like heaven on a plate.' She gave a long, lazy sigh, 'Come to think of it, I am rather hungry.'

Cathy also had a little grumble. 'That's your fault, Daddy! You didn't even give us enough time to have a bite to eat in the café. That chocolate bar I bought on the way out was disgusting. It tasted like dried-up leather, as though it had been left lying all forgotten in the bottom of a drawer or somewhere.'

Dave gave a little chuckle. 'I've never heard such a miserable, moaning lot as you three! For goodness' sake, forget the chocolate bar or whatever and concentrate on the fact that we are off to spend a few days by the sea, in the sunshine, all together for once. All you lot can do is moan, moan, moan! All I want is to simply enjoy being at the seaside with my family.'

'You're right!' Marie said. 'And we truly are very grateful, aren't we, girls?' She looked at the other two. 'Go on then, you two! Tell him how happy we are, to be going away . . . all of us together.'

And so they made much of being grateful for their lovely break along with excessive bowing and grovelling to the sulking driver, who eventually was made to laugh loudly.

The first view of Blackpool was, as always, the Tower, slender but magnificent, pointing into the sky. The whole family searched it out, competing to see which one of them would spot it first. Although the Tower was visible from a few miles inland across the flat landscape, it signified the start of the final approach to the seaside and the journey's end.

Cathy's stomach was bubbling with anticipation, and Marie was nearly as excited as they picked out the impressive structure on the horizon.

The traffic slowed to a crawl. Although it was quite late in the season, Blackpool was ever popular and the roads into the famous resort were notorious for their traffic queues. There was nothing for it but to be patient and enter the busy, colourful noisy town at little more than walking pace. At last Dave turned the weary-sounding car onto the Promenade and, as always, Cathy gave a little gasp of pure pleasure at the sights and sounds that greeted her.

With her nose pressed to the car window, she grew increasingly happy at the sound of the music playing at a fairground close by and quickly wound down the window. A babble of voices rose up from the many excited children playing on the magnificent stretch of sandy beach below.

Cathy was grinning as she reminded herself it would not be too long before she and Ronnie were together.

Just thinking about that made her loving heart skip a beat.

A large and powerful chestnut-coloured horse trotted by, its proud head held high as it clip-clopped along the front, drawing behind it a brightly painted landau, carrying four smiling people.

Cathy supposed that they were a family: mum and dad, and two small, very excited young girls. As the magnificent animal passed by, it appeared to turn its head so as to glance proudly at the admiring onlookers.

However often Cathy saw the proud horses going about their duties, she never tired of watching their amazing strength and powerful beauty.

'Hey!' Marie called out to Cathy. 'Pull your head in from out of the window . . . it's too dangerous!' She indicated the tram gently moving along, some distance from the horses; who were highly trained with regard to safety and keeping a marginal distance from other moving traffic.

As was the horses' master, who was ever alert, and skilfully guiding the horses from the high-bench on the moving carriage.

'Oh, Nan, you're such a fuss. I'm just excited. Just look at them, they really are magnificent, aren't they? Tell me, where else might you see anything like them but here in Blackpool?'

'Yes! You're absolutely right, my darling.' Marie felt the same way as Cathy. 'I'm so glad I'm back for another few days, but with all the family this time. It's been a long time since we were able to do that all together, and it's just so wonderful!'

While the women were discussing plans for what was left of the day, Dave pulled up, and there was a rap on the window. 'I'm sorry, sir. But you can't sit here, I'm not sure if you're aware but you are actually headed up a one-way street.'

'Oh Good Lord!' Dave groaned. 'I'm sorry, officer. To be honest, I didn't even see the sign. We've just travelled for hours, and we're searching for a guesthouse, I'm really sorry.'

The policeman peered into the car to see the three rather tired-looking women looking up at him, with big sorry eyes. 'Right, well I should book you. But you'd best move on before I change my mind. And keep your eyes on the signs in future.'

Dave wound up the window. 'Well I never.' He

shook his head. 'We were damm lucky there.' He closed his eyes for a second or two before resting his head on the headrest.

Dave was now calling their attention. 'Look there!'

He gestured to a nearby guesthouse, where every windowsill was overflowing with colourful flowers tumbling from wooden boxes.

'Look at the sign on the wall.' He drew their attention to the round, painted board attached to the wall alongside the front door. 'It's Beach View. I think we've arrived, at long last.' He pulled up outside.

Anne agreed. 'But, just in case, I'll go in and make sure!'

As she climbed out, a sense of anticipation rippled through the car.

Within a few minutes, Anne was back, a smile on her face that told a happy tale.

'Right then!' Clambering back into the car, she closed the door. 'Everything is absolutely fine . . . It's all been confirmed as I arranged.'

'Good work, that woman!' Marie felt a whole lot easier. 'So now all we have to do is find the pub where Ronnie is working.'

'Ah . . . I have news on that as well, Mother.' Boasting a wide smile, Anne explained, 'After I had settled everything else in the guesthouse I asked the owner if she knew of a pub called The Pitstop, somewhere along the front. Here you are. The woman in the guesthouse wrote down the directions for us.' She produced a piece of paper.

'Well done, love!' said Dave. 'So now, hopefully, we can get on and find Ronnie, eh? I'll be glad to leave the car and stretch my legs. Then maybe, when we've located Ronnie, I might find something substantial to eat.'

'Yes, I agree!' Marie felt shattered.

'I wouldn't mind a pint of something cold, too.' Dave said. His throat felt dry as a desert.

'Me too!' everyone else agreed in unison.

'Mine's a sherry!' Marie was first to place her order.

'I'll have a sarsaparilla!' Cathy clapped her hands in eager anticipation.

'And mine's a sherry!' Anne was ever partial to a nice sherry.

'Right then, wifey!' Dave said to her with a smile. 'Why don't we drop the cases off first?' He gave a long yawn.

'I won't deny it. I'm really tired. In fact I could do with a short nap.' Closing his eyes for a second, he gave a weary groan, 'I've a good mind to park the car round the back and go up to our room now. I need a nap even more than I need that pint. Why don't you lot go and find Ronnie, and I can catch up in a while? What do you say?'

Both Marie and Cathy were all right with that. 'You both look really tired,' Cathy told her parents. 'Nan and I will be fine.'

Marie agreed. 'Yes, that's a good idea. And when you've had your nap you can come and meet up with us, and maybe we'll all have a meal at the pub. What do you say to that?'

Everyone was happy with those arrangements. 'Right then, you two . . . we'll take the cases, you go off and we'll catch up a little later on,' said Anne. 'Oh, and don't either of you wander too far from the pub. Are you listening, Mum? Do not wander off, and try to find Danny Magee. Stay with Cathy and Ronnie till Dave and I appear.'

'Okay, I promise, I'll stay to chaperone them.' She winked at Cathy.

'Good.' Anne took out her little notebook, and quickly copied the telephone number onto a torn-out page. 'Here, Mum, it's the number of the guesthouse in case you need to call us for any reason. And I have the number to call the pub if needed. The landlady at the guesthouse looked it up for me.'

'Let's meet in an hour, is that okay?' Dave suggested.

Cathy and Marie got out of the car, happy to stretch their legs at last, and Dave drove Anne round the back into the guesthouse car park.

'Oh, Nan! I'm so excited about seeing Ronnie!' Cathy hoped he was all right, and that he would be as happy to see her as she would to see him. She didn't seriously doubt it for a moment.

'They both looked tired,' Marie told Cathy. 'I'm

glad they're taking some time out, they look like they need it.'

'But, Nan, you're the oldest. It should be you having a rest.'

'Ah, but you see I'm a tough old bird. Don't you worry about me, sweetheart. I'm just fine,' she chuckled. 'In fact, I'm thinking I might put on my bathers and take a dip when we've found Ronnie. That'll give the young fellas something to admire.'

And the two of them went on their way, arms linked, and laughing out loud.

CHAPTER SIXTEEN

'FOR PITY'S SAKE, Ronnie! Get down from that ladder before you fall off and break your neck!'

The boss was convinced his trainee barman was far too eager to please, but he was a good worker, possibly one of the best the publican had ever had. Ronnie had proved himself to be a worthy candidate for the vacant position of full-time barman.

Moreover, the customers liked him, and that was important.

'Sorry, boss. I was just trying to secure this blind.' Ronnie pointed to where the blind was sagging down at one side. 'Shall I take it down before someone accidentally traps their fingers in it?'

'Hmm . . .!' The landlord took a look at the blind. 'Yes, you could be right, lad. We're closed for a while yet, so I imagine there's time to deal with it before we get busy. Go on then, do your best, and try not to lose a finger yourself, while you're at it.'

'Right then. And what do you want me to put up in its place?'

'Nothing. Not for the minute, anyway. I'll have a word with Nancy. She's been moaning about the damned blinds since I bought them two years back. And you're right about the possibility of someone getting their fingers trapped. The edges of those slats can be sharp. Slice a finger off, they could.'

He shivered at the thought of such an accident. 'Aye, lad! You get it down, son. In fact, while you're at it, why not clear them out of both windows? Nancy will agree with that.'

'And when I've got them down, where would you like me to store them?'

'Oh, I'm sure the wife will have ideas as to what she wants to do with them. She has an opinion about most things to do with the furnishings and I don't think she'll be wanting to dress the windows with blinds again, but let's leave that to her good self, eh?'

Ronnie nodded. 'Right then, boss. When I've got them down, I'll roll them up and tie them together safely. Where will you want me to put them out of harm's way?'

'Oh, that's easy. For now just lie them down in the corner of the shed, and we'll see what the wife decides.'

'Right, boss, it's as good as done.' Feeling comfortable in this decent man's company, Ronnie set about the task in hand.

A few minutes later, Ronnie had the blinds carefully folded. He slung them over his shoulder and carried them outside, where he set them down, safely tucked away in the shed, behind some stacks of old chairs, a couple of stained tables and an unopened box of beer mats.

The landlord was watching him through the back door, while considering the careful manner in which Ronnie had followed his orders. I've found a good'un in young Ronnie, he thought. I hope he's not one of those fly-by-nights who turn up for a few days and then they're gone, never to be seen again.

The landlord thanked Ronnie, then added, 'From now on when you address me, I would appreciate it if you call me by my name – Sam – and not "boss".' He wagged a finger. 'As I've mentioned several times, lad . . . the name is Sam, and that's what you call me. Do you reckon you could do that?'

Ronnie smiled. 'Yes! I reckon I can do that . . . Sam.'

'That's it!' The landlord smiled. 'There you go, son, it wasn't too hard was it, eh?'

'Not at all . . . in fact that's a good strong name, for a good strong man of character.'

The landlord chuckled. 'All right, don't go over the top, 'cos flattery will get you nowhere.' He pointed to the windows, now bare. 'Shift yourself, young man. I reckon it might be a good idea to clean them windows now you've taken the blinds down and revealed all the smudges.'

'I shall tackle it right now . . . Sam.' Ronnie emphasised the landlord's name, before rushing off to find a bucket and cloth. 'I'm onto it,' he promised the older man, 'and when I'm done cleaning the windows, you will not believe your eyes at the difference.'

'I'm sure I won't, especially if you don't shift yourself soon and get on with it.'

'Aye aye, Captain!' Ronnie cheekily tipped the brim of his flat cap.

'And don't leave any smears behind, young fella-me-lad, 'cos I intend to inspect the windows from top to bottom when you're done.'

'Of course you will, I would do the very same if I was in your shoes. And you won't find any smears left behind when I'm finished.'

The big man's leathery face was crinkled in a merry grin. 'You cheeky little sod, you remind me of myself when I was your age. I believed that I could conquer the world all by myself, but it doesn't work like that. We all deal with what we've got, and right now I've got a pub to run and barrels in the cellar waiting to be seen to. So much for conquering the world; getting to grips with this pub is enough for me.'

'If you need a hand, just shout,' Ronnie said. 'It won't take me long to get these windows looking spotless.'

'No, you're all right, lad. You just carry on there. I'll manage on my own down the cellar. I've done it for more years than I care to remember. You just get on and do your stuff. And think on, I want them windows shining like new. And don't forget I'm still considering whether to keep you on or not. I always take my time when I'm recruiting staff, and right now I'm still chewing the situation over, so stop the chatter and get on with your work.'

With that, he turned away in the direction of the cellar.

With the landlord gone to his own errand, Ronnie set about polishing the windows, merrily humming a song as he worked. He felt comfortable here, in this homely place. Sam was a decent boss, and the job on offer suited Ronnie right down to his worn boots. The one thing missing from his life was Cathy.

It wasn't long before the landlord returned. 'Right then, lad . . .' He stood before the windows, legs apart and a look of determination on his round, weathered face. 'Let's see how you've done, eh?'

As he perused the finished task, his smile got wider. 'Well done, lad! I could not have done it any better myself.'

He took a long look at the two big windows. He ran his finger round the edge of the window frames, and he stood a moment, with his hands on his hips, and his face bright and smiley as he admired Ronnie's work. 'Brilliant! That is absolutely brilliant!'

He stepped back to get a look at how much better the place was without the blinds. 'I will never know why we put up them blinds. Just look at the light coming into the room. By 'eck, you've done a right good job, lad. And when the missus comes back from her weekly shop I reckon she'll be over the moon at the difference it makes in here.'

With a huge smile on his face, he again inspected the job well done. 'I'd forgotten how much better it was before the blinds took all the daylight. The view was never the same after we had the blinds . . . rolling them halfway down, then closing them when the sun shone too bright, and folk were always tampering with them. Well, now they're gone, and I for one will not miss them.' He chatted on. 'After seeing how smart and open it is now, with the sunshine pouring in, I reckon the wife will not want blinds ever again.'

After another long look at the windows and the light flooding in, he said to Ronnie, 'It won't be long before we open. We'll get the regulars coming in, and the day-visitors too. Give it another hour and you won't be able to move in here.'

He rubbed his hands in anticipation of the tills ringing out behind the bar. 'For now, though, I'd best get on, what with all the other chores waiting for attention.'

He smiled as he took another look at the windows. 'Just look at the difference,' he purred. 'The view has opened right up, just take a peek out there. You can see right across to the Promenade and the beach beyond. Wonderful, just wonderful.'

He took a moment to peer across the busy road,

with the horses and landaus, and the trams, and the hordes of visitors crowding down to the beach. 'I missed all that,' he told Ronnie.

'You can see what's going on now.'

He gave a cheeky little wink. 'Hey, she's not bad, is she, eh? A bit older than myself, but I bet she were a classy sort in her heyday. Mind you, she's still a looker, and she has a really nice smile.' He gave a muted little wolf-whistle. 'Oh, but just look at the young'un beside her. More your age than mine, but a little beauty all the same.'

While Sam went off to attend to his work, Ronnie absently peered through the windows to see the hordes of holidaymakers strolling by.

He was about to turn away, when his attention was caught by the two women mentioned by the landlord just now. There was something familiar about them. Heavens, for a moment he'd thought they were Cathy and Marie, but that couldn't be true, could it?

As he strained to catch full sight of them, the younger woman turned about and Ronnie got the shock of his life. Cathy? He looked again, but the traffic passing between him and the people on the Promenade was so heavy it was difficult to see individual figures clearly.

And then the older woman turned and Ronnie's heart missed a beat.

'Is that Marie? Good Lord! Am I seeing things?'

The traffic was horrendous. What with the many cabs and horse-drawn landaus, along with the myriad holidaymakers whose numbers were swelling by the minute, it was difficult to see from one side of the street to the other.

Ronnie couldn't risk losing sight of them. Beginning to panic, he rattled on the window, but while some people nearer turned his way, neither Cathy nor Marie could hear him.

In desperation, he ran to the front door. The two familiar figures were gone, and the heavy traffic was filling the main street to such a level that it was difficult to make out anything across the road.

And then, in that anxious moment, he saw her again briefly. It was his Cathy! His heart turned upside down as he ran to the kerb, trying to pinpoint her amidst the moving throngs of pedestrians.

'Ronnie!' Cathy had seen him at last, and her voice carried above the crowds and the traffic. 'Ronnie!'

And now he saw her again, and she was looking straight at him. 'Cathy! Stay there!'

Ronnie looked right and left for a break in the traffic, but it was dense and slow-moving, reckless people sometimes dodging between the cars but most milling on the pavements until they reached a crossing. He realised he would have to do the same and he was about to call to Cathy to go further down to where he could cross to meet her when he heard a very loud bang and people started screaming. An accident, Ronnie guessed straight away, but, alarmingly, it sounded too loud to be a prang between two slow-moving cars, and very close by. He scanned the street in the direction from where the dreadful noise was coming and, as people started to run towards him, he saw one of the famous seaside landaus had overturned onto its side and, somehow, the horse had got loose and had bolted, trailing reins and shedding the broken shafts of the landau as it went. The poor animal was wide-eyed with terror and was causing absolute mayhem. People from every side began to run for safety, some to the beach, while others headed for the side streets.

'Cathy,' Ronnie called out, as she and Marie appeared to be in danger of being separated. 'Get down to the beach, both of you . . . hurry!'

He tried to get to her, but it was not possible with cars turning about or dodging down the side streets, and with people rushing to get away from the frantic horse, it was increasingly difficult to keep an eye on either Cathy or Marie.

When, a moment later, he caught sight of them holding onto each other, he called out again, 'Cathy! You and Marie must get down to the beach, if you can!'

Marie nodded and grabbed Cathy's hand tightly, and made an effort to lead her towards the safety of the beach.

Suddenly, without warning, Cathy broke away and was running towards Ronnie.

'No, Cathy! Go back!' Ronnie ran forward, frantically struggling through the crowd to get to her, but it was difficult, with a sudden surge of people trying to get away from the horse. Cathy had broken through the crowd at her side and was coming straight at him, while both Marie and Ronnie urged her to go back.

But it was too late.

The horse was galloping up the middle of the street and was not about to stop. In an instant, the frightened animal had swerved round Cathy, but she was caught by his hind legs as he kicked out, and sent spinning backwards through a gap between two cars and into a wall. The horse galloped on, bucking and kicking.

Rushing to Cathy as fast as he could, Ronnie gently eased her down on to the pavement so that she lay as comfortably as he could make her, Marie took off her jacket and bundled it beneath Cathy's head as a make-shift pillow. But as they patted her hand and talked to her, it was obvious to both of them that Cathy was badly hurt and that she was already deeply unconscious.

Within minutes, the piercing screams of an ambulance were audible and a crowd of concerned onlookers waved the emergency service over to Cathy, while Marie and Ronnie kept patting her hand and trying to wake her.

The people moved aside to let the ambulance crew through, and the capable team quickly assessed her situation, and were swift to settle her into the ambulance.

They secured her safely, and with Marie and Ronnie

sitting on the small bench in the back of the ambulance, they took off at great speed.

Throughout the journey, the ambulance attendant carried out emergency procedures on Cathy, and to Ronnie and Marie it was distressingly obvious that Cathy had indeed sustained life-threatening injuries.

They hardly took their eyes off Cathy's damaged young body. She made no sound, while Ronnie could hear Marie softly murmuring a little prayer.

Ronnie remained very still and silent, his sorry eyes trained on Cathy's face, looking for the slightest movement or sound that might tell him she was alive.

Instead, she lay worryingly silent, her eyes closed, and her body making no movement.

Reaching out to touch the back of her hand, he was so afraid. She was too still, too cold.

Fighting back the tears he shifted as near to her as he was able. 'I'm here, sweetheart,' he whispered. 'Stay strong. I promise you, Marie and I will not leave you.'

'We'll be arriving any minute now,' the ambulance man assured Marie and Ronnie. 'When we stop, we need to get her straight into emergency. They'll be watching for us. You two follow on, but let us go as quickly as we can.'

Within moments of their arrival at hospital the ambulance crew had lowered Cathy's stretcher down from the ambulance, and she was swiftly taken into the building, where a team of doctors was ready and waiting for her.

The ambulance driver then took charge of Ronnie and Marie. 'It's all right,' he said to Marie who was silently sobbing, her sore eyes trained on the door of a small but seemingly well-equipped room, behind which Cathy was being taken care of. 'The doctors here are marvellous. They'll know exactly what to do.'

Ronnie took hold of Marie's hand. 'Keep strong, Marie,' he whispered although he was every bit as broken as she. 'She's in the best place . . . all we can do is pray and be strong for her.'

Marie simply nodded, her eyes blinded by tears as she trained all her attention on the door behind which the medical team were gathered about Cathy, using all their expertise to tend to her considerable injuries.

The ambulance driver went to make ready for his next call-out and a nurse appeared, asking softly if Ronnie and Marie needed anything, maybe a hot drink to nullify the shock.

The minutes passing seemed like hours, and neither Marie nor Ronnie had any desire to move from that spot.

Finally, Marie got up and walked the corridor a while, sat down, then head down, she was walking back and forth again. Like Ronnie she kept a silent watch on the door of that clinical room, behind which Cathy was being tended by the doctors.

Ronnie was fretful. His hands were shaking, and his heart felt numb as he continued to gaze at the door.

He prayed like he had never prayed in all his life. Eventually he could not stay still any longer, and he too paced up and down, his head bent down to his chest. That was his Cathy in there, and he was helpless. No one came out to tell him and Marie what was happening.

Now he was standing with his face to the wall, his arms stretched out as he flattened his hands against the wall, while quietly sobbing.

'Oh, my God!'

Suddenly, he rushed to take hold of Marie's hand. 'The family don't know what's happened!' He shook his head in disbelief. 'We have to contact them straight away! With everything that is going on we haven't even told them.' His voice broke with emotion. 'Cathy is in there, probably fighting for her life, and her parents don't even know.'

'Oh, dear Lord! I haven't been able to take everything in. My mind must have gone blank.' Marie began shaking her head. 'Oh, but what will it do to them? They'll be shattered.' She could not keep back the tears and started to cry noisily.

'Please, Ronnie . . . will you do it, son? Will you tell them? Oh, God help us . . . be careful how you tell them, Ronnie. They'll be devastated. But how can we make it any easier for them? It's not possible. They will have to be told, but gently please, Ronnie, if you can?'

Digging into her handbag, Marie hastily retrieved the torn-out notebook page where Anne had written the telephone number of the guesthouse. 'Call them now, please, Ronnie.' There was a row of telephone cubicles, she remembered, near the door. 'You could phone from there.' She handed the page to him. 'Just say they're needed. Whatever you do, you must not tell them the full truth over the telephone.'

She dipped into her purse. 'Here you are, son.' She handed him some change, but then she had a thought, 'Would it be any easier, if we asked that nurse whether we might use the office telephone? It would be much quicker and more private, don't you think?'

The two of them glanced over to the office nearby, to see a nurse on the telephone, and with her free hand busily writing on a sheet of paper. After a minute or so, she replaced the receiver and was heading their way.

'Are you wanting to call anyone?' she asked Marie. 'You can use the telephone in my office, if you like. If anyone comes in while you're on the phone, tell them that Matron Armstrong gave you permission. You can make your call in the quiet and privacy of my office.'

Marie thanked her, quickly explaining, 'Cathy's parents don't yet know about the accident and we desperately need to contact them. It would help Cathy so much to see them there when she opens her eyes . . . ' Choking with emotion, she fell silent, but then recovered herself sufficiently to ask when they might know what was happening with Cathy.

'I'll try and find out what's happening,' the nurse promised. 'We won't know too much just yet, but rest assured, someone will be out shortly to give you an update.'

As the matron hurried away to other duties, Ronnie lost no time in making the call.

Nervous and ever tearful, Marie waited outside the office immensely grateful that he was here with her.

A short time later, Ronnie emerged to meet a barrage of questions from Marie. 'Are they all right? How long will it be before they get here? Oh, dear Lord, they must have been shocked to their roots.' She began softly sobbing again, 'It's all such a terrible business, Ronnie. I pray to God that Cathy gets through this.'

She glanced about her, beginning to panic. 'Why hasn't someone come to see us to let us know what's happening? You would have thought that someone would update us, they must know how worried we are.'

Ronnie gave her a reassuring hug. 'Don't get yourself in a state, Marie. I'm sure someone will be out soon to talk to you . . . update you. Meantime, let's try not to panic. I'm sure she is in the best of hands.'

Marie nodded. 'I suppose you're right. Let's hope there are no insurmountable problems. Yes! Let's pray that everything will be all right, eh?' Taking out her handkerchief, she dabbed at her eyes to wipe away the falling tears. 'I'm sorry, son, but it really is too hard to think of Cathy in there in pain. Oh, Ronnie!' Shaking her head, she mumbled under her breath, 'It's all my fault . . . a punishment for my sins.'

Ronnie could make no sense of what Marie was saying, and he could not envisage her ever having sinned in all her life.

Her curious comment flew out of his mind, however, when suddenly there was a flurry of activity in the room where Cathy had been taken. Someone went in – another doctor, by the look of it, for he wore a white coat – and then someone else, who looked like a porter.

Soon afterwards the door flew open and Cathy was being wheeled at a fair pace down the corridor and away. Marie and Ronnie had time to see that Cathy was fixed up to drips and was still unconscious. No one stopped to speak to them and, desperate for news though they were, they knew better than to delay what was obviously the journey to an operating theatre. After that, Marie again took to walking up and down, and Ronnie let her go without comment. Maybe she needed to keep moving, he told himself. He went to look out of the big window, growing concerned that there was no sign of Dave and Anne.

Marie also was beginning to grow concerned, but she told Ronnie when he came wandering back to her, biting his nails, 'The roads may still be impassable in places. Maybe they've been diverted and it will be taking a bit longer for them to get here than we would expect. Don't worry, son, I'm sure they'll be here any minute.'

'Yes, I'm sure they will,' Ronnie agreed and sat down to wait with ill-concealed impatience, gazing tearfully down the corridor where Cathy had been taken. Beneath his breath he said a little prayer for her to be brought back to them safely.

'Marie?'

'Yes, sweetheart?' For the umpteenth time the two of them glanced along the corridor. 'How long will it be before someone comes to tell us what's happening with Cathy?'

'I don't know, Ronnie. But I'm sure they'll come and tell us as soon as they can. Until then, we have to be patient. We must stay here, where they can find us. I know it's not easy, but try to think the best – that they are doing all they can. They will bring her back to us, we have to believe that!'

Her voice melted into sobs, and now she was in his arms. 'Oh, dear Lord, Ronnie, I'm trying hard to be brave, but I'm so afraid. So frightened for my lovely girl!' Clinging to him, she quietly sobbed, and he heard her muttering that she'd left it too late and she'd never forgive herself. But it didn't seem the right moment to ask her what she meant.

Suddenly, Anne and Dave were rushing towards where Ronnie and Marie sat huddled and crying, and their faces were a picture of emotion. Marie got up and hurried to meet them, and they all hugged and cried together.

When everyone was seated and calmer, Ronnie answered their questions as best he could. 'All we know so far is that she was rushed to the operating theatre. The matron told us that we should get some feedback on her condition soon.'

Just then the matron arrived to see them.

She explained that Cathy had been treated for broken limbs and other injuries. 'She's only just awake and no doubt she will be feeling uncomfortable and anxious. The nurse is reassuring her now. For the time being, please be patient. Someone will come and take you to her, in due course. The doctor has suggested only one visitor at a time, and for no longer than a few minutes. She needs the quiet for now. I'm sure you understand.'

Everyone readily agreed, greatly relieved that Cathy was out of surgery and they might be allowed to see her if only for a moment.

Ronnie offered to wait until each one of the family had seen her and then – if they were all right with that – he would then go in to see Cathy for a minute or two. Of course that was absolutely fine with everyone, and they thanked him for his thoughtfulness.

It was not long before Matron returned, and Anne and Dave were the first ones to be taken to see Cathy. And though in her heart Marie knew that it was right, it cut her to the bone to be left waiting in that corridor with no right to see her Cathy, her girl.

Marie saw how lost and lonely Ronnie was as he paced up and down, seemingly deep in thought.

For a moment she was reluctant to disturb him, but then he turned to look at her, he gave a slight nod of the head, along with a sad little smile.

In that moment Marie thought of Ronnie's sister, Beth. The two of them had always been close, and just now he really must be missing her. Beth would have known how to reassure and comfort him. Marie was reminded of the worrying sight of Beth that morning, there in the cold, without even a coat on. Just why was she out there like that, and so very early in the day?

Was her sour-tempered husband the cause of it? Had there been a row and he had actually shut her outside on purpose?

With Cathy to worry about, Marie tried her best to block out the sorry image of a sad-looking Beth shivering on the doorstep of her house. But her thoughts went back to Dave and Anne, who were in with Cathy at this very moment, and she was deeply torn as to what she should do about her own dark secret regarding Cathy. She'd burdened them all with her secret for so long and relied on their support while she did nothing but dither about what was right or wrong. God, should Tony know that his daughter was lying here helpless in a hospital bed?

She knew now that she could not leave it for much longer to tell Cathy the secret of her birth . . . but not just yet. Not until Cathy was strong enough. Thinking back to Beth and her earlier worries about her friend, Marie thought to broach the subject of his sister with Ronnie. Maybe he'd have news of how Beth was coping with her husband's moods lately, and if it was good news she'd be pleased to have her mind put at rest when she had so many worries.

'Have you heard from Beth recently?' she asked.

'No, I haven't been in touch for a couple of weeks now,' Ronnie said, 'what with the new job and all . . .'

'I can understand that,' Marie sympathised. The last thing she intended was that Ronnie should see her enquiry as any kind of criticism. 'I'm just thinking that maybe, what with her being the only family you have, and because she and Cathy get on so very well, you may want to call her and fill her in on what's been happening. I think she'd want to know, even though the accident is such terrible news. It wouldn't be fair to keep her in the dark.'

She deliberately didn't mention that she was worried about Beth and wanted to know if she was all right. If Ronnie telephoned he'd find out anyway, she hoped. It was no use planting more worries in his mind if all was okay with Beth. There was every chance that once Ronnie had spoken with his sister, and Beth had calmed him with her wise and supportive words, then Ronnie would feel better, too.

'Maybe I should call her now, while I've got the chance,' Ronnie said.

Marie agreed. 'Well, you've probably got time enough to do it before they let you go in to see Cathy. But don't worry her, just say Cathy's had an accident, and that she's in hospital. She's now back from surgery and, even better, we've just been told that she's awake. We'll be allowed to see her in a little while. But it might be best if you don't tell Beth about the accident in detail. It might worry her even more.'

'Beth will be upset though. She always was quick to tears, and as you probably know, she doesn't get much love and care from that no-good husband of hers.' His voice hardened. 'Why she ever married him in the first place, I will never know.'

He fell silent, as though he was thinking what to do for the best.

'Look, Ronnie,' Marie said, 'I do understand what you're saying. If you would rather not contact Beth until we've seen Cathy then I shall leave the decision to you. Where your sister is concerned, you know best.'

Ronnie thought a moment longer.

'No, Marie, I'll call Beth now. I promise not to say anything that might alarm her unnecessarily.'

Seeing the matron's office was empty, Ronnie sneaked in and vowed to make it a quick call. He didn't fancy feeding coins into a public call box and speaking to Beth where anyone could hear, especially as he didn't trust himself not to break down.

It was Beth who answered the phone and Ronnie was glad he didn't have to speak to Mike. He really did dislike that man.

Beth's voice was small and nervous as she gave her name, as if she had shrunk and her confidence had evaporated, but when she heard Ronnie on the other end she rallied.

'Oh, Ronnie, I am so pleased to hear from you . . . so pleased. I've been thinking about you lots and keeping my fingers crossed that things were working out for you.'

'Well, kind of,' said Ronnie. 'I'll tell you about me another time but I'm afraid I'm calling now with some bad news. It's about Cathy . . .'

He told Beth briefly what had happened and she was very upset, just as he had predicted. Then it was Ronnie's turn to put on a brave face and try to reassure her, and talking up what little he knew of Cathy's progress helped to bolster his own spirits. By the time he had finished speaking he was feeling stronger himself, but Beth was still tearful and back to the tiny little nervous voice.

'You are okay, aren't you, Beth? I mean, I have to go now – I've borrowed the matron's phone and I shouldn't really be in here – but I don't want to leave you feeling bad. I'm sorry to have to ring with such awful news.'

'It's not your fault, Ronnie. Don't be silly,' Beth said, sniffing.

'But you are all right?'

'Yes . . . yes, of course I'm all right—'

As she broke off, Ronnie thought he could hear Mike's voice in the distance, bellowing for attention in his usual overbearing way.

'Look, Ronnie, I have to go now. Please give my love to Cathy, and let me know how she is when you've seen her, if you can? And kisses to Cathy and Marie from me.'

'Of course I will. And you take care, Beth.' At the sound of Mike shouting again Ronnie rolled his eyes. It wasn't hard to guess that Mike was continuing to give Beth a hard time. 'And if I hear Mike's been causing you any grief I'll be down there and sorting him out. So just you tell me about that. Promise?'

'Look, Ronnie, I really have to go. Love to Cathy. Love to everyone. Ring me soon . . . bye.' And she rang off.

Ronnie replaced the receiver on Matron's telephone and hurried out of her office, his mouth tight at the thought of his lovely sister being bullied by that vile man she'd married. But when he saw Marie sitting where he had left her he painted on a smile for her.

'Ronnie, how did Beth take the news?' Marie asked worriedly.

'As you might expect,' Ronnie told her. 'But she was much relieved that Cathy was out of the operating theatre. Oh, and she asked me to give you and Cathy a kiss from her . . . which I will be happy to do.' And he promptly hugged Marie as hard as he could.

'I can't recall ever having prayed before – I mean really prayed – but I've been praying for Cathy ever since it happened.' He closed his eyes for a brief second. 'Seeing her lying there, broken and unconscious was something I will never forget as long as I live.' He sucked in a tearful sigh. 'I really thought I had lost her, Marie.' As though ashamed, he turned away. 'I'm sorry I should not be talking like that.'

'You must not be afraid to say what's in your mind and heart, Ronnie,' Marie told him. 'It was a shocking thing for you to witness, and I think you are both brave and strong of heart. I'm so very proud that Cathy has someone like you to love and be with . . . hopefully for a very, very long time.' She gave him a motherly hug. 'If ever two people were meant for each other, it's you and Cathy.'

Ronnie gave another big sigh. 'I can't help thinking that Cathy was lucky. She must have had a guardian angel looking after her.'

He could see it all over again in his mind's eye. 'That horse could so easily have killed her. I daren't even think of it. Honestly, Marie, I swear I shall have nightmares for a long time yet . . . seeing her being kicked like that. I was helpless, it happened so fast and the crowds were pushing and shoving, desperate to get away. I swear I will be forever grateful that

Cathy was somehow snatched away from worse peril in time.'

Too choked to answer, Marie acknowledged his dark memories with a nod of the head, and her strong arms about his broad shoulders.

'You'll get through it,' she murmured. 'We all will. I promise.'

Ronnie was grateful for her wise words and the prospect that very soon, they would be able to see Cathy, even if only for a moment or so.

~

Marie's thoughts momentarily fled to Tony who, unknown to the poor girl lying unconscious in the next room, was Cathy's rightful father.

For the next few minutes Marie tried her best to push Tony out of her already troubled mind, but it stayed with her, niggling and worrying her. Should Tony know that Cathy was lying in hospital after such a horrific accident? The thought of Cathy caught up in all that panic, the horse bolting, the traffic in confusion, Cathy being surrounded by doctors and rushed into hospital and into surgery, it was utter mayhem. She knew Cathy was a fighter but she looked so small and broken. And the dilemma would not leave her. She tried to devise a situation which might let Tony know of Cathy's predicament in a rounda-bout way, and leave it open for him to follow his own conscience. All manner of concerns and alternatives tore through her mind about how to tell him, without making it widely known.

She knew that he loved Eileen, and that he would be deeply torn as to what he should do. In her heart, she believed that he should know, because at the end of the day he was Cathy's father, and nothing would ever change that.

But the truth was, Marie knew now that, before she told Tony, she would have to tell Cathy. But, supposing that Cathy survived this horrific ordeal, she could not risk a further shock to her system until Cathy was strong enough to learn the secret that had haunted Marie for all these years.

And so Marie decided that since it was in the hands of those doctors, and the Good Lord, as to whether Cathy would ever come home again, she would just have to wait for Cathy to give her a sign that she was ready to hear the terrible truth.

CHAPTER SEVENTEEN

AFTER TALKING WITH Ronnie on the telephone, Beth sat on the arm of the chair, the telephone in her hand and her head spinning at the shocking news of Cathy's accident in Blackpool.

'Who was that?' Dabbing his face to clear the odd hairs that still clung to his skin after shaving, her bad-tempered husband questioned her again when she didn't answer immediately. 'Who was that on the phone? Don't you dare ignore me!'

'I'm sorry, Mike. I was distracted. I can't help thinking about what Ronnie just told me. There's been a terrible accident.'

'Don't give me that! You're after putting me in a bad mood again, aren't you? Oh, yes! You're a cunning little swine, you love to wind me up, don't you, eh? You get me angry, put me in a really bad mood, and then you have the damned cheek to blame me when I find the need to chastise you!'

His temper rising by the second, he crossed the room and reached out to grab a hank of her long hair, before roaring at her, 'What the hell is it with you, eh?'

He yanked her hair again and again, revelling in her cries of pain. 'I asked you a question, bitch! Who was that on the telephone? Some fancy man was it, eh? Sneaking behind my back, are you?' His temper knew no bounds. 'What are you up to, eh? Answer me, dammit!'

'I'm not up to anything! That was my brother, Ronnie.'

'Liar!'

'No, I'm not a liar!'

Smiling at her squeals of pain, Mike continued to yank at her hair, while bending down to whisper in her ear, 'What does your precious brother want then? Got some kind of secret between the two of you, is that it? Cooking something up, some kind of trickery to make me out a fool, is that it?'

Pressing his face hard against hers, he was enjoying her pain. 'I know he doesn't care much for me, but I don't give a sod about that because as you well know, I loathe him every bit as much as he loathes me.'

He took her by the shoulders and spun her round to face him. 'Well, now?' He smiled wickedly. 'I want the truth! Out with it – and you know better than to tell me lies – what did he want, eh? Your precious brother, what did he say? I can always tell when you're lying.'

'I am not . . . lying!' Upset after hearing of Cathy's accident, Beth was slow in answering. All she could hear was Ronnie's voice in her head, telling her that Cathy was hurt and in hospital.

'Well?' Mike shook her viciously. 'Out with it! The truth, mind.' Leaning down he stared hard into her face. 'Well . . . come on then. What did he tell you? Come on then, bitch! Have you gone deaf and dumb all of a sudden or what?'

Then he had his two hands around her throat. 'Poor little thing.' He smiled nastily into her face, 'I can't for the life of me wonder why I ever took you on, I must have been crazy. Why the hell did I ever get mixed up with you and your family, eh?'

Taking hold of her he began shaking her, but with a huge effort she broke away and fled out of the room and along the passageway to the front door. She had to get away, but Mike was close on her heels. Panic-stricken, she struggled to get the door open, he threw her aside and kicked it shut.

She struggled to get by him but he grabbed her by the arms and fought her back from the door. 'Woah! Desperate to run off with your fancy man, is that it? Well, who am I to stop you? Go on, bugger off, and good riddance to you. But in future, just keep well away from me, and if you rubbish my name to anyone or cause me any trouble, I swear you will pay for it, believe me. Oh, and don't forget, it's me who's been paying the mortgage these past years, which makes this house mine.'

His dark eyes smiled as he thrust his face close to hers and told her softly, 'It's you who's leaving, not me! And if you make any kind of trouble, or try taking my home from me, I'll give you a fight you will never forget. Don't try sneaking back in here,' he warned her in a quiet voice, 'and don't fight me for this house, because, trust me, you will be fighting a losing battle!'

Moving even closer to her, he lowered his voice to a menacing hiss. 'If you and your precious brother try to get one over on me, people will get hurt. You could get hurt.' His smile was wicked. 'Oh, you might not care if I planned to hurt you . . . but I'm sure if it was your precious brother, Ronnie, who had some kind of an accident . . . well now, you would not like that at all, would you?'

Beth remained silent. She knew what he might be capable of.

Enjoying her fear, Mike taunted her with his hands about her throat. 'Don't test me, my lovely,' he purred, and when he leaned forward to kiss her, she backed away as best she could.

'Oh, dearie me! Is your husband so repellent that you can't even kiss him?' he leered. 'Oh my! You really hate me, don't you? I bet you'd like to see me dead, wouldn't you? It would be terrible, though, wouldn't it, my lovely, if your dear brother was attacked one dark night by some people I know — really bad people who owe me big time!'

When she tried to back away, he clutched her to him. 'Oh, yes! Bad people who would do anything to keep me sweet.'

His wicked smile turned Beth's heart over with fear. She knew he had friends who were capable of anything, and she also knew that if he took a mind to hurt Ronnie, nothing would stop him.

'You know I only have to raise my little finger, and Ronnie is in deep trouble, you understand, sweetheart?'

When she gave no answer, he smiled and went on, 'I promise, I will not hang around to pick up the pieces when my people are done with him. And there you would be, homeless and alone, and only what was left of your precious brother, to take care of you.'

He kept her pinned to the wall. 'So tell me – or am I not allowed to know what your precious brother told you, eh? An "accident", isn't that what you said? Well now that's a real shame, and what kind of "accident" was it? A bad one, I hope!'

For what seemed an age, Beth stubbornly kept her ground, refusing to answer and fuel his cruelty until he threw a spiteful, unexpected punch that knocked her off her feet.

'Get up, you're not hurt!' He kicked her as she lay on the floor. 'I said get up!'

When she tried to struggle to her feet, he yanked her up and slammed her against the wall. With one arm across her neck, he reached for the door with the other. 'If you say one word against me, I swear your precious brother will be no more. You have my word on that! You and me . . . we're done with. Don't try finding me, because I'm moving away. The house will be sold.'

Quietly opening the door just wide enough, he looked out to check that the street was empty.

Satisfied there was no one to witness it, he took Beth by the shoulders, while smiling into her eyes. 'I do love you,' he promised, 'but you have been unwise to underestimate me! We're done. Finished with. I've had enough of your lies!'

His meaning was clear.

He grabbed her face between both hands and kissed her full on the mouth.

When she struggled with him, he held her even tighter. 'Just remember, you'll always be my wife, though. Mine. Death do us part. No tricks. And like I say, don't ever forget, this is my house. It's in my name and was bought with my money. Don't ever try coming back here, because you will regret it, d'you hear me? Stay away! Or face the consequences.'

His dark threats were clear enough to Beth. And now his spiteful smile fell away, and in silence, and without an ounce of compassion, he yanked open the door, and he threw her out into the night.

A FAMILY SECRET

By the time Beth had scrambled up from the path where she fell, Mike had already gone back inside and the door was firmly closed and locked behind him. She had nothing, not even a scrap of fight. He'd taken everything.

CHAPTER EIGHTEEN

A SHORT DISTANCE FROM where Beth and Mike resided, Eileen and Tony were settling down to enjoy their hot cocoa before getting ready for bed.

As a rule, the two of them might have been chatting together, or chuckling about this and that, and generally putting the world to rights. But lately, Eileen had been less relaxed, constantly fretting over the meeting with Marie in Blackpool a few weeks ago.

Although Eileen still loved Tony after all these years, because of his liaison with Marie she could never quite trust him, and never quite forget what had happened.

For the sake of her own sanity and the hope of keeping her marriage together, Eileen had stopped asking questions long ago. She wanted the issue closed, and she was ashamed and hurt whenever she thought of how her husband and her friend had betrayed her.

Thankfully, Marie had kept well away from Eileen. On the odd occasion when she and Marie saw each other across the market stalls in town, or walking in the park, each would simply nod an acknowledgement and move on.

At home, Tony had never mentioned the night Marie came to call on Eileen, and found only him there, willing to offer sympathy to the widow, and a great deal more. Indeed, on the one occasion when Eileen might have touched on the reasons as to why it happened, Tony had adamantly refused even to discuss it.

And so, ashamed and angry, she had deliberately pushed the memory of that time away into the dark shadows of her mind in the hope of putting it all behind her for ever.

Let the past stay in the past – with any hidden skeletons there may be.

The alternative was to lose her marriage, along with the man she had married . . . for better or worse.

Sipping her cocoa and nibbling a digestive biscuit, Eileen wondered, as she had many times over the years, if Marie had actually caught sight of her on that particular night, while hurrying away in shame.

The back-street route she had taken from Eileen's house in what appeared to be a panic was badly lit, and frequently occupied by loud drunkards looking for a fight or a loose woman. Why had Marie made such a dangerous and foolish choice, walking alone through that dark and infamous alley? Only guilt or panic could have spurred any respectable woman into taking that alley.

Eileen was convinced that Marie had caught sight of her and in panic she had turned down the nearest escape route.

On arriving home from visiting a friend that particular night, she had questioned Tony as to why Marie had been round at their house. 'What did she want? And why was she in such a panic on leaving that she hurried away down that rough alley? I'm sure it was when she caught sight of me.'

Tony had given what he imagined to be a quick and simple answer, without even glancing up from his newspaper. 'I'm not sure, love. Although, she was a bit quiet, I must say. I made her a cup of tea, as you would have done, and we sat and waited for you while chatting about this and that, and then she just up and left.' He had folded his newspaper and prepared to retire for the night.

'Listen, Eileen, sweetheart,' he had said, looking nervous. 'Tell me the truth, you're not upset at Marie being here alone with me, are you? I mean, I couldn't just turn her away, could I? She was here to see you, not me. But I do wish you had been here. I hope you're not angry with me for letting her in, are you?'

He was gabbling like a man who might have something playing on his mind. 'I mean, what else could I do but invite her inside? I honestly thought you would be home any minute. What I'm saying is, there was nothing wrong. We just talked for a while and then she up and left in a rush.'

He'd quickly changed the subject. 'Anyway, how was your old friend, Gloria, isn't it?'

Without waiting for an answer, he had turned and made for the door to the hall, and Eileen had heard his tread on the stairs.

It had been clear to Eileen that Tony was trying too hard, possibly to convince her that he and Marie had done nothing wrong.

After that, her suspicions had been confirmed when Marie had come to tell her that she had been pregnant, the baby was Tony's but that she'd got rid of it. After that, of course, the friendship was shattered and Eileen had barely seen Marie in all the ensuing years even though they lived in the same town.

When, less than a year after that traumatic meeting, the news was out that Marie's daughter had given birth to a baby girl, it had raised all manner of suspicions in Eileen's troubled mind.

Eileen hadn't really given it another thought, why would Marie confess to something so awful if she'd planned on having the baby? But that suspicion niggled now as whether the child truly was born of Marie's daughter. And she now strongly believed that the girl was Marie's – Marie and Tony's – but for everyone's sake, Eileen was forced to put her suspicion to the darkest corners of her troubled mind. She had sworn Marie to secrecy about there even being a pregnancy. Whatever Eileen herself believed, Tony must never know.

Eileen had been content to sweep all knowledge of Marie's so-called granddaughter under the carpet. She wouldn't have recognised the child in the street and nor was she interested in doing so. If she had any natural curiosity in seeing what Tony's child – if Tony's she was – looked like, she firmly suppressed it.

And then, by some quirk of fate, the girl was brought to Eileen's attention.

Eileen's friend, Beth, whom she'd met in the library and who shared with Eileen a taste for historical romances, had a brother called Ronnie. He was a nice young man but a little unsettled in life. He was always popping into Beth's house, even though he was lodging in a different part of town. He was a very attentive brother to Beth, who was married to a *very* difficult man, and he was often round to see her and to cheer her up. Ronnie had a pretty young girlfriend – had had for well over a year now – and it looked like Ronnie was crazy about her. He'd brought her round to see Beth a few times when Mike, that unpleasant husband of hers, wasn't there, and Beth and this girlfriend of Ronnie's, Cathy, had become good friends.

Of course, Beth had told Eileen all about this lovely

girl that Ronnie was going out with, and Eileen, piecing together the information over a few weeks, realised that, without doubt, Ronnie's girlfriend was the girl she believed to be Marie and Tony's love child.

Naturally she kept this information to herself. At first she was in a panic to think Tony might meet Cathy but then she got a grip of her common sense and decided there was little need to worry, and certainly no need even to mention the girl to Tony. There was no reason why, if he ever heard of this Cathy, Tony should think she had anything to do with him.

'Hey, woman of mine!'

Eileen's rambling thoughts suddenly fell away in the wake of Tony's call.

'Good grief, woman, you were so deep in thought, you seemed miles away.'

He hugged her tight. 'I'm really tired. If you don't mind, I'll say goodnight and get off to bed.'

'Go on then. I won't be long behind you,' Eileen promised.

With Tony gone, she glanced across the room to a framed wedding photograph of herself and Tony. She would never forget that magical day. She'd been so immensely proud and happy that a fine man like Tony had chosen her to share his life. He'd been so handsome that all the girls at school had wanted to date him. And he'd been kind and funny, making everyone laugh with his witty remarks. The life and soul of the party – that summed up Tony; it was hard to believe now. In the early days they'd been so very happy, although sometimes now Eileen's one great wonder was never having had a child. If they'd had a child, would he have strayed? Would he still have been that vibrant man she married, not the quiet disappointed man he was now?

Her meandering memories were shattered as Tony blundered into the room yet again.

'Oh, Eileen, there you are, my love.'

'I thought you'd gone to bed!'

'I did, but I can't get to sleep with you down here.'

'You get off to bed, and I promise I'll be up soon, all right.'

'If you say so!' Crossing the room, he gave her a fond peck on the cheek. 'Don't be too long, though. You know I can't get off to sleep unless I've got you beside me.'

'Go on, you big softy. Just go.' Eileen gave him a playful push. 'I've got a few things to do yet.'

'All right then.' He was halfway up the stairs when the two of them were startled to hear the telephone ringing. 'Who the devil's that at this time of night?' Tony turned to hurry downstairs, calling out to Eileen, 'Don't you answer it, love.'

Rushing to her side, Tony put the receiver to his ear, wondering who might be calling this late.

In attempting to stop Eileen chattering, Tony pressed a finger to his lips, and when she fell silent. He said sharply, 'Hello. Who is this?' He was concerned the caller might be a prankster.

Moving closer to the phone, Eileen could hear the person on the other end, but she could not make out who it was or what was being said.

Tony was surprised to hear it was Beth's brother, Ronnie, who was calling. They'd met him a good few times over the years, he was such a good brother to Beth.

'Oh, my word, Ronnie! It's good to hear your voice, but it's a bit late to call? Not that I'm complaining. We were just off to bed.' He listened a bit and then asked rather nervously, 'What's wrong? Eileen said you were away working?'

'Yes, that's right and I'm calling from Blackpool,' said Ronnie. 'I'm sorry it's late, but I had wanted to tell Beth some news, but I can't seem to get hold of her. I've called several times, but there's no one there. Either that, or they're not answering the phone, and I'm getting worried. I spoke to Beth earlier and I said I'd ring back when I had more news. She didn't say that she'd be out and it is late for her not to be at home. I'm beginning to get worried. I would appreciate it if you might call round whenever possible, just to see if she's all right. Would you do that for me, please Tony?'

'Of course I will!'

'Thank you so much!' Ronnie took a deep breath of relief.

'Can I give her a message if I see her? Pass on this "news" you have for her?' Tony offered.

Ronnie took a deep breath and then said, 'Tony, I'm sorry to have to let you both in on bad news, but soon after she arrived in Blackpool to see me, Cathy – you know, my girlfriend – was caught up in a shocking accident on the Promenade.'

Tony was visibly shocked and seeing this, Eileen was jumping up and down to be told what had happened.

'What kind of "accident"?' Tony asked, at the same time trying to shush Eileen.

Ronnie went on to explain how Cathy had been hurt. 'It's been a real shock, but Cathy was hurt badly.' He paused, clearly trying to pull himself together to describe the moment the horse's hooves had come crashing down on Cathy. 'She was knocked down and taken into surgery, she's through the worst of it now and talking to us, albeit for a few minutes at a time. It was some accident, I'll never get it out of my mind, I was right there, so desperate to get her. But thankfully she's going to be all right. Cathy is a strong-minded woman, you know, a real fighter. She takes after her nan. The limbs will heal and the other injuries, it will all take time. She's in the best hands now. The doctors are now saying that Cathy will be good as new in time. Beth knows about her being hurt, but I wanted to pass on this latest news straight away, and it's just so unlike her to be out.'

Eileen now gently collected the receiver from Tony, asking Ronnie more questions.

'Oh, thank God she's going to be okay! She sounds like she'll come through all right, she's in good care with you all by her side. So don't you go worrying about your sister and home. All we can do is say a little prayer and trust in the Good Lord you get your Cathy back strong and well.'

Nervous and tearful, Tony slumped on the stairs, while waiting for Eileen to say goodnight to Ronnie. Suddenly the crippling weight of guilt felt too heavy to carry. He sat there like a frightened mouse, too nervous to make a bolt for it. It was as though he'd locked the subject away in the deep recesses of his mind where he had hoped it wouldn't have to see the light of day.

When Eileen eventually came to him for reassurance, he gave it as generously as he could, while deep down trembling, with dark thoughts of how easily Cathy could have been taken from him before he really knew her. In that devastating moment, he could hardly think straight.

Seeing her husband in much distress, Eileen was understandably tearful, and she said a silent prayer of thanks, because it sounded as if it could so easily have been a whole different story.

Tony pulled himself together and took back the

receiver. The two men talked for a little longer, and then Ronnie confided why he was especially anxious about Beth. 'Honestly, Tony – regarding that man of hers – I would not trust him as far as I could throw him. He's a devious, nasty devil at the best of times. I never have liked him, but Beth seems to need him, so what can I do?'

'Not an awful lot, son. Except what you appear to be doing; mainly keeping a wary eye on her. And don't forget, we're here . . . and you know we will always look out for Beth. I saw Beth earlier today and she seemed all right, but, as I say, I can pop round and check on her.'

He added in a softer voice, 'The thing is, Ronnie, like you, I don't care for that bloke. Oh, it's not that Beth's ever complained about him to me, but now and then he's often butted in on me and Beth in conversation and he seems a bit of an ignorant sort, if you ask me. But I've never seen him ill-treating her, and if I ever did I promise I would be in there like a shot.'

Ronnie was grateful. 'I'm glad you're looking out for her. Mike's a bit too sneaky and full of himself for my liking . . . but Beth won't have it.'

'Aye well, you know what women are like. They won't ever listen will they? But don't worry, son, I'll go round there now, and if Beth is there then I can bring her back here to speak with you in privacy. How's that, eh?'

'No, better not, in case Mike insists on coming round as well and then takes it out on her when he gets her home. No, it's best if I just keep trying to contact her myself.'

'Please give our love to, um, Cathy, and if you can, will you try your best to keep us informed?'

'Of course, and thank you. I'll give your love to Cathy.' He reminded Tony, 'Be careful when you go round to see Beth. I can't trust that bloke as far as I could throw him. I know from dealing with him in the past. You can't believe a word that comes out of his lying mouth. I just need to know that Beth is safe and I can't thank you enough for helping me.' He gave Tony the telephone number at the pub, to be used in emergencies only, and then he was quickly gone, while Tony reluctantly replaced the receiver.

'I don't blame Ronnie for being worried about Beth. If she isn't at home, where the devil could she be at this time of night?'

Eileen had been thinking about that. 'It is odd that she's not answering the telephone.'

'Well yes, unless of course she's gone out with a friend – maybe to the pictures in town.'

'I shouldn't think so. I mean, I suspect she doesn't have many close friends, I suspect that bloke of hers won't allow it. In fact, Beth actually told me one time that he gets crazy jealous even when she goes shopping with her quiet little friend, Molly, from Peter Street.'

While she talked, she made them each another cup of hot cocoa. 'It will help us sleep,' she explained wearily. 'There is so much running round my mind, I don't think I could sleep anyway.'

Tony agreed.

The two of them talked well into the early hours, about Beth, and her spiteful partner, but also about the message Ronnie had brought about Cathy's terrible accident. 'Oh, Tony! Cathy will be all right won't she?' Like Tony, Eileen had been deeply shaken by the news of Cathy's accident. Though neither could tell the other why.

'We have to believe that Cathy is in safe hands,' Tony assured her. 'Heaven only knows what Cathy's family are thinking right now, and on top of that Ronnie's worried about his sister, Beth.'

He was determined to keep his promise to that caring young man. 'I'll go round there first thing in the morning, and if there is neither sight nor sound of her, I'll do my best to find out where she is. When Ronnie calls again, I might have some good news for him, I'm hoping, he might have some good news about Cathy, too?'

'Oh, I do hope so, Tony!'

When her tears threatened again, Tony grasped hold of her hand. 'Trust me, sweetheart, we have to believe that everything will turn out all right for Ronnie's Cathy, and for Beth also!'

He whispered a little prayer, before his thoughts

again trickled back over the years, to when he and Marie had slept together.

Then he thought of Cathy, his own precious daughter, how she had been so assured and friendly at the greengrocer's so that she caught his eye, and then he discovered the extraordinary connection to himself. He felt somewhat privileged, but he was also deeply ashamed and he prayed that he might be forgiven for his badness all those years ago.

He also murmured a little prayer for the two young women who needed help, to regain strength and comfort in their hour of need.

Then he thought of the family and Ronnie also, a fine young man with a huge weight of worry on his mind – maybe too much to carry alone. With that in mind, Tony asked the Good Lord to help Ronnie.

Now . . . with all these uncomfortable thoughts crowding his mind, he glanced at his wife of these many years, the wife he had shamefully wronged.

Eileen had seldom raised the issue of his cheating. She had certainly never mentioned a child. Tony wondered how much she knew and whether for the sake of their marriage and their love for each other she would prefer to pretend she knew nothing. He suspected so and in that case he kept his silence, even though it weighed heavy.

CHAPTER NINETEEN

Eventually, Tony and Eileen went upstairs to their bedroom, at the front of the house.

When they reached the bedroom, Tony, with his old-fashioned courtesy, went ahead to open the bedroom door for Eileen to go in first.

'I don't know if I could sleep just yet,' she said, wearily undressing and climbing into bed, 'not after what Ronnie told us.'

Tony felt exactly the same. 'Well, if you want to chat, we can do that, sweetheart,' he said. 'But if we start discussing all the things that are playing on our minds, we won't get a wink of sleep, and what good will that do us?'

'I know. But I can't help feeling for Cathy. She's such a dainty little thing, and from what Ronnie told us it's a wonder she wasn't killed! Oh, dear me, Tony, it doesn't even bear thinking about.'

'I've been thinking exactly the same. But, from

what Ronnie told us, the doctors have done a brilliant job and she's getting truly expert care.'

Tony felt lost in emotion, nearly losing a daughter he hadn't had the chance to love. He pushed that thought away, feeling lost and alone. He looked across to Eileen, while she tucked herself deeper under the covers. Tony thought he'd best change the subject, recalling another of Ronnie's worries. 'I've been trying to think about where I might locate Beth. I'll set the clock and get up extra early. First stop is the house, it's likely she'll be there in the morning.'

'And if she's not there, what will you do then?' Eileen asked.

'Well, I'll try and talk to that man of hers, see if I can get any sense out of him.' Tony made a face. 'Hmm! I am not looking forward to that, I can tell you. He's a surly, aggravating sort, not at all helpful.'

'Yes, we all know that, but if he starts getting nasty with you, just come away and enquire as to Beth's whereabouts from the neighbours on either side. You never know, they just might have spoken to her, or seen something.'

'Yes, I'll do that.' Tony undressed and clambered into bed, thinking about Cathy.

He surreptitiously wiped a tear away from his eyes with the back of his hand.

Tony looked into Eileen's tired face. 'I do love you so,' he told her softly. 'I can never imagine my life without you in it.'

Eileen smiled her gratitude and each silently said a little prayer for Cathy's recovery. A short time later they were sleeping deeply. Suddenly Eileen sat up straight and shook Tony by the shoulder.

'Tony,' she whispered urgently in his ear, 'Tony, wake up. I think there's someone outside, Tony!' She shook him again, and this time he sat up straight, eyes sleepy and flailing his arms about.

'What's wrong? What's going on?' Switching on the bedside lamp, he turned to her grumbling, 'For pity's sake, Eileen! You gave me the fright of my life, whatever are you doing? What's wrong?' He rubbed his knuckles into his eye sockets. 'I was fast asleep. What's happening? Why did you wake me?'

Then Tony heard the same high-pitched wailing that had woken Eileen a minute or so earlier. 'What the devil was that? There! I knew it . . . damned things! Marauding, bloody cats,' he growled through his teeth. 'Clattering and banging round the bins at this time o' night. It is! It's them damned cats again!'

Groaning and complaining, he scrambled out of bed. 'You stay there! And turn the lamp off so I can see what the devil is going on out there.'

He continued to grumble, as he edged himself towards the window. 'I bet all you like that's what it is: them damned cats, chasing each other round the rubbish bins. It's the mating season. That's what they're up to, and no mistake.'

He looked out but could see nothing. He listened,

but the night was now silent and so he crept back to bed.

'All quiet now. Maybe we can get a little sleep before morning. I've promised Ronnie that I will track Beth down and I'll need to be up early.'

Eileen nodded. 'Well, I was thinking about Beth. Do you reckon she might be at home now, possibly making up with her fellow after a row maybe?'

'I have no idea, but yes, it's possible. We'll know tomorrow, because I shall be round there early.' Turning over on his side, Tony gave a little mumble. 'Hmm! That's if I ever get any sleep!'

'Sorry, love.' Eileen bade him a gentle goodnight.

But he was already snoring loud enough to keep Eileen from falling asleep just yet.

'Well, goodnight then, husband!' she stifled a chuckle. 'Out like a light, eh?'

Thinking she ought to close the curtains which Tony had left apart, she made her way to the window, and grasping a curtain in each hand, she prepared to shut out the night.

My, it's like a ghost town out there, she thought. She looked up the street and down, and she was amazed. What, no legless boozers singing their way home in full voice? No drunks being sick in the gutter? No sweethearts hand in hand as they wend their way home? In fact, she had never seen the street so deserted.

She glanced up and down the quiet street, but

there was no sign of life anywhere – certainly no meandering cats looking for a mate.

Clutching a curtain in each hand, she prepared to pull them together and go to catch up on her sleep when something caught her eye. There was something out there in the street after all.

Nervously, she carefully drew the curtains together, leaving open the tiniest chink through which she peered.

Through the gap, she saw a flurry of movement in the bus shelter across the street.

Somewhat worried, she carefully slid the two curtains together again. Best be careful, she thought nervously. I bet it's the bad lads who pinched the flowers from the pub window box and threw them all over the place the other week. When Tony went out and gave them a piece of his mind they greeted him with shocking language, which truly riled him.

Knowing she could not easily be seen from up here, however, Eileen was overcome with curiosity and once more she peered through the chink in the curtain. Hmm! Sometimes, it's as if the parents don't seem to give a thought to where the kids are these days or nights, she thought, warily closing the curtains to the smallest chink. If it's kids playing about I had best not let them see me or they'll more than likely start throwing stones up here.

With that in mind, she decided to draw the curtains, but she remained listening.

She heard the boys laughing and play-fighting, and then she heard a man's angry voice, which startled her, and them, as he yelled: 'Clear off, you lot, or I'll set my two bulldogs on yer. Go on! Bugger off. If I let them loose now they'll run you down and rip the arse right off you. Right! I'm counting . . . and once I let them go it will be too late to call them back!!'

To Eileen's horror, as she again peeped out, he screeched 'One!' Holding his dogs back, he carried on, 'Two!'

Before he could continue, the boys were off at the run, and they kept running until they were out of the street and out of sight altogether. The roar of vulgar laughter from the man, as he saw them off, curdled Eileen's blood.

Thankful that everything had fallen quiet in the wake of the many retreating footsteps, Eileen again dared to open a chink in the curtain, but when she peeped out she got the shock of her life.

In the flickering light from the street lamp, she recognised Beth, who seemed to be desperately trying to flee from the bus shelter where she'd been hiding since being turned out on the street by Mike, and waiting for morning so she could rouse Eileen. A big man used his excited dogs to keep her trapped.

At that point, heedless of her own safety, Eileen yelled out as loud as she could, 'Hey, you in the bus shelter!'

When the startled man looked towards where

Eileen was hiding behind the curtain, she called out again while staying hidden. 'The police will be here any minute! Leave her alone! Clear off, or you'll find yourself in a prison cell!'

She almost leaped out of her skin when Tony's big hand fell on her shoulder and drew her away from the window. 'It's all right, he can't easily see you from there.' He gently eased her aside. 'But what the devil are you playing at, putting yourself in danger like that?' He shook his head in disbelief. 'Go on, sweetheart, you get away from the window. I'll see to this.'

'Look there, Tony!' Eileen called his attention to the shocking sight she had seen. 'Look who he's got with him!' She gestured across to the bus shelter. 'It's Beth . . . and he won't let her go. He's drunk and a bit crazy, and he's got bulldogs – at least two of them – big savage things. He was going to set them after some boys who were aggravating him.'

After easing Eileen away from the window, Tony glanced across the street. He could see Beth, who was being held under the lamplight, while the man appeared to be threatening her, and now he was yelling up at anyone who might be listening, 'This is my woman, and I'll fight to the death for her, so, if you know what's good for you, you had best stay away!'

His dogs were pulling at their leads, seemingly eager to rip somebody apart.

Tony knew he had no choice but to get down there, and do whatever he could to get Beth away safely.

He explained to Eileen, 'He's drunk out of his skull! There's no telling what he's capable of. Look, Eileen, I'm going down there.' He glanced to where Beth had been pushed further along the bench in the bus shelter, 'Look at her! She must be frightened out of her mind!'

Eileen begged him to call the police.

'That won't help Beth now. There isn't time. Any moment, he'll be away with her. Like I said, he must be drunk out of his skull.'

Tony was enraged to see the drunkard manhandling young Beth, and he was now itching to deal with the coward.

'I want you to lock the door behind me . . . do you hear?' he told Eileen.

Eileen, however, feared Tony might get hurt. 'No, please . . . if you go out there, he might hurt you and Beth, just to show you he can. He's a maniac. Be careful, Tony! He's bound to set the dogs on you. I don't want you to go out there. Please, Tony. Let me call the police!' Tony was adamant. 'By the time the police get here he will have vanished, with Beth as his trophy! He has to be stopped. He needs to be taught a lesson. Give me a few minutes, and do not call the police unless you really need to. Do you understand, Eileen? Only if you think it's necessary.'

Eileen gave a half-hearted nod. 'Be careful, Tony. He's drunk and he's got them dogs at the ready. Please, Tony, let me call the police.'

'Not yet,' Tony insisted, putting on his clothes as fast as he could. 'If you think it's getting seriously out of hand, then go ahead and call the police. Trust me, people like this fella are basically cowardly when it comes to a serious confrontation and often it's far better to deal with the situation yourself, if you think you can,' he assured her.

He now instructed Eileen, 'Don't let him see you, but just keep an eye on him. He won't see me coming after him until the last minute but if he decides to run like the coward he is I need to know which way he's gone. And like I say, try not to let him see you at the window. And don't worry about me. I'm old enough and angry enough to deal with him.' Wisely, Eileen did not even attempt to dissuade him and a few moments later, Tony had gone, downstairs to the kitchen, where she heard him grab something from the cupboard and then hurry out onto the street.

Tony was both surprised and curious to find two other men walking purposefully alongside him, each of them long-time residents of the street.

Bill Lawson was a big man, with big fists. His buddy, Harold, was smaller, quicker, but built like a little tank,

'Come on then, chaps!' the little fellow called out. 'We've a job to do.' And with that sound instruction he proudly led the way down the road towards the bus shelter.

From upstairs, Eileen stole a peep through the window, and when she saw that Tony had got help, she recalled his advice and kept out of sight, relieved he was not taking on the ruffian alone.

However, when she heard Tony challenging the man in a harsh and threatening manner, she feared a skirmish might start.

She whispered a frantic prayer that Tony and his helpers should not get hurt and that Beth might find a chance to somehow break away from there.

As the inevitable fracas and shouting started, she nervously kept watch, terrified for Tony's safety. When the man saw the small posse heading towards him, in a way that told him he was in for one hell of a fight, he started yelling at the top of his voice.

'I mean it! Get back, or I'll have the dogs tear you apart!'

When he realised they were not in the mood for turning, he continued yelling. 'This is none of your business! Turn around, or I swear I'll let the dogs chew the bones of this young woman!'

'Is that so?' Tony calmly took a few steps towards the man, his voice deliberately quiet, but heavy with portent. 'Don't even think of letting the dogs get anywhere near her unless you want the same or worse!' he warned.

Suddenly snatching the tearful Beth to him, the man dragged her out from the bench with a dire warning to her rescuers. 'Trust me! This woman means nothing to me, but if you don't turn about and get the hell out of here I swear she won't have the same pretty face that she had before you lot interfered!'

Ignoring the threats, the three men continued towards him, and they were not altogether surprised when the bulldogs were released and heading straight for them.

'I did warn you,' the man laughed. 'The dogs are hungry tonight! So now it's you lot first, and then the young woman.' To prove his intent, he dragged the crying Beth out of the bus shelter, and held her under the light from the street lamp.

'She's a pretty little thing, don't you think?' the coward taunted. 'So go on. Get the hell outta here. For her sake, you do not want to get on the wrong side of me.'

Tony and the other two men remained silent as they continued to creep nearer to the bus shelter where the dogs were snarling.

'Get back! I warned you!' Pushing Beth roughly before him, the bully called his dogs to heel.

But then one of the dogs stopped and turned, excitedly sniffing the air, and now the other dog had spun round and was heading towards the pavement opposite, where the three men were waiting their chance.

For a moment, the dogs ran about in confusion, until they heard Tony calling them, 'Here, doggies! Come on! Look what we've got! Come on, over here!'

Suddenly the dogs were running straight for Tony who began throwing his arms about and calling them to him. 'Good boys! Come on, come on!'

When they were only inches away from him, he flung two big, fat, juicy chops as far away from the bus shelter as he could.

In an instant, the dogs were going crazy as they followed the smell of meat, which had landed well away from where Beth was cowering, while her captor chased after his dogs, swearing and cursing hell and damnation on the men who had plied the dogs with meat.

Meanwhile, the three men grabbed the opportunity to quickly snatch Beth away and rush her to a safe distance down the street, from where they watched in relief while helpless with laughter.

The shamed bully, screaming like a madman, rained all manner of wicked threats on each and every one of them, only to be laughed at.

In between his manic threats, he screeched at the squabbling dogs, who took absolutely no notice of him whatsoever, being far too busy fighting each other for the fat juicy chops. Their cowardly owner threatened retribution if they did not heed him 'right now, this minute!', and the more they defied him, the angrier he grew.

'Get over here, you cowardly bastards!' The ruffian's raised voice echoed along the street. 'Come on, I'm ready for you any time!'

To his utter frustration and embarrassment Tony and his mates continued to humiliate the coward with their fits of laughter as the man tried every which way to call his rebellious dogs to heel. Tony was busy reassuring the nervous and shaken Beth, although once in the strong, safe arms of Tony she began to relax.

And as the howling screams of anger and rage echoed down the street, Beth's rescuers retreated into the garden of Tony's house, while laughing every bit as loudly as the bully continued to shout and threaten.

'I'll have you yet, I know who you are and you ain't seen the last of me. Hell and damnation to the lot of you.'

Then the man was threatening his dogs, 'First thing tomorrow, you're off to have the chop, yes, that's what I said. It's the chop for you lot, and I mean it! Call yerselves fearless bulldogs, huh! I don't think so. More like bloody chickens. If my mates could see what cowards you are they'd never let me forget it.'

And when Tony started making a noise like a chicken, the other two men fell into fits of laughter, while the ruffian threatened hell and fury if he ever set eyes on them again!

Eileen had the kettle on and soon a fortifying cup of heavily sugared tea was in Beth's hands and Eileen fussed round her, mopping her tears and smoothing her hair while making 'There, there . . .' noises.

Questions about how Beth's ordeal had come about could wait until the morning. Now was not the time to have the poor woman reliving it.

Tony, Bill and Harold did a lot of slapping each

other on the back and were generally pretty gung ho in a modest sort of way. Harold declared this was his finest hour since the Armistice, and Bill then recalled he'd got an old service revolver in his wardrobe and he wished he'd brought it out with him, but maybe it was for the best that he hadn't remembered it in time. Eventually the men calmed down and, with Beth's thanks ringing in their ears, Bill and Harold went to the front door to make sure the madman with the dogs had gone, then slipped away to their own homes, leaving Tony and Eileen to fuss over Beth.

Eileen turned to Tony, who now seemed taller, straighter . . . more like the imposing figure she had married.

'Well done, my darling,' she murmured, putting her arms around him and holding him close. 'I'm so proud of you.'

Tony in turn held her to him and sighed with satisfaction. He had thought never to hear such fulsome praise from her again.

'I'm always proud of you,' he replied. 'Now let's get Beth settled in the spare room. It's been a busy night so far, but I'm sure we'd all like to get some sleep before the morning if we can.'

'Do you feel you could sleep after that awful ordeal?' Eileen asked Beth gently. 'I've always got the spare bed made up ready. Come up with me and we'll get you all nice and comfy.'

'Thank you, Eileen. You're really very kind. I don't want to put you to any trouble.'

'It's no trouble, love,' Eileen assured her guest, leading her out towards the stairs. 'I'll lend you one of my nighties. There's no hurry for you to get up in the morning. Just take it as it comes.'

Watching Eileen with her arm around Beth's shoulders and listening to her gentle words, Tony thought Eileen would have made a wonderful mother. And he, what sort of father would he have been if he'd known about Cathy?

After a somewhat restless night, Eileen and Tony were alerted by the shrill tones of the telephone echoing from downstairs. 'Who the devil is that?' Tony checked the bedside clock which showed the time to be just coming up to seven a.m. 'Who could be calling us at this time? I'll never get back to sleep now.'

Eileen was more concerned about their guest. 'I expect poor Beth will have been woken up as well, and I was hoping she might get a few more hours of sleep after her ordeal.'

Trying to put the memories of last night out of her mind, Eileen went quickly downstairs, where she picked up the receiver. 'Hello? Who is this?' she asked suspiciously. Eileen had a bad feeling that the man who had terrified Beth might have got hold of their number somehow.

Ronnie's welcome voice made her smile. 'Oh,

Ronnie. Oh, how good to hear your voice . . . thank you for calling. How is your Cathy?'

Before Ronnie could answer, Tony was right behind Eileen, making gestures to indicate that he needed to speak to her.

Lowering his voice to the softest whisper, he leaned towards Eileen and whispered in her ear, 'Eileen, while I have a little chat with Ronnie . . . can you keep an eye on Beth for a few minutes? Tell her that Ronnie is on the telephone but it might not be a good idea for her to tell him what's been happening out there, especially when he's got more than enough on his mind what with Cathy and everything.'

Eileen nodded. 'I understand, and I'm sure Beth would love to talk with her brother for a minute or so. I'll explain what you've just said, though, and I'll talk to Beth about Cathy. And don't worry, I'm sure she will not want to burden Ronnie with what happened last night. She's a kind and thoughtful young woman. Oh, and give my love to Ronnie, will you, sweetheart? Tell him I hope Cathy is all right, and I pray that somehow or another, for her sake and the sake of her family, they might be able to arrange a transfer to a hospital closer to home.'

Then Eileen went to Beth, and explained that Ronnie was on the phone, and that when the two men had finished putting the world to rights, Tony would call her down, so that she and Ronnie could catch up on everything. 'But please don't mention about your dreadful ordeal last night. Ronnie will be furious, and right now he does not need to be fretting and planning revenge.'

Beth fully appreciated what Eileen was saying. When Beth got to talk to Ronnie, she assured him that everything was fine and that he had no need to worry about her. In fact the news was good because she had left her troublesome husband, and had moved out.

'Eileen and Tony have told me that I can stay with them until I get myself sorted out, which I will, because I have never been so determined as I am now.'

She asked after Cathy and her family. 'Please give them my love, and a big hug for you, my lovely brother. Oh, and please tell Cathy that I miss her and that she has to get better as quickly as possible and that when she does get better the two of us will go shopping for bargains. I know she has a good eye for a bargain. But first she has to get better soon, because I miss her and I have heaps of gossip to tell her, and I really do think that the two of us need to get together and put the world to rights like we used to.'

A few moments later, Beth said goodbye and the house fell silent with her, Eileen and Tony feeling heavy of heart.

It was Beth who broke the silence. 'I don't like the idea of Cathy lying in a hospital bed so far away, with broken limbs and other injuries. What can I do for her? When can I go and see her?'

'It's not that easy, Beth,' Tony explained. 'From what we know, she is in a good hospital, but Cathy has a long and uncomfortable road ahead of her. She knows her family are there and I'm sure she knows that everyone will each do whatever they can to make her life easier and help her recovery.'

Beth agreed. 'And my poor Ronnie must be going through it to see Cathy in such a bad way. I fully understand why you did not want Ronnie to know what happened out there on the street last night. You truly are two wonderful friends to both of us.'

Thinking that she owed them the absolute truth, she confessed that it was her bad-tempered and spiteful husband Mike who had thrown her out on the street.

A short time later, feeling weary, Beth had to excuse herself. 'I'm really tired. Is it all right if I leave you two and go back to bed?'

'Of course!' Both Tony and Eileen were also feeling the worse for wear. 'In fact, I think I will too,' said Eileen. 'It isn't yet half past seven and I've no need to be up after such a disturbed night.' They both decided that bed was the place to be.

In no time at all, the house was quiet, except for the hollow snores that echoed through from the direction of Tony's cosy bed.

'For pity's sake, shut up! I can't get to sleep with that noise going on!'

That was Eileen's voice.

And the ensuing silence was absolute bliss.

PART FOUR

Sunshine After The Rain

CHAPTER TWENTY

THE DOCTOR WAS a kindly man, with a wealth of experience of broken limbs and recovery procedures, and now after she'd been a month in hospital, the doctor had arranged a meeting to speak with Cathy and her family, about her progress and long-term outlook.

'I have two pieces of good news for you,' he started. 'As you already know, Cathy is doing very well on her crutches. She is working hard to help strengthen the muscles and damaged fibres. I am pleased to tell you that the muscles in her legs are well on the mend, and have strengthened quite considerably since she moved from the wheelchair to the crutches. Her thigh muscles have strengthened, and are now well able to carry her weight while she's walking and performing the stretching exercises as advised. In fact, her wounds in general are healing quicker than I had expected, and as a result, her confidence is increasing by the day.'

He concluded with a smile, 'In fact Cathy is raring to go home. A home environment will only encourage her to get stronger and eventually to do away with the crutches. We have managed to secure her a month of daily appointments with the physiotherapist at your local hospital.'

He went on to explain, 'They now have a new exercise wing, recently installed, and a dedicated wing mainly for patients with the same kind of injuries as Cathy has. The series of day-visits will strengthen her muscles and get her legs working strongly. I hope within weeks she might even be able to discard at least one of the crutches altogether. Already her right arm and leg have significantly strengthened with the treatment she has recently undergone with us.'

That was wonderful news, for both Cathy and the family.

For Marie, however, always at the back of her mind was the fact that Cathy must very soon be told the truth about her shameful beginnings, and the wicked lies that she had been allowed to believe throughout her young life would be revealed. Despite the guilt she felt about Cathy and Tony, while she was lying there, broken as a rag doll, Marie knew Cathy had to know the truth. Even though it could destroy all of the happy memories she made growing up. Even though Anne and Dave would risk losing the girl they called their daughter. Marie owed it to Cathy now she was stronger.

After receiving the glad news about Cathy being

released soon, Dave went to sit and talk with her. With her blessing, he needed to return home to his many pressing responsibilities.

His boss at work had been entirely understanding when Dave explained how he must take time off in order to see Cathy through the worst of her long stay in hospital but now he needed to get back to work. Dave had been fiercely adamant he must stay near Cathy until she was truly out of the woods, but now she was on the mend, he needed to get back to work, and the house had been empty for long enough. It had been decided between Anne and Dave that someone needed to be at home, looking after everything. And as Dave said, the guesthouse wasn't going to pay for itself, and this way they could save themselves an extra room and they would keep it for as long as was necessary.

Marie and Anne stayed on at the guesthouse, and for most of each day and part of the evening, they remained by Cathy's side, making plans. They were so relieved now that Cathy was more like herself, and eager to get home.

Finally the day came when Cathy was to be allowed home, armed with all the details of the local hospital she must attend.

Anne waited with her, for the doctor's notes, and a last briefing about Cathy's ongoing treatment at the next hospital, but Marie felt a pressing need to distance herself from the procedure. She felt deeply concerned that the moment the family had dreaded over many years had finally caught up with them.

With Cathy's heart settled on marrying her beloved Ronnie, Marie was very much afraid of whatever turmoil was waiting to be unleashed on the innocent and trusting young woman. She would need her birth certificate to wed, and there the truth of her birth would be spelt out in black and white.

There was no place to hide, and so Marie prepared herself as best she could, rehearsing the moment when Cathy would learn the sordid truth. In a strange way, Marie felt as though a great weight was about to be lifted from her soul.

But what of Cathy?

Time and again over the years, and especially now, Marie had put herself in the shoes of Cathy, a kind and lovely young woman who had done nothing wrong. How would she ever deal with having been made to live a lie all these years? To believe she had an honest and decent family about her, and whom she adored without question, when in truth it was all a selfish fabrication.

Marie had been haunted over all this time, and would continue to be haunted until she was taken from this earth, and made to answer her shocking sins to the Good Lord.

With that thought playing on her mind, she

rejoined Cathy and Anne, clutching a cache of documents to give to the offices at the new hospital.

'I just phoned the guesthouse before we went in,' she told Cathy. 'Your father is travelling back up right now to pick us up.'

That final night in the guesthouse before the drive home, Marie's guilty mind would not let her rest, and so wrapping her dressing-gown about her, she sat at the bedroom window and looked across to the sea, now dark and deep in shadow.

She heard the laughter of merrymakers along the Promenade, and smiled when some happy drunk suddenly started singing in a raw, common sort of way, which was painfully beautiful.

And then, feeling deeply emotional, Marie began to cry, and could not stop.

After a while, she got to her feet, suddenly frantic to shake off her dressing-gown. And now she was scrambling to get her clothes on again, along with her coat and scarf. For some reason, she felt she had to get out of the room and as far away from here as her weary legs would carry her.

Taking her key, she tucked it inside her coat pocket, and went quietly out the bedroom door and down the stairs to the front door. After locking the front door behind her, she softly stole away like a thief in the night.

'Good grief!' The landlady had seen Marie through the lounge window and quickly alerted her snoozing husband in the armchair beside her. 'Look, it's Anne's mother, Marie. Where the devil is she off to on her own, and at this time of night? Should I go and wake her daughter?'

'Good Lord, no! She's old enough to look after herself that one. Don't forget the family have been at the hospital for most of the day. Marie probably needs to get out and breathe the sea air. And if she fancies a break for a while, that's up to her, love. It's been a worrying time for the family since Cathy's accident. I'm not surprised Marie can't sleep, poor thing.'

Unaware that she was being watched, Marie walked down the street, then across the road.

She had no idea where she was going, or when she might be back, but she could not bear being cooped up in that small room any longer.

So she kept walking until she stopped to rest on a low, bumpy, stone wall that skirted the Promenade. After a few minutes, she was up and off again, and a minute later, she again stopped to sit on the wall, her short legs dangling, and her body shivering in the damp sea air.

She looked across and down to the beach. It was so incredibly lonely and quiet and frightening in its endless magnitude.

A minute later she was up and away yet again,

walking, on and on to nowhere, totally unaware of the people still about, many casting curious glances as they passed her by.

Finally, when she stopped, Marie was surprised and gladdened to realise that she had walked all the way up to the old cabin where the big Scotsman, John Ferguson, and his mate, Danny, kept their worktools. So far she had not seen hide nor hair of either of them. Her priorities throughout her stay had been Cathy, and the family.

Suddenly feeling cold and exhausted, she looked to see if the two men were anywhere about, but there was no sign of them, and neither should there be, at this godless time of night.

Standing nearby, of course, was the Blue Bench, and Marie went to it and sat down.

She smiled at the thought of Danny Boy with his loud, melodic chuckle, and the bright, mischievous sparkle in his eyes. She had definitely developed a fond spot for Danny. He made her laugh so hard that sometimes, when he was in his funniest moods, she would even end up crying.

Just now, with a mood of sadness and huge loneliness overwhelming her, she felt Danny's warm, cheeky presence, and she glanced about her, hoping and wishing for him to be with her, in this crowded, lonely place.

For a fleeting moment, she actually felt his nearness, his sense of fun and those twinkling, laughing eyes. She had such strong memories of laughing together with him that her heart seemed to swell with a rush of warmth, which made her ache even more with loneliness.

Suddenly, she desperately needed to see him, to laugh at his silly jokes and enjoy his crazy sense of humour.

The very thought of him lifted her spirits. Danny was a caring friend, a genuine, honest man, often serious, often madly, outrageously funny, and so loving, in a naïve, childish way.

She needed him right now – this minute – with his cheeky smile and funny banter that lit up her heart.

If he was to suddenly arrive right here and now, she would feel wanted, and loved, and forgiven for all the bad, stupid things she had done in her life.

How could she ever erase the bad things she had done? How might she deal with the guilt she had carried all these years? Loneliness had crept up to shadow her life until now she had no idea which way to turn, no real idea how to start again. Shockingly bad things touched Cathy because of what Marie had done, and for that she would never forgive herself. Never! She had no one to blame but herself for not being honest, for not being good enough. She was a coward through and through, and now she seemed to have lost her way.

She was frightened, struggling in the dark with no one to help her.

How might she sort out the thoughts in her head, the toxic mixture of guilt, shame and deep regrets, which were now hopelessly tangled?

And now, shifting about on the Blue Bench, she wrapped her arms about her and, leaning her head back, she closed her eyes and thought of the really bad things she had allowed into her life: making a baby with a man who was married to her friend, when her husband was barely cold in his grave. When she thought of Cathy she felt ashamed, and yet she was also proud of having given birth to such a lovely, caring soul. Her Cathy was the miracle.

'Oh dear Lord, thank you for bringing her back to us.'

She started sobbing, softly at first, and then she could not stop the tears. With her arms wrapped about her head, she simply let the tears flow. She felt like a failure, a cheat and a sinner who should never have been born.

Suffocated by every dark thought, she bent her head forward and, clutching herself, she sobbed uncontrollably.

'Hey, come on now, woman. This is not the place to be showing all and sundry what a shocking state you're in.'

Startled by the familiar voice, Marie quickly wrapped her coat about her, hoisting herself to the edge of the bench. Then she was crying with relief when she saw her old friend. 'Danny Boy!' Suddenly she felt wanted, warm and safe. 'Oh, Danny, I'm so glad to see you.'

Marie opened her arms to him, and taking off his long coat, Danny placed it over her own and wrapped it about her shivering body.

'Ssh, now!' He eased her to her feet. 'Let's get ye inside. I heard about yer girl, Cathy,' he said softly, 'and now I hear she's doing all right, thank the Good Lord!'

When she began sobbing again, Danny quietened her. 'Ssh! Come on, me darlin', I'll take ye to the pub where I work in the evening. The landlord's a good man. He'll not turn us away.'

Hugely relieved to see Danny, she walked with him, wiping away her tears as she went.

'You should leave me here,' she told him, 'I've done such bad things in my life.'

'Aw, come on now, darlin', sure, haven't we all done bad things at some time or another? We all need to live and learn, and if you're truly sorry, it will all come right in the end.'

He wrapped his strong arm about her and carefully shepherded her across the street and along the pavement, towards the brightly lit pub, where he happily worked part time among the loud people and the strong smell of booze and food, and the merry men who took their pleasure at the snooker table and the dart board and the frothing pints that kept coming.

And where, most of all in this place of merriment, with his arms about his woman, Danny Boy now found his heaven on earth.

When Danny explained a little of the situation to the landlord, he was only too willing to help them.

'But you really should let your family know where you are,' he told Marie. She agreed, and told him the name of the guesthouse.

'Please, could I speak with them on your telephone, otherwise my daughter will begin to worry?'

When Marie phoned Anne to tell her where she was, Anne was frantic. 'Oh, Mum! Why didn't you wake me? I didn't even know you had gone out until the landlady got worried and told me. I was about to get dressed and come after you. Stay where you are and we'll come and get you, right now.'

'Go back to bed, love . . . I've been offered a room here, for the night,' Marie explained. 'I'm sorry to have worried you.'

Then Anne spoke with the landlord and agreed to collect Marie in the morning. But then Danny suggested that he would borrow the landlord's car and bring her straight back after she'd had a bite to eat. 'Is that okay with you, Anne?'

Of course Anne agreed. She was happy for Marie to be in Danny's capable hands, especially as he had always made a show of adoring the ground her mother walked on.

Anne had always considered him to be a rough diamond, the genuine article, and she had seen with her own eyes that Danny Boy, behind the jokes and the blarney, had always loved Marie from afar.

The landlord made them each a hot toddy, and left them in the bar chatting and planning, and catching up on everything that had passed since they'd last met. There seemed to be a lock-in going on, because it was past closing time, yet the pub was full and very lively. It soon became apparent that each had missed the other so much . . .

'Ah, sure it's good to see ye, me darlin'! My life was not even worth the living without ye!'

'I missed you too, Danny,' she confessed boldly, 'and I don't think we should ever lose touch.'

'Absolutely!' Danny did a little Irish jig, and when he was done he felt so breathless he could hardly speak, although he managed to get out the words that really mattered. 'How about the two of us get married, eh?' He gave a cheeky wink, but the look in his blue eyes said he was completely serious.

'What!' Marie wrapped her two hands about his face, while smiling into his blue Irish eyes. 'Danny Boy! I thought that I might not see you, so full of woe has this visit here been, and here you are, spouting love and marriage. And do you know what?'

'What's that then, eh?'

'I think this should tell you how I feel.' And she gave him the biggest, longest kiss ever.

'Wow!' Somewhat breathless, Danny gave a huge smile. 'You little hussy!

When he grabbed her and bent her backwards for a long, breathless kiss, a mighty cheer rose up to the rafters from the merry boozers, who got to their feet and clapped until they could clap no more.

'So! You bandy little Irish divil, you swore you would get your woman in the end, and you did an' all!' That was the landlord.

They all raised their drinks and wished the unlikely pair 'A long and happy life together!'

Danny Boy was so excited he grabbed hold of Marie and danced her across the floor, and round the bar, and up and down the short flight of steps at the door, and when he grew breathless he stopped to take a gulp of air, and then he was off again, swinging his woman round and round until he fell over dizzy and took her with him.

'I swear I've not had a drink this night,' he promised, 'I'm just dizzy with love for you, that's what it is!'

Of course, not a man jack in the place believed one word of it. They all chuckled, as the landlord merrily informed Marie, 'He's telling the truth. He has not had one single drink. In truth, he's had at least four that I know of!'

With the roar of jibes and merry laughter, Marie could have sworn that the building actually trembled under their feet.

The evening was a runaway success, with lots of tuneless singing and bandy-legged dancing. And then the naughty jokes started and the drunken laughter, and the wild, comical jig that Danny launched himself into.

It was a crazy, awful, noisy, and wonderful evening. And Marie thought she had never been so happy.

Even with the merriment and the cheery Danny now filling her world, Marie was ever mindful of her approaching duties and responsibilities to Cathy. But before she was even able to tell the truth to Cathy, she needed to confide the truth in the man she had now promised to marry.

That was a huge step for her to take, but a necessary one because although Danny was often prone to wildly fanciful a tale, or to tell the porker of a lie now and then, Marie had a feeling that he would be mortified to learn the shocking secret of the woman who had promised to be his wife.

Danny was a good and decent man at heart, and once he knew the awful truth – that she was a liar and a shamed woman who had given birth to a child fathered by the husband of her best friend – Marie worried that he might not want her any more . . . She could not have been more wrong.

CHAPTER TWENTY-ONE

THREE MONTHS HAD passed so very quickly, and Marie was both nervous and excited that the day for her and Danny to be married was now only one week away. Cathy's recovery had been painfully slow and Marie still had not found the inner strength to take Cathy aside, and tell her the truth of her birth, acknowledging her part in the cruel manner in which Cathy had been allowed to believe that the parents she adored were not in fact her parents at all.

Marie grew more nervous as the days rushed by. Many times she had made the hard decision to confess the truth to Cathy, but each time she thought she might be ready to broach the subject, her shame stopped her from speaking, and now the wedding day was almost upon them, and she was beginning to panic.

She knew in her heart and soul that she could not walk into that church and allow Danny to put a wedding ring on her finger when she still carried the heavy weight of her sins.

Marie had earnestly prayed time and again to find the strength to do what had to be done. She must not take her own happiness before she had given Cathy the truth of her beginnings.

More than anyone, Cathy deserved the truth.

Now that Cathy was back on her feet, she was determined at last to do the right and proper thing, even if it meant losing Danny, the man she had loved all these years, and only recently realised how much he truly meant to her. Time was fast running out, but now, at the eleventh hour, she would not change her mind.

Marie was certain of only one thing in this crucial moment . . . Cathy had done nothing wrong. And she deserved the truth, however shocking. It was now or never.

~

'Come on, you girls!' The wedding day was now just twenty-four hours away, and Anne was busy carrying out her last-minute responsibilities. 'This is your last dress fitting before the wedding tomorrow, so come on! Get your backsides in here, you two!' she called Beth and Cathy to heel. 'We should have tried the bridesmaid dresses on again yesterday, but with all the rushing and planning and chasing our tails, it's been absolute mayhem!'

She called to Marie through the kitchen door. 'You're next, Mum . . . so don't go anywhere!'

'I don't need another fitting, Anne, you've already altered the hem twice: once to take it up, and another to drop it back to where it was!'

Anne shrugged. 'You put me in charge of the dresses . . . so kindly let me get on with my responsibilities.'

After both bridesmaid dresses and Marie's wedding outfit had been refitted, they were to be put away safely for the big day.

'Right then!' Anne instructed the three of them. 'Looks like we're all set. So you two girls hang your dresses behind the door in the bedroom, and you, Mum,' she gestured to Marie, 'you can hang your outfit in my wardrobe if you like, it won't get interfered with there. Yours looks lovely, Mum. I'm so glad you changed your mind and chose the light blue straight skirt and jacket instead of that pinkish thing. It really did not suit you at all.'

When Beth and Cathy had gone out of the room, Anne quietly closed the door behind them, while drawing her mother towards the far side of the room where they might not be overheard. 'Mum . . . did you manage to have a talk with Cathy?' Her voice was ominously quiet and serious.

Marie shook her head, feeling terrible, 'Not yet, but I have it all in hand.'

Anne gave a long, anguished groan. 'Oh, Mum! You

promised you would tell her yesterday, and the day before that, and the week before that! If you're not careful, you'll miss your chance and then it will be all too late. She has to know the truth. She deserves that much at least. Oh, I realise it must be a daunting thing to be telling her, but you're getting married tomorrow . . . you need to get it all off your chest today. Please, Mum. You have lived with this far too long, you stopped living. Don't leave it for another moment. I would tell her, but you won't let me, so do it, Mum!'

Anne was shocked that Marie was still procrastinating. 'Go and open your heart, and tell her about having lost Dad . . . your beloved man . . . and that he was everything to you. Explain to her, you were in a really bad place at the time – you were distraught, not thinking straight. And for the first time in your life, you did something that you have always regretted. You adored Cathy from the start but you have punished yourself ever since.'

When the tears began escaping down Marie's face, she quickly wiped them away. 'All right! I'll go and find her and I will tell her the truth. But do not ask me to make excuses because there is no justification for what I did, and there never will be!'

Seeing the pain in her mother's sad face, Anne went on softly, 'Our Cathy is a warm and loving young woman. I'm sure she will understand. She's a kind and sensible girl, and you are her world. So, please, Mum – for all our sakes – go and find her now!'

Marie was deeply uneasy. 'By rights, I should have told her long ago, but I was a coward, and I still am. But the day before the wedding? You know how excited and happy she's been, looking forward to being a bridesmaid. Oh, Anne, don't make me tell her now. She's so excited, and full of joy. If I told her the truth now, I would only be hurting her terribly . . . taking something away from her that she sees to be very special, and that she is an integral part of. It would be an unforgettably cruel thing to do, destroying her joy and excitement of being a bridesmaid for the very first time. She is so proud, Anne . . . proud of being a part of this family – our family—'

Marie's voice trembled with emotion, and now she dropped to the sofa and, covering her face with her two hands, she told Anne softly, 'I don't want to hurt her yet again. I don't want to make her upset and shocked at what I must tell her, not today. She's been so looking forward to it.'

Marie broke down and sobbed like Anne had not seen her cry since her father had passed away, leaving her mother bereft and so incredibly lonely without him. Going to the sofa, she sat beside Marie. 'You're absolutely right, Mum. It would be wrong – it's taken so long for Cathy to recover from the accident, and this day has been a light for her to look forward to.'

Marie gave a heartfelt groan. 'I should have told Cathy years ago, but the thing is, I'm afraid that when she hears the truth of what I did, she will absolutely hate me.'

Anne understood her mother's anxiety. 'I understand, Mum, I don't want you to hurt her, any more than you need to. She's my little girl too. But I know her, and we'll get through this as a family. Together, we can face anything. So, after the wedding – maybe a day or so after – you must tell her the truth. As we're all going to Blackpool after the wedding there will be time and opportunity to confide in Cathy there, and if you need me to be with you, I promise, I'll be there. I know what you've been through and I am nervous of how Cathy will take the news of what happened all those years ago, and why she was never told.'

~

Beth was bouncing with excitement about Marie's wedding. It was to be a beautiful romantic day, two people who adored each other being united after years of friendship. Danny was being welcomed whole-heartedly into Marie's family; everyone was charmed by him and could see what a good husband he would be to partner Marie into her old age. But for Beth, one of the best things about being a bridesmaid was that she, too, felt welcomed into Marie's family. They had long been friends but to be given the honour of attending the bride on her special day filled Beth with joy.

Beth had come down from Blackpool on the train to spend a few days with Marie before the wedding. It was the first time she'd been back since she'd left for the job that had restored her confidence and given her independence, and she was dividing her time between Dave and Anne's house and the wedding preparations, and Eileen and Tony's. It was good to see that dear couple again and she would never forget what they had done for her when she was at her very lowest.

Beth's new life had all been down to Ronnie and Eileen. He'd been keen to have Beth near him and far enough away from Mike and his bullying ways that she need never see that vile man again. Eileen and Tony, who had been so very good to her, agreed that she might want to make a new start somewhere where she wasn't perpetually looking over her shoulder.

'But what would I do in Blackpool?' Beth asked Eileen, one morning as they drank coffee and ate the shortbread Beth had made. 'I have no skills as an entertainer and I haven't ever worked in a shop either. I know I need to find a way of supporting myself – I don't want to be a burden on anyone – but I've never had to do that before and I . . . well, I'm worried I don't know where to start.'

'Tony and I have been thinking about this,' said Eileen, taking another shortbread biscuit, 'and I do believe the answer is right before your eyes.'

'What do you mean?' Beth looked around the neat drawing room.

'I mean that wherever people get together they want food, and you're the best baker I know. Since you've been staying with us we've got used to home-made cakes for elevenses and at teatime, and fresh bread at lunchtime. Heaven knows, we'll miss you when you do decide to move on, but we'll miss your baking as well,' Eileen laughed.

Beth smiled, pleased that the baking she did for her friends was appreciated. 'Thank you, Eileen, but I don't really know where to start.'

'Well, I do,' Eileen replied. 'I'll be on the phone to Ronnie at the pub this afternoon, when it's his break. He was only saying the other day that Sam and Nancy were wanting to do food but they hadn't got the time to organise it. Seems to me that young Ronnie might well earn some brownie points by organising it for them. A few sandwiches at lunch-time, with home-made bread – even cheese and pickle's a treat when the bread is good – they could start with that and see how it goes.'

'Work at the pub? Work with Ronnie? Oh, that would be brilliant!' Beth's eyes shone. 'Ronnie likes Sam and Nancy, thinks they're fair employers, so I know I'd get on with them.' She jumped up from her chair and went to get the notepad on which Eileen wrote her shopping list.

'I'll just jot down a few ideas so I'm ready when I

talk to Ronnie later.' She took a deep breath. 'Probably I should speak directly to Sam or Nancy if Ronnie thinks this is a sound scheme.'

'That's the spirit,' Eileen beamed.

She would miss Beth when she was gone. These few weeks with Beth in the house had been like having a daughter of her own. Now Beth was over the worst of her ordeal there was a lively and youthful feeling about the place. But Eileen knew Beth could not stay forever, and it did her heart good to see the lovely young woman begin to spread her wings and fly.

Sam and Nancy asked Beth to go up to meet them and make a few sandwiches to show what she could do. They hired her on the spot, and Beth was now living in Blackpool and sharing lodgings with Ronnie. She'd never been happier, and word was already getting round that The Pitstop served the best sandwiches in town. Nancy was even talking about expanding the range. She and Sam were counting their blessings – as well as their profits – and chief among those blessings were Ronnie and Beth, no longer waif and strays but a huge part of the popular pub's success.

CHAPTER TWENTY-TWO

THE WEDDING DAY began with a moody sky and a light shower, and a house filled with great excitement.

'Come on, you lot!' That was Dave. 'Get up, you lazy devils! You've got four hours to get yourselves looking beautiful before the carriage awaits you, so come on, chop chop! Outta bed and up with the lark, eh?'

And even before he had finished yelling orders, everyone was up and about, with the girls being so excited, they could hardly contain themselves.

In record time, they were all washed and tidy, and far too excited for breakfast.

'There will be loads of food after the wedding,' Anne promised, as she put the kettle on, 'but we can't start the day without a cuppa!' And everyone agreed.

Within a surprisingly short time, everyone was dressed and ready to leave.

'Hurry up . . . you girls!' Anne ushered everyone into the front room, where she set about fiddling with the girls' hair, and checking the lovely dresses and pretty shoes.

'You all look wonderful,' she gushed, as she then lined them up in the hallway where she handed them their bouquets. Once out on the pavement, she checked everything again, while the neighbours gathered, and clapped the pretty bridesmaids as they came out of the house, and were carefully ushered into the big car Dave had hired for the occasion, and which he was to drive himself.

And now they were on their merry way, waving out of the window, as the small crowd continued to clap and cheer. Someone had unearthed a box of confetti and the neighbours scattered it after the car and over each other.

'I hope they have the decency to sweep it up afterwards!' That was a tired Dave, finding a reason to grumble, even on a momentous day like today, with Danny and Marie ready to tie the proverbial knot for life.

'You seem unusually quiet, Marie.'

Dave had noticed how Marie had been continually glancing out of the side window throughout the short trip to the church, and she had hardly spoken a word to anyone, which was unusual.

'Marie?' He looked across at her.

'Yes, Dave?'

'Are you all right? I mean you're not having second thoughts, are you? Because Danny is no doubt waiting for you to arrive, and you're looking particularly lovely,' he added with a reassuring smile.

Marie smiled back at him. 'I'm fine . . . honestly. A bit tired, if anything, but then I didn't really get much sleep last night. And to be honest, I kept wondering whether I'm doing the right thing in getting married. I mean, in some ways I don't really know Danny, do I? Oh, I know I've spent a lot of time in his company, and he's told me his family history, but although I've known him for years, when you think about it, there's been many years I haven't known him, hasn't there?'

'Oh, don't worry, you've just got a little panic going on. It happens to the best of us. I imagine you're no different from any other woman – or man, come to that. Once we're all dolled up and wondering how it might all turn out, the jitters get to you, making you think of all manner of unlikely things that might or might not happen. Look, Marie, I really don't think you have anything to worry about. I've seen you and Danny together many times now, and I have to say, I honestly believe that you two were made for each other.'

Dave was no fool. He knew well what had unsettled Marie.

She had not yet told Cathy about the true circumstances of her birth, and the sorry truth that went with it.

Dave himself was also upset that Marie had not yet found the strength to speak with Cathy, and he knew Anne was as well. Looking across to the passenger seat, he was sorry to see her so far away in her thoughts, especially on a day like this, when it should be one of the happiest moments of her life.

But rather than let her suspect his true thoughts, he quietly assured her, 'I know how you feel, Marie. It's one of those days when everybody is on edge – excited and looking forward, while wondering if everything will actually turn out for the best. We just have to believe it will, and I don't see any reason for you to worry, because you found yourself a genuine man in Danny.'

He was relieved to see her tiny smile. 'Thank you for that.' Marie felt more confident, 'You're right, it's just nerves, but I feel a little more settled now.'

'I should think so too! It's obvious Danny worships the very ground under your feet. He thinks you were made for him, and he tells everybody who will listen that you are a wonderful and caring woman, and from the first minute he clapped eyes on you he decided that you were the only one for him, the apple of his eye.'

He gave a chuckle, 'Mind you, the poor bloke has not yet suffered your terrifying musical snores in the middle of the night.' Laughter echoed throughout the car.

'All right, sweetheart?' Glancing in his mirror again, Dave stole a glance at Cathy, while feeling bad about the bombshell that she would shortly be made aware of. It was vital Marie's secret was revealed sooner rather than later, so especially since Cathy and Ronnie had grown even closer over the weeks while she was recovering from her injuries.

Only this morning, Anne had confided in him that she and Marie were still talking about how and when to reveal the truth to Cathy.

He had to suggest they might work that one out between themselves. By now, over the years, he had said it all, and today there was no time for talking.

He had been considering the matter a lot of late, and he had many times thought to take Cathy aside and reveal the truth of her birth to her. But as Cathy was Marie's child he felt it only right that she should be the one to choose the right moment, if indeed there would ever really be a 'right' moment. He privately thought the 'right' moment had long since passed, and that he and Anne had indulged Marie's indecisiveness, but he knew better than to say what may split his family forever.

Now they were arriving at the church, Dave stopped the car, got out and opened all the car doors, so that the passengers began to alight, along with the flowers and the bouncy, lace dresses. Last out was Marie dressed in her new outfit, and looking proud and girly-shy as Dave gave an appreciative little whistle. 'By, that Danny Boy is a very fortunate man, don't you think?'

He ushered them all out onto the pavement amazed that not one little flower had been crushed in the process. 'My word! Oh, but you look lovely, all of you!'

Proud as a peacock, Dave escorted them to the church porch, and when everyone was ready, the nod was given and the organ music started. Then – amazingly, in Dave's opinion – the proud procession went forward without a hiccup.

As well as the haunting organ music, the air was filled with 'Ooh!'s and 'Aah!'s As everyone turned to look at the exquisite, bright outfits, and the pretty flowers. Ronnie was there, looking immaculate if somewhat uncomfortable in a smart new suit for his role as usher. And Big John was bursting with pride to be best man to his oldest and dearest friend.

Feeling nervous, Marie looked up at the bronze figure of Jesus nailed to the massive cross above the altar, and a tear rose in her eyes. She felt as though he was watching her, blaming her for sinning in such a terrible way, all those years ago. Wicked and unworthy was how she felt then. It was almost as though she had no right to be here, in this holy haven of truth and innocence.

Then she saw Danny, and a surge of love wrapped

itself about her sorry heart. Danny was here . . . for her. He loved her with truth . . . he took her as she was. When she'd told him about her secret he'd held her hand and soothed her telling her that he'd love Cathy even more now. And that was that. Tears threatened, and then began to flow down her face until she found it difficult to breathe.

As Marie reached his side, Danny looked across to her, and his warm, loving smile washed away all her fears and all her painful regrets. For the first time in a long time she felt truly loved.

Marie's heart was filled with love, and gratitude that she had met such a man in Danny. A warm and honest man . . . a man who loved her, and with whom she could happily spend the rest of her life.

But not until she had done what she should have done many years ago. Confessing the truth to Cathy was a daunting, fearsome noose about her neck, and she wished with all her heart that it would soon be over, and that Cathy might somehow find it in her heart to forgive her.

She gazed on Danny's smiling face, and in that fleeting, precious moment, she felt that the Good Lord was ready to forgive her. All she had to do was find the strength to tell Cathy every shameful detail.

Somehow, somewhere, amidst the goodness and love currently surrounding them all, Cathy must know the true circumstances of her birth. Not tomorrow, or another day, but today! Here in this beautiful church, where sins might be forgiven and love might grow, she made her decision.

For the first time in many sorry years Marie felt calm, and somehow ready.

The service began, and with every promise, she gave of herself, as did her Danny. Very soon, they were man and wife. For the first time since she'd given birth to her precious Cathy, she felt strong enough to have a future.

Marie could hardly believe it was over so quickly and they were led to the small room to the side of the altar where they each signed their names in the register with the promise that they would be true to their marriage, and to each other.

Then they were walking down the aisle, with smiles all round and the joyful 'Wedding March' ringing in their ears as they emerged into the bright morning. Danny took Marie in his arms and swung her round, to the sound of clapping and cheering from the wedding guests.

Marie made a silent vow to the Lord that, before the day was over, Cathy would be told her real mother's secret. When all the festivities were over, she would take Cathy aside and tell her everything. She adored Cathy, and she was so desperately afraid that when Cathy was told she might turn away in hatred and disgust from the woman who had tricked and lied to her for all these years.

If that happened, Marie's own life would be as nothing to her.

Cathy and the rest of Marie's family were eagerly waiting to hug and kiss and congratulate the two of them, while everyone gathered in turn to admire the two brand-new wedding rings, sparkling in the dry air.

And when Danny Boy took her into his warm embrace, Marie thought how lucky she was but she couldn't help glancing across at Cathy, smiling and happy, and totally unaware of the bombshell waiting to fall on her.

On their arrival at the reception, a sumptuous feast in a woodland lodge, a great roar of clapping and congratulations greeted the newly-weds, who thanked everyone for being with them on this special day.

The caterers had made a wonderful spread, and when the guests had enjoyed their fill, it was time for the speeches. Danny's in particular was greeted with laughter. After the formalities were well and truly over, people sat and talked, or they wandered outside to stroll in the pretty woods.

With a handful of guests already making their way home, Marie felt a need to get away into the silence and glory of the woods around them in this wonderful place. She had a lot on her mind at that and the moment she had waited far too long for had arrived at last. She was deeply emotional.

While the bridesmaids laughed and chatted, and

other guests went walking, Marie drew Danny aside, out of earshot of anyone else, to a secluded bench.

'I need to speak with Cathy alone for a moment, if that's all right,' she began.

'Go ahead, sweetheart. I'm glad you have finally found the courage to tell her, and thank you for confiding the truth in me also. We should not have any secrets between us, especially now. We have each other, and that's all I need. So, go on. And keep a brave heart. I'm sure Cathy will be all right, maybe after a while. But you must be honest with her.'

They talked through again about the news Marie had to tell Cathy: about Marie's indiscretion all those years ago, how she had slept with Tony, and bore his child, and that the child was Cathy. When Marie fell tearful, Danny let her cry. It seemed to be the right thing to do at that moment.

Cathy had had the best day of her entire life. Not only was Ronnie down from Blackpool for the wedding, and looking just dreamy in his new suit, but she'd been able to spend nearly every minute of this afternoon's wedding feast with him. She knew she looked her best in the flouncy bridesmaid dress of sprigged cotton that Marie had chosen, and Ronnie's appreciative glances were well worth all the care she'd taken with curling her hair and doing her make-up. Her beloved nan was marrying the adorable Danny, an instant Irish granddad and just the best granddad that a girl could hope for. The service had been beautiful and very touching, and the wedding feast just amazing, with all the latest food you saw only in magazines: prawn vol-au-vents and Black Forest gateau.

Now, as Beth went back inside to get a cool drink, Cathy decided to take a little walk in the gentle woods around the lodge and take some fresh air. She set off, humming the lovely 'Wedding March' under her breath, swishing her long frilled skirt and dreaming of when she and Ronnie would have such a day as this.

She had moved away from the worn path and stopped still to watch a rabbit nibbling on some grass in the distance when she heard voices. It was Nan and Danny, and Nan was sounding upset! Cathy wondered what could possibly have made her cry on such a perfect day and she crept closer, deciding whether or not to interrupt them. What she heard rooted her to the spot with horror. She knew she shouldn't be eavesdropping but she was dragged in for the best motives and now, even though what she discovered was the worst thing she could possibly imagine, she could not leave. She had to stay and hear what her nan – no, not her nan, her mother! – was saying.

Suddenly Cathy startled Marie and Danny as she appeared out of nowhere, pointing at Marie and telling her in a tearful, shivering voice, 'You lied to me! I hate you. Hate you. I don't want you any more!'

And then with a look that turned Marie's heart inside out, she turned away and was quickly out of sight, with Marie chasing after her. 'Come back, Cathy, please . . . we need to talk, please, sweetheart, come back!'

When she started to go after Cathy, Danny stopped her. 'Let me go. I promise, I'll find her and I'll bring her back so the two of you can talk.' When in tears, she hesitated, he promised, 'I will get her back. You two have so much love between you. It will be all right, but you have to be truthful with her, sweetheart.'

He hurried away, heading after Cathy, striding into the woods like a man with a purpose, while Marie stood by the bench, looking in every direction to see if Cathy was coming back to her.

After a time, becoming frantic, she walked to the spot where she had last seen both Danny and Cathy disappearing. She then took a few steps into the trees searching in every direction, but when there was no sign of either of them, she went back to the bench and sat waiting, hoping and praying that Cathy would come back to her.

~

Cathy ran like the wind, tears rolling down her face as she recalled what Marie had said . . . that she was her mother. 'It was all lies! My whole life is a lie! Who am I? That woman is not my nan . . . she's my mother! And I hate her!'

A short time later, Danny found her curled up on a bench, her arms wrapped about her knees and her face downcast.

'Go away!' Cathy attempted to clamber off the bench, but Danny caught her by the hand.

'No! Please, I'm sure that what you overheard has shocked you. What she said was true, and all these years she has agonised over it. She tried so many times to tell you, but she was afraid you would reject her . . . and now you have. But please, let's talk awhile, eh? Marie did a bad thing, and she has punished herself for it over all these years.'

'Why did she do it?' Cathy asked. 'Why did she let me believe a lie all these years?'

Danny took her into his arms. 'Let her tell you, sweetheart. Let's go back . . . she's waiting for you. Yes, she did a bad thing, but she has punished herself for it, over and over. So many times she wanted to tell you the truth, but she was afraid you would not want her any more. Please, Cathy! No one will ever love you like she does. She made one mistake, and for all these years she has never forgiven herself.'

Cathy looked up at him, at that lovely, craggy face with the built-in smile, and she knew he meant every word he was saying. 'Why didn't she tell me, Danny?'

'Because she was afraid.'

'Because she was cowardly, you mean?'

'Well . . . yes, I suppose. But she was so afraid of losing you.'

'Well! Now she has!'

Danny asked her softly, 'Do you love your family
. . . all of them, including Marie?'

After a long silence, Cathy nodded. 'Of course I
love her. That's why I'm so shocked that she could
leave me not knowing the truth . . . for all these years.'

'Tell me again, sweetheart?'

'What?'

'Do you love your family – the people you believed
were your mother and father? Did you have a happy
life with them?'

After a long pause, Cathy looked up. 'Yes, I love
them all, but I was living a lie. The shame of it! And
they must all have known. How could they do that
to me?'

'Because they love you too much to let you go.
They needed you, as much as you needed them. You
are their lovely Cathy, wanted and loved. To all intents
and purposes, you were their daughter, not Marie's
daughter, although she loved and cared for you. She
was proud to see you grow up, right under her very
eyes, in her home, where she could have you with
her, and if that is not love . . . I don't know what is.'

He whispered softly, 'You are a very fortunate young
woman, Cathy, growing up in a loving family, always
being taken care of. Knowing that you will never be
alone. Knowing that those good people truly are your
family. They would be broken-hearted and utterly
devastated if you could not love them now.'

A FAMILY SECRET

From a discreet distance, Marie heard his every soft word, and as she listened, her tears fell and her heart was uplifted, to hear Danny's gentle, loving wisdom.

'Listen to me, Cathy.' Danny took hold of Cathy's hand. 'You are a very fortunate young woman. You have a family who love you deeply. You have a future now, with Ronnie, the young man who adores you. And, unlike me, you had a good childhood. I never knew my mother. She ran off and left me and my dad when I was six years old. My nan came to live with us, and in many ways she was my mother, and I loved her dearly. But she's gone now. I still miss her like you could never believe. Listen to me, sweetheart, you truly are a lucky girl. You have always had a loving family about you, with parents and a wonderful grandma who made a bad mistake in having a child out of wedlock. But she was determined not to let you go.

'However difficult it was going to be for her, she was not about to let you be taken away from her, my darling. Instead, she did what she thought was best for you, as did the whole family – your family. And might I say, they have done a wonderful thing in raising you to be the young woman you now are: kind and gentle, beautiful, and just beginning to embark on your own family life with a young man who adores you.'

Cathy turned away from him and sat silently for what seemed an age.

When she eventually looked up, she saw a small, solitary figure in a wedding outfit watching her, always loving her, aching to wrap her arms about her.

Suddenly Cathy was running to her, the tears rolling down her face as she threw herself into Marie's welcoming arms.

'Oh, Cathy, I thought you would not want me any more. I thought you would turn me away . . . ' Marie hugged her tightly. 'I do love you so . . . we all do. And later on, I will explain it all to you – everything – because you have a right to know.'

That very night, when the two of them were sitting in the garden under a darkening sky, Marie told Cathy the truth at last. But when it came to who her real father was, Cathy did not want to know.

'I have my father and mother, and my lovely nan, and so I have everything I want and need, right here. Why would I want strangers around me?'

Marie's heart was filled with love, and maybe also a few regrets. But right now, she felt like the happiest, luckiest woman in the world.

~

On the morning after the wedding, before Marie and Danny set out for their honeymoon in Blackpool, Eileen came to see Marie. Nervously, remembering how they had parted earlier in the year, Marie showed her into the front room. Eileen looked very cheerful, though, which gave Marie hope that she hadn't come to be angry with her.

'I've come to say that I'm sorry,' she said kindly. 'I was bitter and angry when we met in Blackpool and I have been thinking ever since that I should have been more charitable.'

'Well . . . that's very . . . nice of you, Eileen,' said Marie. 'You know how sorry I am for what I did. I can't blame anyone else, and I really wish I hadn't hurt you.'

'I know that, Marie. You're starting a new life with a lovely man and I don't want any disagreement between us to cast a shadow over that.'

'Thank you,' said Marie in a small voice.

'So, what do you say? Can we be friends again, do you think?'

Marie nodded silently as tears sprung to her eyes and she went to hug Eileen. They held each other for a long moment and when they pulled back each was smiling through her tears.

'And I have some good news,' said Eileen, sniffing and visibly pulling herself together. 'Tony and I have plenty of time to suit ourselves since he retired and he seems to have a new lease of life since . . . well, over the past few months. He needs a new interest – there's a limit to how often a man can mow the lawn, after all – and what we both need are new horizons. We're going on a cruise! The Mediterranean! I can't wait. I've never been further than Blackpool in the whole of my life but, you know, Marie, it's never too late.'

'Don't I know it!' Marie said. 'Here's me, a newly-wed, and there's you, travelling the world. I hope you both have a lovely time.'

'Thank you.'

'Send us a postcard.'

Eileen laughed. 'I will. And now I must go. Beth is heading back to Blackpool today and I want to give her a proper lunch before she goes.'

'Danny and I are going there later, too. Maybe we'll see her on the train.'

'She won't want to cramp your style,' smiled Eileen. 'I'm sure you and Danny would prefer to travel on your own.'

After a few more emotional moments, the two parted as friends and went their separate ways, while promising they would meet again.

Eileen gave Marie a parting hug. 'God bless you, sweetheart. You're a good woman, and sometimes even good people might stray from the path and get lost. But when you have a family and friends who love you, you will never be alone.

'Be happy, Marie,' she added softly. 'You've got a good, handsome man in Danny. You make sure and look after him, eh?'

With a little smile, Marie promised she would.

~

When Cathy and Ronnie had their first child, a small image of his daddy, Marie cried all day, and into the night. Danny told her she was a softie, and he would not want any other woman for as long as he lived.

In truth, he wondered what he must have done to deserve such happiness.

Dear Readers,

I'm so happy to share my latest story with you, this was a very special book for me to write. The past year has been full of the twists and turns that life can take and it has brought home just how important and cherished family really is. For Marie, too, I hope you can see the immense love she has for her family, guiding her through the dark times. We never quite know what life will throw at us, how it will all take its toll, but we have to hold on to the hope that everything will come good in the end.

Marie has been carrying the burden of a secret for many years. She fears the truth coming out, knowing that the consequences could badly hurt the people she loves most. Don't judge her too harshly, we all make mistakes and have regrets, but it's our inherent goodness that counts in the end. The characters in the story all show incredible strength and I hope you can see the devotion that they have for one another in the face of guilt and hardship. For them, and for all of us lucky enough to be surrounded by family, it's important to remember that the love of a family is the most precious gift.

I hope that you can welcome these characters into your hearts. For me they are very real, they live and breathe with me. Please do let me know, after you've read this story of love and loss through the generations, what you thought of their journeys.

I love hearing from each and every one of you, and always look forward to the letters that find their way to my door. Just as family is so precious, you, my loyal readers, are much-cherished too. And you're not just readers, but friends and compatriots, and I hope that you can confide in me whenever you feel lonely or sad. I have so much gratitude for the loyalty and love I get from you, and I will strive to reply to your wonderful letters as soon as I can.

I hope that this year will bring you everything you wish for. For me, it will be another stride towards the next book, and I can't wait to share more stories with you.

With all my love,

Jo x